THE DUKE'S CHAMPION

The Duke's Guard Series
Book Thirteen

C.H. Admirand

Additional Dragonblade books by Author C.H. Admirand

The Ladies of the Keep Series
Liberating the Lady of Loughmoe (Book 1)
Bargaining with the Lady of Merewood (Book 2)
Rescuing the Lady of Sedgeworth (Book 3)

The Duke's Guard Series
The Duke's Sword (Book 1)
The Duke's Protector (Book 2)
The Duke's Shield (Book 3)
The Duke's Dragoon (Book 4)
The Duke's Hammer (Book 5)
The Duke's Defender (Book 6)
The Duke's Saber (Book 7)
The Duke's Enforcer (Book 8)
The Duke's Mercenary (Book 9)
The Duke's Rapier (Book 10)
The Duke's Man-at-Arms (Book 11)
The Duke's Lance (Book 12)
The Duke's Champion (Book 13)

The Lords of Vice Series
Mending the Duke's Pride (Book 1)
Avoiding the Earl's Lust (Book 2)
Tempering the Viscount's Envy (Book 3)
Redirecting the Baron's Greed (Book 4)
His Vow to Keep (Novella)
The Merry Wife of Wyndmere (Novella)
Lady Farnsworth's Second Chance at Love (Novella)

The Lyon's Den Series
Rescued by the Lyon

Captivated by the Lyon
A Lyon's Word of Honor (Novella)
The Lyon's Saving Grace

Historical Cookbook
Dragonblade's Historical Recipe Cookbook:
Recipes from some of your favorite Historical Romance Authors

Dedication

For DJ, the other half of my heart…cannot believe it has been five years.

Acknowledgements

A special thank you to my wonderful editor Arran McNicol! I wish the comma faery who whispers in my ear could agree with your comma faery, who must be totally exasperated with mine! Thank you for your excellent advice. I'm so grateful that you're my editor.

For my loyal readers, and new-to-me readers, thank you for reading my books and letting me know how much you love The Duke's Guard Series and my handsome-as-sin Irishmen. Now that Eamon O'Malley's book has been published, there are only four more stories in The Duke's Guard series…the Flaherty brothers. Where have the last two years gone since the first book in this series was published in June 2022? Time flies, and I'd better catch up!

*Seamus is up first. You may remember him from **Tempering the Viscount's Envy (The Lords of Vice, Book 3)**. He and Michael O'Malley were assigned to escort Lady Calliope and her maid, Mary Kate Donovan, from Wyndmere Hall to Chattsworth Manor. Loved writing the scene where the carriage wheels slide on ice, and it lands on its side, hovering over a ditch at the edge of the road. Seamus and Michael pull off an impressive rescue…but that's another story.*

CHAPTER ONE

Seamus Flaherty fought to keep a neutral expression on his face. His cousin, Dermott O'Malley, spun around and stalked off to man his post. Flaherty should tell his cousin that he hadn't asked the man's wife to spend time with him…time she should have been spending with her husband. But bloody hell, he'd been clenching his jaw at the time to keep from groaning in pain in front of witnesses.

"Bugger it! 'Twasn't me who wandered off without waiting for an escort—or telling me that she planned to."

"That's the tale ye told the lot of us, Flaherty." His cousin Sean O'Malley wasn't smiling as he approached. "Georgiana said to tell ye she's bringing a fresh batch of scones."

Speaking of Dermott's wife, Flaherty groaned. "She didn't bake them herself—did she?"

In was obvious Sean, head of the duke's guard at Lippincott Manor, was irritated on his sister-in-law's behalf. "'Twould be more than ye deserve, having to eat Georgiana's inedible scones. Ye let the lass fawn over ye, while 'tis plain to the rest of us, who've been shot before and more than familiar with the extracting of lead balls and healing involved, that ye were well on the road to recovery."

Flaherty shrugged and winced at the pull of the healing flesh and muscles beneath it. "I tried to tell his lordship I'm ready to resume me duties—not spending me time teaching the latest group of footmen how to fight." Frustration boiled inside of him, and his neutral expression slipped. When he felt his brow furrowing, he inhaled and schooled his features. He was impatient and bloody well through waiting. "I understand the earl is keen on hiring more footmen to add to our numbers, but for the love of God, every last one of them thinks he has to fight fair! Who in God's name fights fair?"

Sean's lips twitched. "Every Englishman thinking he'd get the best of an Irishman."

Flaherty was relieved that his cousin's irritation faded. "Ye'd think they'd have heard our tales of glory."

"Aye, as the Irishmen who have been guarding the sixth Duke of Wyndmere and his family since he accepted the mantle of duke!"

Flaherty grunted. "How is it that there are still those who haven't heard of our exploits, and the number of times we've been shot, stabbed, or clubbed over the head while continuing to do our job?"

"Did ye forget we aren't in Ireland anymore, Flaherty? We're outnumbered here. Though in our favor, we have more bare-knuckle champions between the sixteen of us than in the whole of England!"

Flaherty grinned. "It does give us a bit of an edge. Those who think we'd be easy to defeat in their quest to harm the duke or his family find out who they are up against."

Sean scrubbed a hand over his face. "Ye need to put Dermott out of his misery, Seamus. He feels responsible for ye getting shot in the back."

"Twice," Flaherty added helpfully.

Sean blew out a breath and stared at Flaherty before agreeing. "Aye, Seamus—twice. Ye lost so much blood that we feared...feared the worst."

When his cousin's voice broke, Flaherty knew it was beyond time to stop taking advantage of Dermott or his contrite wife.

'Twas selfish of him to boot. "'Tisn't that I'm after trying to make either of them feel guilty. However, if she'd waited, as she promised, for me to escort her—" At Sean's direct look, Flaherty sighed. "Ye're right, Sean. If ye'll have a word with his lordship about me resuming me duties, then I'll be asking Dermott to please tell his wife that I'm nearly recovered."

"Is that all ye plan to tell our cousin?" Sean demanded.

"Nay. I'll be telling Georgiana that I've appreciated her care and concern, but 'tis time for her to pay attention to Dermott. Then I'll plant the bug in her ear that I've heard Dermott's worried her affections have shifted to me."

Sean jabbed his elbow at Flaherty's gut, but Flaherty feinted to the side, avoiding the blow. With a grunt, Sean said, "Meet me in a quarter of an hour behind the bachelor's quarters. That'll be the true test. If ye don't keel over after trading a few punches, I'll speak to his lordship. He'll be more apt to listen to me."

Flaherty ignored the dig about the quarters, which used to serve the men in the guard. Until, one by one, his O'Malley and Garahan cousins married. 'Twas irritating as a thorn in the arse that he could not quite reach to pull out. The reminder that the O'Malleys were the men the duke chose as heads of his various estates never sat well with Flaherty, but to give the devil his due, Patrick O'Malley had worked for the previous duke and never complained all those times he'd had to haul the profligate fifth duke over his shoulder to cart his drunken arse up the stairs to his bedchamber six nights out of seven. Thankfully, the sixth duke—the man they now served—was nothing like his elder brother. In fact, His Grace had repaired the damage to the title and family name. Flaherty, his brothers, and their O'Malley and Garahan cousins had been instrumental in that regard.

"Well now, as yer arse on the line as the man in charge of us, Sean, I'll have to agree with ye." Flaherty shook his head. "I haven't been meself for the last few weeks. I'm not used to being idle. I hate being left out. I need to be in the thick of things."

Sean clapped a hand to Flaherty's shoulder. "Out of all of us who've been injured, ye think I don't understand? I nearly lost me arm to infection, after having it flayed open to the bone."

"But ye didn't, thanks to yer lovely wife, and our cousin Emmett the healer."

"Aye, and Lieutenant Sampson and Dr. McIntyre." Sean gave a brief nod, then left.

Flaherty watched him leave, and guilt assailed him. He should admit to taking advantage of Georgiana's attention. Being shot in the back, while protecting her, shouldn't be held over her head. If he hadn't lost so much time recovering from wound fever, he might have confessed his small-mindedness sooner. His thoughts drifted to a fiery-haired lass and he wondered why Mary Kate had not come to see him after he'd been shot. He'd been courting the woman, and by all counts she was besotted with him.

Flaherty closed his eyes and swore the lass had a perverse way of showing it. "I need to get back to work." He needed to forget the faithless lass with the bewitching eyes. Concentrate on his duties. "'Tis what I signed on for." He thought of his cousins' wives and marveled that every one of them had been unafraid to go toe to toe with the men they married whenever they thought they were right. What a sight that had been!

The lot of them are beautiful and stubborn to the bone. His thoughts immediately went to the woman he hadn't seen hide nor hair of while recovering. The fever had held him in its grip longer than he anticipated. *Bloody hell!* He'd even dreamed that Mary Kate had been beside him, but it must have been the fever overheating his brainbox. Flaherty had been weak as a babe those first few days after his fever broke. Well, he was hale and hearty now, and had made up his mind to confront her.

He decided it was past time to ask Sean for the time away from his duties to pay her a visit. She'd taunted him in his delirium—and in his sleep. It gutted him that the woman always claimed James Garahan was the man who'd saved her life. When would Mary Kate remember the far more dramatic rescue the day

Flaherty had pulled her and Lady Calliope, Viscountess Chattsworth, from the duke's carriage? It had slid on ice and tipped over onto its side, just a half a mile from Chattsworth Manor.

Mary Kate was a winsome lass, with blue-violet eyes, a sunshine smile, and lips as red as a rose. Soft and supple, just ripe for kissing. But women were fickle creatures at best. Why had she deserted him in his time of need if she loved him?

A devastating thought occurred… The lass was still in love with Garahan! *Did she ever love me?*

The last time Mary Kate showed up at Lippincott Manor, he'd just had two lead balls dug out of his hide. Thank the Lord, it had been his upper back and not lower, where it could have lodged in something important, like his heart or a lung. Or lower still…in a kidney! Otherwise, he might not be standing here contemplating what he wanted to say to the beautiful lass.

He could not decide if Mary Kate was a temptress, wrapped up in curves that had his hands clenching and his fingers itching to get a hold of her again, or an angel. The last time he'd kissed the lass was at Grosvenor Square. His gut clenched as he remembered the feel and taste of her mouth. It had been a sumptuous feast fit for a starving man.

'Twas shortly after that James Garahan had rescued the lovely Melinda Waring—whom he married. Flaherty had been jealous of Garahan at the time, wondering if Mary Kate still carried feelings for his cousin. He'd wanted her to remember that she'd been casting her lures Flaherty's way before they traveled to the duke's London town house. When he'd finally caught her alone in the hallway by the kitchen, Flaherty demanded her attention with a kiss that had her melting against him. Her response ignited his passion. God help him, when she kissed him back, his eyes had crossed! Even now, he broke out into a sweat recalling the heat of the fire that burned within him.

Flaherty frowned. The rumors began not long after he'd been assigned to Lippincott Manor, and Mary Kate had remained at the neighboring estate, Chattsworth Manor. Sly talk soon followed, revolving around her haunting the stables whenever the new farrier arrived to tend to the horses. Flaherty scoffed—in his opinion, the man was too puny to shoe horses for a living. He raked a hand through his hair, and winced as the movement stretched the healing wounds in his back. He had best remember to duck the next time some blackguard shot at him.

Resolved to end the mystery, and confront Mary Kate as to why she'd abandoned him, he squared his shoulders and made his way to the kitchen. It was past time to find Dermott's wife and make amends. Georgiana would be there at this time of day. She may not have mastered cooking or baking, but she was always willing to lend a hand in the kitchen. For Dermott's sake, Flaherty hoped some of the cook's talent in the kitchen would rub off on his cousin's wife.

Mrs. Wyatt looked up as he stood in the doorway. "You're looking well, Flaherty. How do you feel?"

He couldn't help but smile at the concern in the older woman's voice. The earl's cook had a big heart that had her voluntarily taking care of every one of the men in the duke's guard. It did not matter if the men were stationed at the manor or any of the other duke's residences.

"Better every day, thank ye."

The Lord works in mysterious ways. His cousins had fallen in love with the women they'd rescued. Flaherty had rescued Mary Kate, and while he'd been attracted to the lass, he hadn't felt compelled to offer her marriage. *And why not?* he wondered before shoving that question aside to address the more pressing matter. Apologizing.

He smiled at Georgiana. "I need to speak with ye for a moment, if ye have the time."

Dermott's wife brushed her hands on her apron. With a glance at the cook, who nodded approval, Georgiana followed him out of the room into the long hallway. Halfway down, he paused and held out his hand, which she took.

"I need to apologize to ye." She was already shaking her head when he insisted, "Ye need to listen. Please?"

When she stilled, he dug deep to pull out the emotions he'd been ignoring. Guilt-laced gratitude. "Forgive me for letting ye think I was still feeling poorly."

Instead of interrupting him, she remained silent. He continued, "I have to admit, I was feeling a bit irritated that ye hadn't listened to me that day and waited for me escort. And more, I was worried that ye'd wandered off when ye knew full well—" He paused to scrub a hand over his face. When she giggled, he grumbled, "What part of ye getting kidnapped, and disappearing to God knows where, do ye find amusing?"

Georgiana bit her lip and struggled to stop laughing. "I didn't mean to interrupt. Please continue."

He held on to his temper—barely. "Where was I?"

"You were about to yell at me."

"Flaherty would not dare raise his voice to ye." Dermott strode toward them and glared at their clasped hands. "Let go of me wife!" Flaherty dropped her hand, and Dermott added, "He wouldn't survive the beating."

Flaherty was about to disagree when Georgiana said, "If you would let Seamus finish, Dermott, I think he was about to apologize after he got through reminding me of events that keep me up nights—my selfish need that day to clear my head with a long walk. I never gave a thought to the danger that had been lurking nearby for days—or the consequences, should one of those dangers lie in wait for one of us."

Turning back to Flaherty, she patted his arm. "Whenever you're ready to continue, I'm listening."

With a brief glance at his cousin, Flaherty said, "I may have been thinking ye needed to feel bad on me behalf for a bit longer, as I wanted ye to remember the consequences of not listening to me." The fear that gripped him that day returned. "Ye'd been kidnapped, and I feared I wouldn't find ye before ye were spirited away."

"I will never forget that you were shot protecting me, Seamus." Tears gathered in her eyes, and he felt as if he'd been kicked in the stomach.

"Don't be crying over a few lead balls in me hide. I'm not dead yet, lass. I'm sorry if I let ye think I was still in pain."

"Ye'd best finish yer apology, Flaherty—I need to have a private word with me wife," Dermott interjected.

"Hah! Ye've got that look in yer eye, Dermott. Ye'd best not be taking time for more than a few kisses. I'm meeting Sean behind the outbuilding in a few minutes." That pulled his cousin's attention away from his wife, as Flaherty intended. "He'll be testing me reflexes and stamina by going a few rounds with me."

Dermott nodded. "Good idea. Then he'll be speaking to his lordship for ye?"

"Aye, and I thought to speak to the earl again afterward."

Dermott pulled his wife close to his side. "The earl will have already heard about the bare-knuckle bout by now and show up for part of it." With his arm around his wife, he nodded and started to walk away.

Flaherty knew he'd best get the rest of his apology said quickly. "I need ye to forgive me for not taking into account yer tender feelings, Georgiana. I would never have wanted ye suffering lack of sleep, or night terrors, on me behalf. I've mended and am ready to resume me place in the guard." She didn't speak right away, and guilt hammered him. "I'm truly sorry, lass."

She slowly smiled. "Of course I forgive you, Seamus. I promise not to ignore instructions from you—or any of the other guards—again. I'm so sorry you were shot on my behalf."

"Twice," he murmured.

"For feck's sake, Flaherty!" Dermott grumbled. "Let it go! Ye're lucky the blackguard didn't aim for yer head!"

"Or me arse," Flaherty added.

Dermott's laugh rang out. "Fecking *eedjit*."

Flaherty shrugged. "If the bugger had shot me in the backside, I'd have hated not being able to sit for the last few weeks."

Georgiana giggled, and Dermott grumbled, "Watch yer

words around me wife's tender ears, and quit monopolizing her!"

Flaherty swallowed a chuckle. "I beg yer pardon for me language, lass." He nodded to Dermott. "Satisfied?" His cousin grunted, and Flaherty asked, "If ye could put in a good word for me with our cousin Sean, I'm thinking I owe Mary Kate a visit. The last time she was here, I was a bit under the weather."

Dermott stared at him for a moment before agreeing. "That ye were. Weak as a newborn babe."

Flaherty growled. "I had just been shot."

"Excuses, excuses." His cousin snickered, pulled his wife into the room at the end of the hall, and closed the door.

Their muffled laughter ended abruptly, and Flaherty felt a hard tug of jealousy. His cousins had somehow managed to not only rescue lasses who were grateful, but who fell hard and fast in love with them. Had he misunderstood Mary Kate's feelings? Would he have fallen in love with her if she had stopped harping on Garahan saving her life—ignoring Flaherty's more daring rescue?

Why couldn't Mary Kate understand that it drove him to the brink of sanity that she always referred to James as the man who rescued her? If only she could understand how badly he needed to be the one she thought of first. Besides, Garahan was a married man! The jealousy was eating him alive.

It was time to tell her how he felt and demand she do the same! He'd not continue to court a woman who had no feelings for him.

CHAPTER TWO

MARY KATE WALKED toward the kitchen, her thoughts twisting in on one another. Had Seamus changed his mind? Did he regret asking to court her? He'd been distant as of late—even before that terrifying day he'd been shot. Hand to heart, she tried to slow the beat with her will, recalling the terror of that day. Yes, he had been weak—and lost a lot of blood—even before the physician extracted the lead balls from his back.

The very thought of how that had been accomplished had her heart pounding and hands trembling again. "Calm down! Seamus is fine. He's recovering—at least according to Michael O'Malley's latest report."

The spoken words did nothing to alleviate her worry. Why hadn't he sent word to her? If Flaherty was truly courting her, he would want to reassure her, wouldn't he? Given the numerous duties his position within the duke's guard required of him, and the time it took to complete them, their courtship had been a bit unusual.

Lately, she had begun to think that there was something else behind his silence. She'd heard the other men call him the Duke's Champion, and wondered how he had earned the moniker. Flaherty was not the only man in the guard who had been given a name. The duke's men at Chattsworth had them, too. Michael O'Malley was the Duke's Shield, and James Garahan the Duke's

Hammer. At Lippincott Manor, Sean O'Malley was the Duke's Protector, and Dermott O'Malley the Duke's Mercenary.

Thinking of her first impressions of the men, she realized each name seemed to be part and parcel of the man's makeup, along with the individual's specific talent and strong points. She had overheard bits and pieces about the men and agreed they exuded the confidence and capability their names imbued them with.

Mary Kate needed to find out what had gone wrong between Flaherty and herself. The fear that the auburn-haired, stubborn giant, with the crooked smile and devastatingly clear blue eyes, knew what she hid from the world terrified her. Did he agree that she wasn't worthy of his regard, his attention, or his love? Her parents were not wealthy, but both Mum and her father worked hard for every penny they earned. She never doubted that they loved her, whether or not she did as she was told, and helped with the household chores until she was old enough to seek employment.

Had he finally decided to distance himself first, before ending their courtship? Was it her fear of discovery that had her oblivious to what Garahan's wife must have felt every time Mary Kate brought up the fact that Garahan had rescued *her* first? How blind she had been to Melinda's feelings—and Garahan's. How could that possibly eclipse the fact that Garahan had fallen in love with Melinda? Did he feel revulsion for her because of her ignorance?

Mary Kate needed to find out, but she also needed to find out why Flaherty was keeping his distance. Had to understand the reasons behind his words and deeds. The unasked—and unanswered—questions plagued her. Was it because of his recent injury? It had been horrific, and one she had not expected him to survive. She'd had him dead and buried, and been grieving his loss, when Dermott delivered the message that Seamus was asking for her.

She'd never understand the way Flaherty's mind worked. He was by turns enamored of her and kissing her senseless at the duke's town house. Standoffish whenever she smiled at another man. After arriving at Grosvenor Square, Mary Kate had learned to smile again, returning to her former sunny disposition. Flaherty spent most of his time frowning. Did she want to spend the rest of her life defending herself when closely questioned as to why she smiled at the innkeeper, the vicar, or the new farrier? Couldn't he understand it was because of the way she had been accepted and treated as if she mattered by the duke's staff, after suffering for so long in Lady Kittrick's kitchen?

Ever since she had been booted unceremoniously out of the woman's town house, literally landing on her hands and knees on the sidewalk, she had been trying to change her way of thinking. She'd escaped a difficult situation, and been given a second chance to work in a different environment. The longer she worked for Lady Calliope, who was a gentle and kind woman, the more she felt as if she had been able to shed the cloak of darkness and depression that had settled upon her as she worked for a member of the *ton* who had treated her as if she were an object, not a person. Neither the cook nor their previous mistress had valued Mary Kate's strong work ethic, the one thing she was raised to believe had the most value—next to being honest and forthright in everything she said and did. She doubted either of her parents had ever worked for someone like her former employer.

The few years she worked in that difficult situation had changed her to the point where she almost believed hard work and toiling for little or no coin, and receiving harsh words, was her due. Until the day she'd been unceremoniously ejected from her previous position. Was it because she'd been berated daily for her pleasant disposition, or mayhap being told to be silent and finish her work? It had been hard to listen to the complaints. After toiling to complete her tasks, being told her work was unsatisfactory demeaned her further. Threats of letting her go without a reference had soon followed.

Those insidious comments and complaints chipped away,

eroding her self-worth, until she believed every unkind—and untrue—claim uttered about her, fearing that any day would be her last. But thankfully, she'd been rescued from that dreadful existence. Thank heavens Lady Calliope and Viscount Chattsworth were the complete opposite of her former mistress.

Luck was on her side the day James Garahan helped her to her feet, promising to help her find another position. The duke's kindly cook, Mrs. O'Toole, had tended to her scrapes and bruises before plying her with tea and scones. Mary Kate would always have a special place in her heart for Garahan's kindness and willingness to help a complete stranger. When he had found her crying on her hands and knees on the sidewalk, she had been despondent, wondering how she would find another job without a reference—Lady Kittrick had nearly broken her spirit.

Why couldn't Flaherty understand it was no more that that? Mary Kate tried to recall if he had ever asked about how she ended up losing her job, but couldn't. And that wasn't the crux of the matter—it was her smiling and happy because of her position at Chattsworth Manor. "I refuse to revert to the shadow of a woman I had become working for that horrible woman!"

"Lady Kittrick's loss is our gain," a soft voice replied.

Mary Kate spun around with hand to her heart. "Forgive me, Lady Calliope. I thought I was alone."

"In a house this size, with servants?"

She could not help but echo her mistress's smile. "True, there have been additions to the staff as of late. Mrs. Romney seems pleased with the new scullery maids. Mrs. Meadowsweet mentioned the new housemaids hired to keep the upper floors in order have helped alleviate the stiffness in her legs and knees, since she does not have to constantly climb the stairs. The poor woman is so grateful to you for rearranging things so her room and duties are all on the main floor." Neither woman spoke of the ages of the loyal, long-term Chattsworth servants—especially the oldest of the bunch, Hargrave, the butler, and the irascible MacReady, who had been acting as the viscount's valet and footman when Mary Kate accompanied Lady Calliope to her new home at the duke's order.

Fortunately, Rowland, the steward, was years younger than the other servants. His job required him to constantly view the estate, visiting the viscount's tenant farmers and keeping track of the crops produced, grain stored, etc. When Calliope's husband had all of two pence to rub together, those few servants had remained without pay. It spoke volumes of the viscount's character, and explained why he would go to such lengths to try to convince the duke to grant him an endowment. Things had not worked out quite the way the viscount had planned, though looking at the couple now, one would think there had been a spark from the start.

Lady Calliope linked her arm with Mary Kate's. "Have I told you recently how very grateful I am that His Grace assigned you as my lady's maid?"

Mary Kate smiled. "Yes, your ladyship. Just the other day, but you do realize that you have it backward—*I* am the one who is grateful to be working for you. You have always treated me as if I mattered, and haven't berated me for inferior work."

Calliope shook her head. "You do remember that I was once in a similar position. I have never understood why people are cruel to others." She bit her lip as if to hold back the rest of what she had been about to say.

Mary Kate had heard bits and pieces of what her ladyship had suffered at the hands of her cousin, working in his household when considered a poor relation. "I have witnessed the good in some, and the meanness of others," she replied. "I have not decided if it is because of something in a person's past that made them act that way, or if it was inherent in their very makeup or ancestry."

Calliope nodded, and Mary Kate remembered hearing that Earl Lippincott's wife Aurelia and her uncle had rescued the viscountess from an untenable situation. She marveled that Lady Calliope's true nature had not been damaged beyond repair by the experience. Marriage to the viscount had had a difficult beginning. Not to mention that horrible duel and the viscount's selfless act, leaping into the fray to protect Aurelia's uncle. The viscount was shot instead of her uncle. It had been the turning point in the early days of their marriage.

"I have yet to decide if it is because of one's environment, or one's makeup," Calliope remarked, "or a combination of both."

Mary Kate was quick to reply, "Mayhap it is both and depends on the character of the person." She thought of the daily interactions between Lady Calliope and the viscount. Seeing them together, one would never know that theirs had not been a love match, but a marriage to save her reputation. Mary Kate still had trouble believing the tale she'd heard. While still a poor relation, Calliope had been at the Duke of Wyndmere's estate in the Lake District, at the top of the grand staircase, when the viscount barreled out of the duke's study into her and knocked the wind out of her, causing her to lose her footing.

Thankfully, the viscount grabbed hold of her and caught her in his arms. The story was that he thought she'd stopped breathing. A number of the duke's staff had been on hand to witness the dramatic rescue and the immediate aftermath. The viscount had placed his ear to her breast to ensure her heart was still beating, and she was still breathing. From the base of the stairs, Mary Kate imagined it had looked like something else entirely, though she would never give voice to that supposition. It would hurt Lady Calliope, and she would never do anything to distress her mistress.

Mary Kate sighed just thinking of the romantic rescue. Then there was Calliope's subsequent rescue of Lord William when the duke ordered him to London to attend to matters, ordering Calliope and Mary Kate to Chattsworth Manor. Between the two of them, they had pushed up their sleeves and pitched in to bring his house to some semblance of order, endearing the remaining servants to her ladyship and forging a friendship with Mary Kate.

Looking back, she marveled at how much had happened

since they first walked into the viscount's home. Putting it to rights was the first action that had brought the couple closer together. So much more had happened since then, leaving Mary Kate to wonder, would she ever have a knight in shining armor come to her rescue? Well, she qualified, Garahan had, but then he rescued Melinda Waring from the horrible situation she had suffered through working in her cousin's tavern in the stews of London. Garahan had fallen in love with Melinda and married her.

Calliope slid her arm free and placed a hand on the stair rail. "I need to check on little William." Her quiet gray eyes studied Mary Kate. "While I do, you can tell me what has been bothering you these last few weeks. You haven't been the same since you returned from Lippincott Manor after nursing Flaherty through the worst of his wound fever."

Mary Kate was too embarrassed to discuss what had happened and had not wanted to confess that Flaherty had ordered her to leave. As if her sitting beside him, bathing his brow, helping him drink—when he refused to do so for anyone else— had not occurred. It had cut her to the quick. He'd broken her heart.

She cleared her throat to tamp down the ache inside of her. Needing to distract her ladyship from asking questions that Mary Kate was not ready to answer, she murmured, "We'd best see what William is up to. He is growing so fast and already grabbing hold of furniture and chairs to hold himself up."

Lady Calliope laughed, a bright, musical sound. "He is the light of our lives. You're right. I'd best be ready, because I have a feeling once he takes that first step, he'll learn to run instead of walk!"

Mary Kate fell silent as they ascended the staircase. Her mind still tried to understand Flaherty's hot and cold treatment. He had rescued Lady Calliope and Mary Kate—and brought up that fact more than once since he had been stationed at Lippincott Manor, while she was working for Lady Calliope at Chattsworth Manor, a few miles away. It was as if he thought she would forget the gallant way he had pulled them both up and out of the duke's carriage when it was lying on its side precariously over that ditch. The strength he exhibited as his muscles tensed to accept their weight as he deftly extracted them, one at a time, from the coach was extraordinary. Yet he hadn't been winded after he set them on their feet outside the carriage, where they waited while he and Michael O'Malley righted the coach. Another feat of ingenuity and strength.

But strength alone was not a reason to let her heart or her head get carried away. Like-minded opinions mattered. Whether or not one wanted to live in the city or the country, and then there was the question of children. Did one suffice, or would Flaherty want half a dozen children? Would he expect her to leave her position as part of the viscount's staff? Just the thought had tears forming. She blinked furiously to keep them from falling.

Calliope paused in front of the door to the nursery. "I'm afraid I cannot wait until you are ready to tell me what occurred when you were at Lippincott Manor for those worrisome days Flaherty's life hung in the balance. You have been carrying a heavy weight ever since you returned, even though he has recovered."

"I… You see… That is—" Mary Kate's eyes welled with more tears, and this time, she could not seem to stop them.

Lady Calliope put her arm around Mary Kate. "Tell me everything!"

When Mary Kate shook her head, her mistress opened the door, pulled her inside, and closed it. With a stern expression Mary Kate had never seen before, Lady Calliope told her, "Do not leave anything out!"

Little William's face scrunched up, and he started to cry. Calliope soothed him and lifted him out of his cradle, kissing away his tears. "I am so sorry for scaring you, my little angel face." When he quieted in her arms, she turned to Mary Kate. "I apologize for sounding harsh to you as well, but I have given you plenty of time to confide what happened between you and Flaherty." Calliope's frown was fierce. "I must have a happy balance in my home, for my precious little one's sake, my darling husband's, and every one of the staff. You are like family to me— and to William. I know it is not the way of things, and how most households within the *ton* are run, but William and I are in full agreement. We owe Hargrave, Mrs. Romney, Mrs. Meadow-sweet, MacReady, and Rowland so much for their loyalty in remaining, even when William had not been able to pay them. Can you not see that you are not just hurting yourself, but all of those around you?"

The floodgates opened and Mary Kate dissolved into tears.

CHAPTER THREE

FLAHERTY TOOK THE jab to his chin as his due. He may have thought he was fully recovered, but Sean's not-so-subtle reminder that his reaction time was still slower than normal had to be acknowledged. He flexed his jaw to relieve the ache from the blow. He ignored the pain in his back. It wasn't as bad as it had been a few days ago—a marked improvement.

Sean dropped his guard and took a step back. "Ye're nearly there, and I'll be telling his lordship. I'm to meet him after we're through."

"Dermott seemed to think the earl would want to watch us practice."

"His lordship was waylaid by Lady Aurelia and little Edward. The lad pulled himself up and used the settee as a handhold while he took a few steps before landing on his rump."

Flaherty grinned. "Well now, that is good news. I wonder if her ladyship is ready for their son to start walking."

His cousin shook his head. "Ma always said once we learned to walk, we ran."

"Aye, me ma said that same to us. Must be our strong Irish genes." Flaherty unrolled his sleeves and donned his frockcoat. "Thank ye for speaking to his lordship on me behalf regarding returning to me post, and the hour or two off to speak with Mary Kate. It may even take less time."

Sean frowned. "Seamus, there's something Dermott and I have been meaning to ask ye."

"Aye?"

"Ye're acting as if nothing happened between yerself and Mary Kate the last time she was here."

"I don't have *shite* for brains, Sean. I know it was hard for her to see me barely conscious and bleeding."

His cousin studied him for a few moments before he shook his head. "Ye have no memory of what happened, do ye?"

"What kind of question is that? Sure and I'm not likely to forget the pain of having those lead balls dug out of me back."

"And after?"

"The stitching me hide back together?"

"Nay…the fever."

Flaherty sighed. "It must have been worse than I thought if ye're bringing it up. The worst of it must have lasted a good day or so."

"More than," Sean murmured. "Do ye remember nothing?"

Flaherty shrugged. "Me dreams were disturbing. Mary Kate was in some of them. The worst was the one where she'd been crying as she left me. Why would she be leaving me, when I needed her?" He paused as his cousin's earlier words sank in. "What do ye mean by *more* than?"

"Ye were burning with wound fever for five days."

He shook his head. "I would have known if it had been that long. Are ye certain?"

When his cousin stared at him without speaking, Flaherty had his answer. He'd been insensate for five long days!

"Why then didn't the lass stay by me side?" He couldn't believe Mary Kate would abandon him in his time of need.

The pained expression on Sean's face spoke volumes. Something had happened…something Flaherty knew he would not want to hear.

"What aren't ye telling me? Did I swear a blue streak when I was in the fever's grip? She has delicate sensibilities, but has heard meself and surely Michael and James swear before."

Sean placed a hand on Flaherty's shoulder, as if to ground him. "The moment yer fever broke, ye told her ye didn't need a faithless woman like her in yer life and to get out."

The gut punch of O'Malley's words had Flaherty denying it. "Nay!"

"I was standing in the hallway speaking to Lieutenant Sampson at the time. We both heard ye as plain as day—loud enough to be heard in the kitchen."

"Why didn't ye stop her?"

"Ye'd started thrashing around and swinging. Sampson and I had to hold ye down until ye quieted. We didn't want the threads to rip—ye'd lost too much blood already. By the time we'd settled ye, Mary Kate was gone."

Flaherty scrubbed a hand over his face and groaned. "Why didn't ye tell me before now?"

"Ye've grumbled to meself and Dermott more than once since Garahan married Melinda and accepted his permanent assignment at Chattsworth Manor that ye didn't trust Mary Kate not to flirt with Garahan—or the new farrier, for that matter. Why would we question it when ye were out of yer head with fever?"

"Aye, but I told ye we were courting. Ye know I've never asked to court another woman!"

"If yer heart was in the courting, ye'd have been badgering me to ask his lordship to spare ye for an hour or two daily just to be with the lass." Sean stared at him. "That's how I felt with Mignonette, though we didn't have the time to court. Our situation was different—a matter of life and losing a limb!"

Flaherty's throat constricted. He was eventually going to have to confide in one of his cousins. His brothers were elsewhere, and it wasn't the kind of missive he'd want to send by messenger. He sure as hell wasn't about to ask Garahan for advice. "From the start, Mary Kate's been waxing poetic about Garahan's rescue instead of me own."

Sean's eyes flashed as disbelief colored his expression, before it disappeared. "Ye're jealous of our married cousin who only has eyes for his wife?"

When he put it that way, Flaherty felt like a fool. What was worse, he'd acted the fool off and on since the green-eyed monster of jealousy started feeding on his feelings for Mary Kate, added to what he imagined was happening. He acknowledged the censure in Sean's gaze and accepted it.

"Ye aren't trying to get a rise out of me by claiming I insulted the lass before ordering her to leave?"

"I wouldn't do that to yerself or Mary Kate."

Flaherty rubbed a hand over where his aching heart still beat in his chest. "That must be why the lass hasn't accompanied Lady Calliope the last two times she visited Lady Aurelia."

Sean nodded. "There's more."

"More than me casting the woman I love aside during me fevered delirium, and the lot of ye letting it happen?"

"Mary Kate was the only one ye *didn't* fight off when yer fever spiked hours after ye were sewn back together. She sat with ye, bathing yer brow, chest, and back. We all knew ye were courting her, and his lordship felt it would help ye heal to have Mary Kate by yer side."

Flaherty's heart felt as if he'd taken a blade to it. "I must have been in a bad way for the earl to set aside propriety. How long did she tend to me?"

"Four nights and five days."

Flaherty's head reeled with the knowledge of what he'd done—'twas his fault the lass hadn't been to see him. To gift him with her smile, and her smoldering looks. Those bewitching blue-violet eyes of hers constantly tempted him to kiss the breath out of her.

The thought that she may never glance that way at him again gutted him. "What have I done?"

Sean crossed his arms across his chest and braced his feet apart in a battle stance. "Not a thing that cannot be mended. Go to her. Apologize and tell her what ye just told me. Ye had no idea ye'd said such harsh things to her."

"What if she won't listen?"

"I'm thinking she might. She loves ye, Seamus. Only a jealous, hardheaded fool wouldn't see it."

"What if she won't forgive me?"

"She may need time, but I believe she will forgive ye. Every last one of us have seen what she feels shining in her eyes whenever she looks yer way."

Flaherty's shoulders slumped under the weight of his cousin's words, added to what he'd said to the lass when in the fever's grip. "I'll never be able to forgive meself if I've killed what she feels for me."

"Stop feeling sorry for yerself! Ye know what ye need to do. Go fecking do it!"

Flaherty rallied to the call and squared his shoulders. "I may be a bit longer than planned."

"Don't return until ye've spoken to the lass, and apologized in front of witnesses."

"Witnesses?"

"Aye, more than one would be best. Oh, and ye may need to grovel a bit. Do ye want to get on yer knees now and practice?"

Flaherty snorted and shoved his cousin out of his way with his shoulder. "Feck off, O'Malley!"

"Want me to ask the earl about a special license?"

For the first time since Sean had told him what he'd said to Mary Kate to push her out of his life, he smiled and sprinted toward the stables. "Aye. I'm thinking I'll have her eating out of me hand by teatime. Ask his lordship if he'll speak to the vicar about marrying us tonight."

As he saddled his gelding and rode toward Chattsworth Manor, he imagined how pliant the lass would be when he drew her close and pressed his lips to hers. One thought led to another as he closed the distance between the estates, and by the time he arrived, he was anticipating his wedding night with the woman who'd tied him in knots from the moment he first laid eyes on her.

"What a grand life we'll lead, lass."

CHAPTER FOUR

MARY KATE'S LIPS trembled as she bravely told Calliope of the last hour she'd spent tending to Flaherty. "I never prayed so hard in my life. My arms were tired, my head ached, but I was afraid to leave his side for fear that he would never open his beautiful blue eyes again."

The memory of that last glimpse into his eyes had fear grabbing her by the throat all over again. The hand that gripped hers brought her back to the present. Calliope's face was shrouded in concern. "What happened?"

Mary Kate cleared her throat. "Sweat began to pour off him, and I was so relieved that his fever seemed to be breaking that I turned from him. I dipped the linen cloth in the cool water and wrung it out, but when I leaned over him to bathe his face, he grabbed my wrist and glared at me."

"That does not sound like Flaherty at all," Lady Calliope remarked.

Mary Kate agreed. "He is normally even-tempered, though I have overheard the men talking about him using the force of his strength and conviction protecting the duke and his family to subdue those who would defame, attack, or destroy them."

"What did you do?"

Mary Kate licked her lips to moisten them. "I was about to ask him what was wrong. He told me..." Her heart ached at recalling his words. But she pushed through the hurt to confide in her mistress, "He bellowed that he did not need a faithless woman like me in his life. Then he told me to get out."

Another large handkerchief was thrust into Mary Kate's hand. Grateful, she mopped her tears and dried her eyes. Hiccupping, she finally looked up and noticed the stone-faced man who had handed her the handkerchief. *The viscount!*

She shot to her feet. "Forgive me, your lordship. I thought Lady Calliope and I were alone."

"I am going to take care of the problem." He spun on his heel, but stopped with his hand on the doorknob when Calliope called out, "After you rein in your anger, William, you'll realize that anything you say at this point would only add more fuel to the fire if you confront Flaherty when your temper is up."

"From the moment the duke assigned Mary Kate as your lady's maid, she has been nothing but kind and generous. She is under my protection as well, and I will not let anyone treat her this way."

When Calliope walked toward her husband with their son, little William reached for his father, who pulled the little boy into his arms. Their son put his hands on either side of the viscount's face. "No."

"No what, William?"

Their son turned and pointed at Mary Kate. "Kate's crying."

It was clear Mary Kate's tears upset their son, and the viscount was clearly loath to have their little one on the verge of tears himself. His loud sigh had Calliope leaning against her husband.

Mary Kate's eyes welled with tears again at the tender sight of the family she loved as if it were her own. She wiped her eyes and dug deep to find her smile. "I'm not crying anymore, William. See?"

The little one rested his head on his father's shoulder on one side, while Calliope rested her head on the other. Her belly clenched, and her chest felt tight.

"If you'll excuse me..." She couldn't say anything else without weeping, and she didn't want to do that after their sweet son had asked her not to.

She escaped before she embarrassed herself further. Servants were not supposed to show emotion at all, let alone break down into a puddle of tears, or shirk their duties. Would they ask her to leave? Would she need to find a position elsewhere? Dear Lord, would the viscount refuse to give her a reference?

Her head began to pound as her worries escalated to the breaking point. She'd been holding back her tears for three long weeks, not wanting to give Flaherty the satisfaction of hearing from either one of the duke's men at Chattsworth Manor that she'd been reduced to tears by the man who had been courting her, then rejected her.

She dashed down the hallway to the door to the servants' staircase and stumbled her way up. By the time she reached her room, she collapsed on her bed, her heart in shreds. Holding the pillow over her aching stomach, she finally let herself grieve for what was never meant to be. It was past time to accept what she hadn't wanted to believe: she didn't deserve Seamus Flaherty's love.

"I'LL BEAT HIM bloody," Garahan promised.

"Though I think he'd be deserving of it," Michael O'Malley said, "'tisn't right to beat on our hardheaded cousin just because he's got *bollocks* for brains. Especially since it's only been a few weeks since he's been shot."

Garahan grunted. "Mary Kate deserves far better than Flaherty."

"Aye," O'Malley agreed. "Who did ye have in mind?"

"Monroe."

"The farrier? Are ye daft?" O'Malley shook his head. "Ye'd

only be asking for trouble. What do we know about the man, other than he treats the horses well?"

Garahan shrugged. "Isn't that reason enough to encourage the man? He has an even temperament and a way with fractious fillies and stubborn geldings. Even though he knows she's being courted by Flaherty, Monroe asks after Mary Kate every time he comes to tend to the horses. 'Tis clear he's besotted with her."

"True enough," O'Malley agreed. "But the lass loves our *bollocks*-for-brains cousin."

"MacReady overheard Lady Calliope and his lordship when he was in the hallway outside of the nursery just now," Garahan confided. "Flaherty already cast her aside. He doesn't deserve her."

O'Malley waited a beat, then said, "'Tisn't uncommon for someone suffering the delirium of a high fever to say things they otherwise wouldn't."

"Mayhap 'tis how he really feels. Besides, Flaherty has always had a jealous bone. Remember the time he was half in love with Fitzroy's daughter?"

O'Malley sighed. "Aye, and he'd heard someone say she'd been out walking with Declan McClaren."

"Flaherty knocked the man on his arse the next time he saw him. Much to McClaren's surprise."

"And Fitzroy's daughter," O'Malley added. "She ended up helping McClaren to his feet and taking him home to her ma for tea."

The men were silent for a moment before Garahan asked, "Are ye meaning to interfere, Michael?"

"Aye, but I'm thinking—" The sound of hoofbeats in the distance had the two men turning to investigate. Garahan slowly smiled. "Well, well… Speak of the devil."

Flaherty dismounted and nodded to them. "Is Mary Kate in the kitchen?"

O'Malley and Garahan shared a look before O'Malley answered, "She's not feeling well."

"What's wrong? She is never ill. Has the physician been sent for?"

"'Tisn't a concern of yers," Garahan replied.

Flaherty marched over to him and grabbed him by his lapels. "Anything that has to do with the lass is me concern."

"That's not what we've heard," O'Malley said. "Let go of him."

Flaherty gave his cousin a hard shake before setting him free. He turned his back on Garahan, which was his first mistake. Not having his guard up was his second. Garahan's right cross leveled Flaherty.

O'Malley walked over and shoved Garahan aside. "Enough! Ye got her punch in. I'll not let yer temper cause friction within our ranks. We're blood, Garahan!"

O'Malley waited a beat before saying, "Best grab the bucket by the horse trough."

Garahan's eyes gleamed. "A grand suggestion, Michael." He scooped up water and tossed it on his cousin, who came to sputtering before lurching to his feet.

"What in the bloody hell did ye do that for?"

"The punch was for making the lass weep. The water was O'Malley's suggestion."

"Flaherty!"

The deep voice coming from behind the three men had them standing at attention.

Flaherty immediately answered, "Aye, yer lordship?"

Viscount Chattsworth's face was devoid of expression. "A word." He spared his men a glance, then said, "Have you been relieved of duty?"

"Just changing shifts, yer lordship," Garahan replied.

The viscount frowned at his men, but accepted the response and turned to Flaherty. "Follow me."

$$\longrightarrow\!\diamond\!\bullet\!\diamond\!\bullet\!\diamond\!\bullet\!\diamond\!\longleftarrow$$

CHAPTER FIVE

FLAHERTY HAD NO idea what had upset the viscount, but had a sneaking feeling that it had to do with Mary Kate. Had he heard what happened? Did everyone but himself know of the debacle? Had no one else ever spouted nonsense, or things they did not mean, when in the grips of wound fever? Surprised that the viscount had not turned toward the house, but the stables instead, Flaherty followed behind him. Best not to speak and interrupt whatever his lordship was thinking.

Chattsworth opened the side door to the stables and entered, nodded to his stable master, and continued over to where the man's pride and joy—Maximus, a huge black Thoroughbred stallion—watched them approach from his stall.

Flaherty had a healthy respect for the beautiful animal, who was huge, strong, and had a temper to match the viscount's. He wondered if he would end up spending time currying the animal when Chattsworth put a hand in his pocket and retrieved an apple. "Sorry I was delayed, Maximus. We'll be leaving for our ride after Flaherty and I come to an understanding."

Having worked closely with the viscount when stationed at Chattsworth Manor, Flaherty knew to wait until the man was ready to speak. As one who spoke to his horse about all manner of things, Flaherty didn't mind waiting. Chattsworth's temper rivaled his, so it would be wise to be patient. It was obvious the viscount wanted to speak with him about Mary Kate. Would the man believe him?

"I hope you are here to apologize to Miss Donovan."

"I am."

"And do you believe that is all that you need to do? Apologize for breaking that young woman's heart? A woman who has been my wife's right hand for nearly two years?"

"Ye have to believe me, yer lordship, that I don't recall saying anything at all to her."

Chattsworth raised one dark brow—the same habit His Grace, the viscount's distant cousin, had when he was irritated. "And you expect me to believe you?"

"I don't lie."

The viscount growled, but did not contradict Flaherty. All of the men in the duke's guard were trustworthy. "Am I to believe that it had to do with wound fever?"

"Aye, yer lordship. One lead ball in the arm is dangerous, as ye well know—but two in the back..." Flaherty hoped the man remembered how he and O'Malley had helped the viscount off the dueling field after the viscount had leapt onto it to prevent murder. The viscount had been watching and saw Chellenham turn around at the count of fifteen—*not* twenty. He prevented the dastard from shooting Lord Coddington in the back. Lady Aurelia, his wife's sister-of-the-heart, would have been inconsolable if anything had happened to her uncle.

"You are a man of honor, Flaherty, and I know you would not intentionally hurt a woman's feelings—"

Flaherty interrupted, "Especially the woman I've been courting."

The viscount frowned. "You've been courting her for months. Your cousins married within weeks of rescuing the women who captured their hearts. Why have you waited?"

Flaherty did not want to sound like a lovesick *eedjit*, but wasn't that what held him back? Would the viscount think him weak of heart for carrying a jealous grudge against his own cousin?

"The longer you wait, the harder it will be to confide," Chattsworth said. "Especially if you've been holding it in for months."

"Mary Kate's always saying how Garahan was the one who saved her—when all he did was help her up off the footpath outside Lady Kittrick's town house."

The viscount's surprise was evident, but only lasted for a heartbeat, then he returned to a neutral expression. "I see. If I remember correctly, Calliope mentioned how frightening it was when the duke's carriage slid on ice and ended on its side over that ditch. You were the one to pull her and Mary Kate to safety."

Flaherty met the intensity of Chattsworth's gaze. "Aye."

Maximus finished the apple and nudged the viscount's shoulder, gaining a chuckle out of him. "Fresh out of apples. How about a carrot?" The horse's ears twitched, and Chattsworth snorted. "That means yes."

"Yer horse loves carrots almost as much as apples." Flaherty's throat felt tight at the thought of repeating the harsh words he did not remember uttering, but he shoved past the feeling. "In truth, I may be jealous of Garahan being the first to rescue the lass, but mine was more urgent—her ladyship and Mary Kate could have been injured if we hadn't had the coachman holding the team while Michael held me legs, and I pulled the ladies free."

The viscount fed the carrot to Maximus. When the animal finished off the treat, Chattsworth turned back to Flaherty. "If I could hazard a guess, I would think that the first rescue may be more prominent in Mary Kate's mind because it was symbolic."

"I'm not following yer line of thinking, yer lordship."

"She was rudely ousted from her position within her mistress's household, as if she were a stray animal with no feelings. Her humiliation had to have been severe. Garahan treated her as if she mattered. Like the rest of the men in His Grace's guard, Garahan would never treat a woman as if she had no value. Every one of you treat all women—no matter their station in life, or what has happened in their past—as if they are important.

Worthy of your regard. Precious."

"'Tis me hard head that has had trouble convincing meself that she isn't pining for Garahan."

"Has she acted in a way that would have you thinking that she does?"

For the first time, Flaherty actually thought about her actions—forgetting the whole "who rescued whom" first. "I'm thinking she smiles at him too much."

"She has a sunny disposition, which, according to Calliope, blossomed after a few weeks working here at Chattsworth. Mary Kate is generous with her smiles, Flaherty. Even MacReady has mentioned it gives him a bit of a lift first thing in the morning when she greets him."

"'Tis her eyes," he confessed. "They bewitched me from the start."

"Just her eyes?"

"Her fiery hair slips from its pins and just begs to be..." He closed his mouth before he sounded like a complete *eedjit*.

"Calliope was so excited when you first asked permission to court Mary Kate—not that you needed approval, though it was good of you to do so. My wife tells me that Mary Kate spoke of you constantly, until she returned from Lippincott Manor a few weeks ago."

"How do I regain her trust, when I don't remember losing it?"

The viscount bade his stallion goodbye and motioned for Flaherty to follow him out of the stables. Walking toward the manor house, Chattsworth replied, "You might want to begin with that last question. Then remind her that you'd had wound fever for five days. She was exhausted from caring for you— which you don't remember, and how could you? It may be that you did not bellow at her at all, but had a sharp tone, and again, why would you not? The pain from having two lead balls extracted had to have been excruciating. I know for a fact how *one* lead ball feels."

Flaherty lifted one shoulder and then the other, testing the healing wound. "Still pains me, but I hope ye'll keep that to yerself, yer lordship. I'm needing to get back to me duties to the earl. I can deal with the discomfort—besides, I held me own against Sean going a few rounds an hour ago."

Chattsworth chuckled. "Most men would simply take their horse out for a ride to test their endurance, not engage in a bare-knuckle bout." He stared at Flaherty. "But you are not most men—not a one of you are."

"Faith, I'm glad ye recognize that fact, yer lordship. 'Tis how we keep ourselves ready to defend all comers, in all circumstances—well, that and keeping our weaponry skills sharp."

"I'll have Calliope speak to Mary Kate and let her know you are here. My wife will be able to cajole her into seeing you. I'll ask Mrs. Romney to prepare a tea tray and deliver it to the small sitting room near the library. It's one of Calliope's favorite rooms, and I know she and Mary Kate spent time there while I was in London tending to His Grace's affairs."

"Will there be scones?"

Chattsworth laughed. "Aye, with jam and clotted cream."

Twenty minutes later, Flaherty and the viscount were in the sitting room deep into a discussion of Emmett O'Malley's recent rescue and marriage to Michaela Colborne—the angel of the streets—then nearly dying. To hear Darby Garahan tell it, Emmett *had* died. Though Tremayne had been skeptical, even Michaela's father, Dr. Colborne, was inclined to believe that a miracle had happened.

Calliope arrived alone. "Mary Kate is willing to speak to you, but not at the moment."

Flaherty felt the blow to his heart. Had he lost her affection as well as her respect? "I see."

The viscountess walked over to where the men stood and slipped her arm through her husband's. "She has been lying down with a cool cloth on her eyes. Though she may not want me to tell you, you should know that her eyes are so red and puffy from crying, she can hardly open them."

Flaherty felt as if he'd been horsewhipped. "That's me fault, too. I've made her cry. If I'd been in me right mind, I never would have lashed out at her." He sought Calliope's gaze and rasped, "Ye believe me, don't ye, yer ladyship?"

"After caring for William after he'd been shot—and you remember what shape he was in—you and Michael O'Malley were there at the time and helped him off the dueling field."

"I do remember."

"I cannot even remember half of what William muttered when the fever set in, though his did not last as long as yours."

"The half that ye do remember, did he seem out of character?"

Calliope softly smiled. "Yes, and I'll be certain to relay that to Mary Kate when I go and check on her in an hour. She was so exhausted that she was drifting off to sleep by the time I closed her door behind me."

"Shouldn't someone be sitting with her? What if she gets up and has trouble seeing, or faints from lack of food?"

"I've already made the arrangements, but will check on her myself shortly."

"Thank ye, yer ladyship." Flaherty turned to the viscount and thanked him. "I should be returning. There's a new group of footmen who still need more training. Tomorrow I'll be returning to me regular shift."

"Would you be able to come back tomorrow around teatime?" Calliope asked. "I believe that will be enough time for Mary Kate to have rested and be ready to speak with you. I know that she'll listen to what you have to say...provided you begin with the apology."

"Aye, yer ladyship. I'll be back."

A flicker of hope in his heart buoyed him. Surely the lass would listen to what he had to say, and forgive him, provided that Lady Calliope spoke to Mary Kate about how the viscount had acted when he suffered from wound fever.

Riding back to Lippincott Manor, he felt as if a tiny portion of the guilt-laced sorrow weighing him down had lifted.

"Lord? 'Tis Flaherty again—Seamus Flaherty, just so ye aren't thinking it's one of me brothers. I could use yer help convincing the lass."

CHAPTER SIX

MARY KATE WAS embarrassed that Lady Calliope had witnessed her abject misery. While she and her ladyship had formed a wonderful working relationship, the viscountess had offered more...friendship. Would Mary Kate's neglecting her duties earlier force them to let her go?

Worry had her wondering if she should have confided in her ladyship a few weeks ago. Would it change the outcome? Mayhap she had misremembered how Flaherty had sounded when he railed at her. He had to have been in excruciating pain at the time. But what if she had recalled the exchange exactly as it had occurred?

Lifting her chin, she resolved to accept the outcome. Either she would be able to continue working for Lord and Lady Chattsworth, or they would have no choice but to let her go. If that be the Lord's will, then Mary Kate vowed to accept their decision to let her go with equanimity and grace. Surely they would not turn her away without a recommendation.

Would they?

She poured the now-tepid water from the pitcher into the bowl, dipped the sliver of rose-scented soap in the water, and washed. The water normally soothed her, but not today. She dried her face and hands and smoothed her gown—the few wrinkles could not be helped. Hopefully, her tear-ravaged face would not add weight to their decision, if it was to let her go. A glance in the looking glass over the washstand had her accepting the fact that it would take hours for the swelling around her eyes to go down. The red rimming her eyes and coloring the end of her nose would not disappear for at least a few more hours.

Mary Kate knew she needed to speak with her ladyship before any more time passed. She had to have been in her room for at least an hour. A whole hour away from her duties, right when little William would be eating his midday meal and then be put down for his nap. Lady Calliope usually needed Mary Kate's assistance during the early afternoons more than she had a month ago. The poor viscountess had been so tired of late, leaving Mary Kate to wonder if her mistress could be expecting again—not that she would ever ask such a personal question.

The only reason she had been brave enough to put that delicate question to her ladyship the first time was that the poor woman had been unable to rise in the mornings without losing the contents of her stomach. Yet the rest of the day, she appeared hale and hearty. Mary Kate had suspected that Lady Calliope had been carrying the viscount's heir, yet when she mentioned the possibility to her ladyship, Lady Calliope's shock had been palpable. Mary Kate remembered her expression of wonder as she confessed that the thought had never occurred to her. Her ladyship's tears of joy had warmed Mary Kate's heart.

Resolved to put the question to Lady Calliope, and not let the matter fester inside of her any longer, Mary Kate opened her door. No one was about on the third floor at this hour, so there was no need to avoid anyone. She made her way down the servants' staircase to the nursery, where she knew she would find her mistress. As she drew nearer to the door, she heard the little boy asking for her. Guilt slashed through her.

She knocked on the door, and entered when bidden. "Lady Calliope, please accept my apology. I have never neglected my duties before, and will do my utmost never to do so again."

The viscountess looked up from where she sat rocking her

son. "What if another man dares to do or say something that breaks your heart again?"

Mary Kate shook her head. "What makes you think—" It would be ridiculous to continue to pretend Flaherty had not broken her heart. Looking directly at the viscountess, she rasped, "I shall never allow myself to fall in love again."

Calliope's lips lifted into a small smile. "Speaking from experience, I know how difficult that would be to do so. Tell me, Mary Kate, have you truly fallen out of love with Flaherty?"

"How could I when—" Mary Kate felt her face heat at the knee-jerk response that had burst from her lips. Shock had her mouth gaping open for a moment, before she collected herself enough to snap it closed.

The viscountess's smile widened. "Do you not remember how brokenhearted I was when you and I arrived here? William had left me at Wyndmere Hall, after pledging his life to me before the vicar and witnesses. My hopes and dreams curled up, withered, and died when he turned and walked away from me."

"I have not forgotten. Your sorrow hurt my heart."

Calliope traced the tip of her finger along the curve of her son's cheek as he rested it against her breast. "That was the first time William broke my heart—the second time was when I overheard the staff mention that he was in London tending to the duke's affairs. William had not seen fit to confide his whereabouts to me. That he could not escape my presence fast enough after we were wed was evident, but the fact that he was within a days' ride and had not let me know hurt." She paused to press a gentle kiss to her son's forehead. "I never thought I would be able to forgive him, but my heart had other ideas. Especially after we talked and realized that the duke sensed we would be at cross purposes. William needed to marry an heiress to save Chatts-worth Manor, and I hoped to marry for love."

Mary Kate forced herself to speak past the tightness in her throat. "And it came to light that the duke ordered his lordship to London to take care of the duke's affairs there, while the duke packed you up and sent you here to Chattsworth…with me."

"Guarded by two of his trusted guards, Michael O'Malley and Seamus Flaherty."

Mary Kate sighed. "The duke had no idea what state his lordship's home was in."

Calliope agreed. "Nor did His Grace realize the extent of the turmoil surrounding my father-in-law's disappearance at the time. Thank goodness the truth came to light and William's father returned safely."

"It was a day of celebration," Mary Kate agreed. "Are you encouraging me to be patient and give Flaherty a chance to explain why he would say such awful things to me?"

The viscountess nodded. "It is never wise to jump to conclusions, especially when one doesn't know the full extent of the circumstances regarding any one situation. More often than not, we are judging by past experiences that have colored our way of thinking."

"You have given me a lot to think about, your ladyship."

"Then you'll speak to Flaherty when he returns tomorrow?"

Mary Kate frowned. "How can you be so sure that he will return? He has ignored me for weeks!"

"Ah, but the poor man had been shot protecting Dermott's wife and was healing, which is no small feat after suffering wound fever. He did not realize he was ignoring you. I have no doubt he thought it was *your* choice not to see him."

"What a bumblebroth this situation has become," Mary Kate murmured. "Do you think the explanation is as simple as that? Could it have been his fevered brain's imaginings that had him speaking to me that way?"

"From what I know having been under the man's protection, I would be inclined to believe just that. Grant him the opportunity to at least speak to you, Mary Kate. I believe he truly loves you."

"Then why would he constantly bring up Garahan's name in our conversations, asking me if I still harbored feelings for the man?"

"How many times have you brought up Garahan's name yourself, whenever you wax poetic about how he saved you the day you were so rudely ousted from Lady Kittrick's home?"

Mary Kate opened her mouth, then closed it. How could she answer that question without sounding hypocritical?

As if her ladyship understood, she rose from the rocking chair and walked over to the cradle, settling her son down for a nap. "Now then, I believe tea and something sweet is what we need to soothe frazzled nerves and feelings. Don't you?"

At the suggestion, Mary Kate walked over to the corner and gave a tug on the bellpull. A few moments later, there was a knock on the door.

Rather than answer, and take a chance that she would wake William, Lady Calliope walked over to the door, opened it, made her request, and closed the door. "Now then, why don't you have a seat and tell me what else is worrying you."

Mary Kate walked over to the grouping of chairs on the other side of the room and sat. Waiting for Lady Calliope to do the same, she wondered what else to say.

"Why don't I tell you what I have noticed?" Calliope suggested.

Feeling as if she had had every emotion wrung out of her, Mary Kate could only nod.

"You are quick to mention Garahan as the man to have rescued you—even in front of his wife—which I would ask you to stop doing. Especially given that we are both aware of the beatings Melinda received before Garahan rescued *her*. As far as I know, and unless you tell me differently right now, you were never in that type of situation. Haven't you noticed how quiet Melinda is whenever you are around? Do you not think she compares herself to you, trying to see you through her husband's eyes?"

Perplexed, Mary Kate asked, "Why would she do that?"

"Why would you continue to ignore the courageous way Flaherty and O'Malley saved us from injury when they pulled us to safety after the accident by never mentioning it? Why only speak of Garahan?"

Before Mary Kate could answer, Calliope continued, "If I did not know you as well as I do, I would think that you are trying to outshine Melinda—who, from all accounts and what I know of her situation, would never speak of what occurred that necessitated her being rescued, nor why James Garahan felt the overwhelming need to save her."

Mary Kate's eyes welled with tears yet again. "I would never intentionally wish to harm Melinda with my words or actions."

Calliope reached for her maid's hand and gave it a quick squeeze. "I know that you would not. That is the only reason I hesitated to speak of it before now. Unfortunately, it has become quite obvious to everyone concerned—*except for you*—that you are oblivious to the pain you have caused, and dare I speculate tension between Garahan and his wife?"

The knock on the door interrupted what Mary Kate had been about to say. Relieved by the interruption, she shot up from her chair and answered the door, letting the footman bearing the requested tea tray in. She set out the tea as Lady Calliope directed and closed the door behind the footman. Putting off continuing the difficult discussion, Mary Kate stopped to check on the little William.

Satisfied he hadn't been disturbed from sleeping, she rejoined her mistress. Continuing the unusual tradition of taking tea with the viscount's housekeeper and the cook when they first arrived at Chattsworth, she and Calliope often enjoyed tea together. In the beginning it had been a way to learn about the estate from those few servants who worked for the viscount.

Yet it had also helped the two of them to know one another better and to forge a friendship that included escapades that had nearly driven the viscount mad with worry. Though his growing love for Calliope had had his lordship forgiving her for not following his instruction and remaining behind—especially when her ladyship had learned of the duel.

"Forgive me, Lady Calliope, I—"

"I am not the one you should beg forgiveness from," Calliope reminded her.

Mary Kate's stomach ached. She wondered just how many times she had brought up the subject of being rescued in front of Melinda. "She must hate me."

"I do not believe she is capable of hating anyone," Calliope murmured. "Though if she were, her cousin, who so horribly mistreated her, would be the person fully deserving of it."

"Do you think Melinda would accept my apology? I know it must seem as if it is too little, too late."

"I am quite certain that she will. Now then, drink up, and I shall tell you of my plan for you to smooth things over with Melinda and Flaherty."

Mary Kate's eyes widened at the mention of the man's name. "I do not owe him an apology. He—"

"It never hurts to swallow one's pride and apologize, even if one does not believe one has been in the wrong, but wronged."

"But he—"

Calliope set her teacup on its saucer and placed it on the table between them. "I do believe a bite of something sweet may be what you need to stop protesting and see that you must apologize to both Garahan's wife and Flaherty. Only then will you have opened yourself up to the healing that needs to take place before you will even listen to Flaherty's explanation."

Mary Kate knew when to speak and when to listen. She nodded.

Satisfied, the viscountess passed her a plate with a generous slice of butter cake on it. "Eat up, then we shall make our plans for when you will meet with Melinda, and what you will say to begin to mend fences with her. She is a lovely woman and has suffered so much at the hands of those who should have been protecting her."

The viscountess's words hit home. "You would know more

than most how that would have affected her, having suffered yourself."

Calliope's gaze met hers. "Yes, I do. Now then, here's what I think you should do…"

CHAPTER SEVEN

AS HE HEADED back to Lippincott Manor, Flaherty's head pounded in time with his gelding's hooves. Though he could not put his finger on when, he thought he'd detected a hint that Lady Calliope was hiding something from him—aside from Mary Kate Donovan. If he could describe the feeling, it would be as if the skeletal finger of the banshee skated up his spine.

Shoving that to the back of his mind, he cleared his thoughts of all that he had heard since rising that morning. The first thing he intended to do upon returning was to demand that Sean tell him the whole of what happened, from the moment he'd lost consciousness when the physician started digging for the first lead ball. As he followed the road leading to the manor house, Flaherty had a feeling the tale was incomplete.

The woman he'd been courting believed that he had tossed her out, and he could not remember doing so. He knew the truth was there, somewhere in the middle of what she believed and what he believed.

Dermott approached as Flaherty dismounted. "Ye don't look like a man who's about to wed the woman he loves."

Flaherty was still mulling over the fact that he hadn't even seen the lass, let alone had the opportunity to ask her to marry him. He was man enough to admit that it would have been an awkward conversation, being as how he would have had to lead off with the apology he owed her. In truth, he wasn't so sure that he had insulted the lass, but then again, why would his cousins make up a tale like that when it would hurt Mary Kate?

Flaherty led his horse into the stable for a rubdown. One of the earl's stable lads was there to take over the chore, which might have had something to do with the fact that Dermott had been dogging his steps, demanding to know what had happened. Once the gelding was preening, his hide rippling with pleasure at being combed, Flaherty confided, "The lass wasn't in any shape to speak to me."

"Has something happened to her? Surely we would have heard, because their ladyships are thick as thieves and both have formed friendships with their lady's maids," Dermott reminded him.

"Lady Calliope said Mary Kate had been weeping." Just the thought that it had been because of the harsh words he could not remember saying had Flaherty falling silent.

"Then ye aren't in need of the license or the vicar tonight?"

Flaherty's hand curled into a tight fist as the guilt of causing the lass pain sliced his guts to ribbons. He didn't realize he'd fisted his hand to level his cousin with a punch until Dermott leaned to the side to avoid the blow.

"Well now," he rumbled, "I'm guessing yer reply is a no, then." With a shake of his head, he continued, "Sean has the footmen assembled for today's lesson in hitting their target."

Duty calls. "I hope at least one of them will hit the target I set up for them today."

"Ye'd think at least one of them would have had experience firing a weapon," Dermott remarked. "When will ye switch to a pistol? The footmen should be comfortable with both rifle and pistol if they're going to be protecting the duke's family."

"That they should," Flaherty agreed. "Would ye mind telling his lordship that me plans have been put off for a day or two?"

"Aye." The understanding in his cousin's eyes helped to ease some of the worry that the longer the lass hid from him—and now that he had time to reason it out, he was certain that she had been avoiding him—the harder it would be to convince her that she was mistaken. Added to that thought was the tiny seed of doubt that took root: Mary Kate Donovan would not accept his offer of marriage.

Flaherty did not have the time to worry about what might happen—he was expected to continue training the footmen. He sure as *shite* could not do that if he was bemoaning the fact that the slip of a lass had a hold of his heart, distracting him from his duties. O'Malleys and Garahans let themselves be distracted by a pretty face—Flahertys did not!

He entered the building by the rear door and swiftly made his way toward the kitchen to see if Mrs. Wyatt had left him the promised scones. The cook's expectant gaze had him internally flinching as he answered her unasked question. "I'm to return tomorrow. Mary Kate was not free to see me."

Mrs. Wyatt's expression all but shouted her thoughts. Instead of giving voice to what she was thinking, the woman said, "It sounds as if you could use a bit of jam on those scones I set aside for you."

Flaherty appreciated that she'd changed the subject. Thinking of her mouthwatering scones, he smiled. "I would love nothing more, but I'm certain Finch has the next group of footmen ready and waiting for me to take them through their paces today."

Mrs. Wyatt wrapped two warm scones in a linen cloth, handed it to him, and frowned. "I overheard the physician remind Mrs. Jones that you could return to your normal diet and activities, provided you did not overdo it."

When he did not reply, she sighed. "By the time you've finished instructing the footmen, the second batch of meat pies will be ready. I'll set some aside for you."

He grinned at her. "You are a treasure, Mrs. Wyatt. Thank ye." Passing through the door to the main part of the house, he nodded to the butler who had been waiting for him.

"Ah, there you are, Flaherty." Finch waited a beat. Though

the older retainer did not ask, it was obvious from the expectant look on his face that he hoped Flaherty would share news of when he and Mary Kate would marry. The man was doomed to disappointment. Flaherty shook his head at the butler, who gave a brief nod, then turned to instruct the footman stationed outside the earl's library to assemble the next group for target practice.

When they were alone, Finch remarked, "Miss Donovan has a kind heart. I do believe she just needs a bit of time to realize it was the fever talking."

"Does everyone but me know what I said?" Flaherty demanded.

The butler squared his shoulders and lifted his chin, as if it would make him appear any taller than his five feet, eight inches of height. "Miss Donovan was the only person able to calm you when you were tossing and turning, burning with fever."

The butler's comment added another dagger to Flaherty's heart. "I swear I don't remember telling her to leave."

Finch met and held the Irishman's gaze long enough to have Flaherty fighting the urge to squirm. "Even the strongest of men cannot control the rambling of their minds when a fever takes hold. I believe you."

The sound of footsteps approaching had the butler falling silent and Flaherty turning to greet the men. "Well now, I hope ye're ready to take on the new target I've asked Sean to set up for ye."

The group followed him down the hallway to the side door that would lead them to the outbuilding where he had been living since being permanently assigned the duty of guarding Earl Lippincott, Lady Aurelia, and their son.

As promised, his cousin had set up two targets for the men to use. One at a reasonable distance, and the other a bit beyond. He hoped to hell that at least one of the men would be able to hit their mark. "Now then, lads, we'll be starting with pistols and then moving on to rifles. Who wants to shoot first?"

The first two footmen hit the edge of the target. The third

managed to get closer to the center. Finally, the last man hit just to the left of dead center. Flaherty cheered, "Well done, lad! I'm thinking ye've been practicing, though, for the life of me, cannot imagine when ye've had the time."

The younger man shrugged, while the others ribbed him good-naturedly about his hidden skill. Flaherty knew from experience that the lad had not magically been imbued with the talent. He was used to firing a weapon.

"Not everyone who is employed in a position was trained or born into the job. At times, a man accepts any job that will help feed his family."

"Is it true that you are a former soldier?" one of the men asked.

Flaherty shrugged. "Officially, that would be no." He pitched his voice low to add, "Unofficially, I have been known to lead a mission or two back home, but ye did not hear that from me lips."

The men readily agreed, which was a relief. Flaherty knew not to speak of his political leanings as a lad. The bitter memory of losing his Uncle Patrick O'Malley—falsely imprisoned and later exonerated, only to die in his brother's arms hours before they were released—was still fresh in his mind. The Flaherty connection to the O'Malley family was through his ma's side. His grandma was an O'Malley. Every member of his family, as well as his rebellious countrymen, would fight to the death not only for their freedom, but to protect their families. Not one of them would ever boast of their exploits—nor their da's or grandda's—for fear of calling attention to what was better left in the past.

Flaherty walked over to the table where he'd set out the weapons and munitions they'd be using. He lifted the Kentucky long rifle, turned, and began a detailed explanation of how the rifle compared to the Brown Bess musket.

"Is that an American rifle?" one of the footmen asked.

"Aye. Me O'Malley cousins live on both sides of the Atlantic. This beauty was a gift to me cousin, Patrick." Flaherty set it down to hold up the English rifle. "Though the Brown Bess is a handy weapon to have, the Kentucky long rifle uses a smaller caliber .50 compared to .75. What's more, 'tis more accurate—up to four hundred yards!"

The footman who'd hit his target said, "I'd like to shoot it."

"Let's see how you aim and shoot it, then, Sterns."

The youngest among the footmen held out his hands and just stared at the long, sleek maple barrel as Flaherty placed it in his hands. "Ye'll need to stop admiring this beauty long enough to learn how to load her."

Sterns watched, listened, and loaded the rifle. When prompted, he glanced at Flaherty.

"Use the rear sight to line up the front sight, aim, then fire."

The young man shot and hit the target dead-on.

"Excellent! We've got a sharpshooter among us, lads," Flaherty proclaimed. "Who's next?"

A short while later, the group helped collect the weapons and Flaherty looped two rifles over one shoulder. The other two he'd have to carry.

"I can help you carry them," Sterns offered.

"Won't Finch be looking for ye by now, lad?"

"Aye, but he'll ask the others where I am."

Between the two of them, they stored the weapons in the guards' quarters. Before Sterns left, Flaherty thanked him again. "Ye've fine aim, lad. I'll be letting his lordship and Sean know that ye'll be me top choice to have on hand should we need an armed guard protecting her ladyship." The footman's grin had Flaherty chuckling. "Best let Finch know ye're returning to yer duties. I don't need himself chasing me down demanding to know what kept ye."

"Thank you, Flaherty!"

He nodded and watched as Sterns loped toward the rear door. Flaherty's upper back ached, but he rolled his shoulders a few times to relieve the pain and followed behind the footman. Once inside, he sought out Sean first. He'd give his report, and his cousin would relay it to the earl. It had been an hour well spent, as they'd identified another footman with fine aim who knew his way around both pistol and rifle. An excellent advantage should any more of the duke's enemies come calling.

Flaherty would bet a week's worth of Mrs. Wyatt's scones that it wouldn't be too long before another of the duke's many enemies would come slithering around, looking to cause confusion and delay. If and when they did, the duke's men would be ready.

CHAPTER EIGHT

THIS WAS GOING to be harder than Mary Kate envisioned. It wasn't uttering the words "I am sorry" with conviction that worried her—it was the fact that she had unknowingly been striking out at Melinda Garahan. A woman who had been victimized and mistreated by her own family. A story so close to Lady Calliope's that it hurt Mary Kate's heart to know that she was the one who had been causing strife in Melinda's life, and more—hurting the woman's heart.

At Calliope's suggestion, Mary Kate carried the tea tray into the small room at the end of the hallway and placed it on the table set out for their use. She couldn't sit. Waiting had always been something Mary Kate did not do well. She paced until she heard a light footfall. Bracing herself, she stood where Melinda would be able to see her as she approached the door.

"Oh." Garahan's wife stopped in the doorway. "I didn't expect you to be waiting for me. Am I late?"

"Not at all," Mary Kate assured her. "I'm early. Won't you sit down? Mrs. Romney has prepared this lovely tea for us. Lady Calliope will be joining us shortly."

Melinda hesitated, then entered the room and sat down. Relieved that Garahan's wife had not ignored her request to join her for tea, Mary Kate sat across from Melinda and poured her a cup. "Would you like cream and sugar?"

The other woman did not answer right away. She seemed anxious, leaving Mary Kate to wonder if she had caused her to feel that way. Needing to get the hardest part over with, she set down the teapot and quietly asked again, "Cream? Sugar?"

Finally Melinda replied, "Yes, thank you. Er…Lady Calliope said that you had something you wanted to talk to me about."

After passing the sugar and cream to Melinda, Mary Kate picked up her teacup, sipped, and set her cup back on its saucer. Not knowing how to begin, she simply blurted out, "I am so sorry!"

Melinda blinked and set her cup down. "For what, exactly?"

Mary Kate had no idea what to say at first and wondered if the other woman was baiting her. But the perplexed look on Melinda's face had her replying, "I should not have constantly brought up Garahan's rescuing me months after it happened. After he rescued you, it was obvious he was in love with you. And then after you married—" She bit her lip and shook her head, unable to continue as guilt plagued her. Mary Kate glanced up only to find Melinda was not looking at her, but staring down at her lap.

Needing to explain, she rushed out, "I had been treated so abominably by Lady Kittrick's cook and her other servants that I felt as if I were constantly being ridiculed…chastised…meant to feel as if I were nothing more than a scrap of dirt they tried to wipe off the soles of their shoes."

Melinda looked up at that. "How did you find the courage to leave?"

Mary Kate sighed. "I didn't."

"But you said James rescued you," Melinda insisted. "I don't understand."

"Lady Kittrick was in a rage over something…come to think of it, she was always angry. That particular day, she took it out on her cook, who took it out on me. One thing led to another, and before I realized what was happening, Cook had me by the arm and was dragging me down the hallway to the side door. She shoved me out onto the sidewalk."

She glanced up and noticed that Melinda was still looking at her, listening. She'd best get the rest of her apology out. "I landed hard on my hands and knees and was still in a state of shock that I'd been booted out—without a reference. I had no idea how I would find another position without one."

Melinda reached across the table and patted the back of Mary Kate's hand. "That's when my James found you."

A tear formed and slid past Mary Kate's guard. She cleared her throat. "Yes. That's when he found me, coaxed me to my feet, and led me over to the earl's carriage."

"And he took you to the duke's town house, where Mrs. O'Toole took care of you?"

"Yes, the duke's cook is the kindest of women. I was unsure if I should be going anywhere with a man I did not know, but there was something about Garahan. It's hard to put my finger on it, but—"

Melinda interrupted her, "There was something in his manner that immediately had you trusting him."

"Yes."

"I felt the same way, though I fought against trusting him. I'd trusted too easily before, and it landed me in an untenable position of working for my cousin, who wanted me to..." She trailed off.

Mary Kate, seizing the opportunity, reached for Melinda's hand and squeezed it. "You do not have to say another word. Garahan convinced you to go with him, promising that he would find you a position with better pay in a respectable establishment."

Relieved not to have to continue, Melinda nodded.

"Can you forgive me for harping on it for so long? I should have let it go, but the longer I thought about it, the more convinced I was that it was a turning point in my life. He had been there at the exact moment that I needed him to be. That he passed me off to O'Malley to drive me to the duke's townhouse was the part I am forever forgetting to mention."

Melinda's smile was brilliant. "James has a way of making you feel as if you are the only person in the whole world when his eyes meet yours. I know. He has the power to turn my mind to mush—and when he kisses me…"

Mary Kate smiled. "The last time Seamus kissed me, every thought just leaked out of my brain."

Garahan's wife stared at Mary Kate for a moment before speaking, "You really do care for Flaherty, don't you?"

"I do, though God only knows why after what he said to me."

"Oh, but you have to forgive a man when he's suffering from wound fever. Sometimes they say awful things…and sometimes wonderful things. It depends on the type of wound."

"I have never heard anything more preposterous," Mary Kate mumbled.

"Garahan was saying crazy things the last time he got knocked on the head."

Mary Kate chuckled. "I understand that is a regular occurrence with the men in His Grace's private guard."

"True," Melinda admitted. "But sometimes he's not affected by a good whack on the head, like when he and Michael O'Malley are sparring, practicing their bare-knuckle skills."

"I see." At least, Mary Kate *thought* she did. "Has Garahan ever suffered from wound fever?"

"Not to the extent that Flaherty has. You must have been beside yourself with worry for him."

She felt her throat tighten with emotion she could not give in to. She could cry later. "I was."

"I hope you can find it in your heart to forgive Flaherty. From what I've heard Garahan and Michael say, he would never treat a woman that shabbily…especially one he has been courting since that day I first met you at the duke's town house."

Mary Kate felt herself flush, remembering the way Seamus kissed her—that first time. Her brain had simply shut down. "Maybe I should."

"Don't let your misplaced pride or sense of injustice hold you back from the man you so obviously care deeply for."

"Am I that transparent?"

"To someone who is in love herself?" Melinda asked. "Yes, you are. Give him a chance to apologize and make it up to you. You will not regret it."

Mary Kate sighed. "Will you forgive me for being so unkind?"

"I already have."

"You have?"

Melinda nodded. "You do not have a mean bone in your body. Mayhap a thoughtless one or two, but not a mean one."

"Er… Thank you."

They were both smiling and chatting amiably when Lady Calliope arrived with Mrs. Romney, who was carrying a fresh pot of tea. Calliope's eyes lit up. "I am so happy that you two have had a chance to finally speak to one another and correct this misunderstanding."

"We have," Melinda replied. "Now all we need to do is send word to Flaherty that Mary Kate is ready to speak with him."

Mary Kate hesitated, but a direct look from Lady Calliope had her changing her mind. "Yes. I believe that would be best. Thank you for forgiving me, Melinda. I will be forever in your debt."

Melinda shared a glance with Lady Calliope. "Not if you send word right away that you need to speak to Flaherty."

How could Mary Kate refuse? She looked at Lady Calliope and asked, "Is it too much trouble to send word?"

Calliope beamed at her. "Not at all."

Two hours later, Mary Kate found herself waiting for Seamus Flaherty to arrive.

CHAPTER NINE

"FLAHERTY! GET YER arse over here!"

Flaherty lifted his head and glanced over his shoulder. "Have ye lost yer mind then, Sean? Ye just told me to switch shifts with Dermott."

Sean O'Malley crossed his arms and glared at him, his typical stance when waiting for Flaherty to comply.

Mumbling, Flaherty wondered aloud, "Why in the bloody hell did His Grace decide only O'Malleys would be in charge at each of his estates?"

He must not have been using his inside voice, because Sean replied, "His Grace needed men known for having a clear head in the middle of chaos."

Flaherty snorted. "Oh, aye, and whose head was clear when yer lovely wife Mignonette was in danger?" Before Sean could answer, Flaherty reminded him, "As God is me witness, it wasn't yerself."

His cousin ignored him. Flaherty knew he had no choice but to obey orders—he'd taken an oath. An oath he would die to uphold.

"What has ye barking at me now? I'm making progress with the footmen I've been training, especially Sterns. He's one of the youngest in the bunch, but has an eagle eye. Rarely misses the center of whatever target ye set up for us."

"That's all well and good, but ye're needed."

"Mrs. O'Toole's next batch of scones is out of the oven?"

O'Malley chuckled. "Nay, a summons from Chattsworth Manor. Mary Kate's asking for ye."

Flaherty felt the blood drain from his head to his toes and fought to lock his knees in place. He cleared his throat. "Did the missive say anything else?"

Sean shrugged. "'Twasn't a missive. One of the stable lads was instructed to give me the message and to return immediately to Chattsworth."

"I'd best report to me shift first—I can go over later…"

"Ye'll go now."

"But I—"

"Won't argue with yer older, wiser cousin-in-charge," Sean told him.

"Ye only have eleven months on me…and barely an inch in height. I'll argue any time I feel ye need it."

Sean's face lost all expression, and Flaherty knew he'd pushed his cousin too far. He was only trying to make light of a situation that could control his future—and Mary Kate's. Leave it to an O'Malley to push Flaherty to submit to his orders. Well, normally, if he wasn't twisted up into knots over the lass, he might have done so without a qualm.

Bloody hell, he'd been worried the lass would never deign to speak to him again, let alone let him hold her against his heart and brush the tears from her cheeks, kiss her supple mouth until she breathed out that little sigh she'd made the last few times he'd kissed her. His guts tied into knots when he remembered the sound, and her capitulation, as she melted into his embrace.

He squared his shoulders, nodded to Sean, and spun on his heel. Striding toward the stable, he wondered if she would be telling him she'd forgiven him…or would she be slamming the door into his arse after she booted him out of the manor house and her life?

Flaherty was not a coward—he'd face whatever the Lord had

planned for him regarding the lovely lass. Though he wanted to marry her—and just when had *that* thought become so important?—he knew he would not try to coax her to change her mind if it was set against him.

Sean must have sent word to the stable master, because a gelding was saddled, ready to take him to Chattsworth Manor and his future. He settled on the horse's back, held the reins in his hand, and rasped, "We've been summoned, laddie. Best take me to the lass and pray that she'll forgive me and have me for her husband."

The gelding's whinny of agreement soothed the sharp edge of Flaherty's worry.

With each bend in the road, each copse of trees that he rode past, the dire feeling that had nearly frozen from his feet to his knees spread ever closer to his heart. Pushing thoughts of banishment from his mind, he whispered a prayer: "Lord, 'tis Seamus again…please let the lass forgive me."

Pulling up in front of the viscount's stables, he dismounted and handed the reins to one of the stable lads. "He's been lounging around all morning, so he won't be needing an apple or carrot—" The gelding's short, sharp snort had Flaherty chuckling. "Faith, ye know I always reward ye for carrying me on yer back, laddie." Stroking the animal's neck, he soothed the beast, then said, "If ye have a spare apple or carrot, the lad deserves a treat."

He left his mount in the stables and followed the path to the rear entrance. A footman was waiting to show him into Lady Calliope's sitting room, where the woman who had been on his mind and in his heart longer than any other sat looking out the window that faced the gardens.

"Ye wanted to see me, lass?"

Her head whipped around so fast, he was afraid she'd be dizzy from the movement. "I was not sure that you'd come."

"And why wouldn't I come when the lass I've been courting summons me?" Mary Kate rose from her seat, and he motioned for her to sit back down. "No need to stand up. I'll join ye, if ye don't mind."

She met his gaze and settled onto her chair. "Thank you for coming so quickly."

He did not say anything when his orders had been to come "at once." Surely she remembered making that demand. Didn't she?

She lifted the teapot and held it poised over his cup. "Er...tea?"

"Aye, thank ye, lass."

"No sugar, just cream?"

Ah, so she did remember, though they hadn't taken tea all that many times together. Not trusting his voice to give away the emotions colliding inside of him at his being this close to her, he nodded.

"Mrs. Romney made lemon and lavender scones. Would you like one of each?"

Flaherty's stomach chose that moment to announce itself. He shrugged as Mary Kate giggled.

"I'll take that as a yes." She served him his tea and scones before pouring herself a cup.

"Are ye not having anything to eat?" He wondered if she was suffering to the same extent as he had been. Plagued with lack of sleep, awake and replaying a scene he had no memory of, so he was not certain if he really had barked at her, or if his voice had been stern. Why in the bloody hell could he not recall?

"Lass?" When she did not look up right away, he sighed and said, "*Mary Kate*, how are ye feeling today?"

Her teacup rattled against its saucer until she set it on the table and placed her hands in her lap.

"Ye look pale to me. Are ye not sleeping?"

The emotions in her gaze tugged at his heart and heaped a pile of worry onto his head. He had caused her to fall into this melancholy. 'Twas his fault she was despondent and not carrying on her half of the conversation.

This *shite* had to end. Now! He rose to his feet, reached for her hand, and pulled her into his embrace. "Lass? What's wrong?" She trembled against him. "Can ye not tell me?" He felt her shake her head against his chest. He nearly chuckled, then remembered what he was supposed to do and the need to laugh evaporated. "Mary Kate, will ye accept me heartfelt apology? I do not recall telling ye to leave, nor saying such terrible things to ye."

Her trembling slowed until she was eerily still in his arms. "Never would I willingly hurt yer tender sensibilities, lass. Ye mean too much to me."

Still she did not speak, and thereby refused to accept his apology. What could he say to convince her? He racked his brain until it ached, and then it hit him—he'd respond in kind.

Easing back, he gently placed his knuckle beneath her chin and lifted her beautiful face so he could gaze into her blue-violet eyes. She blinked, and he claimed her lips, pouring every ounce of regret that she'd suffered because of him into the kiss. When her mouth softened beneath his, he coaxed her to kiss him back with a quick nip of her lips followed by his tongue soothing where he'd nibbled.

Her soft sigh was music to his ears. Not wanting to risk conversation yet, when she still hadn't responded, he continued to kiss her. Pleading his case without words, he placed a hand to her waist, encouraging her acquiescence with the pressure of his lips and heat of his body.

Drawn to him like a moth to candle flame, she burrowed into his arms until he groaned with need, as every bit of her curves molded to the hard planes of his body, awakening the desire he felt for the lass. Her soft gasp had him easing his hold on her. Rather than point out the obvious, not willing to have that particular conversation with her until she'd forgiven him and until after they said their vows, he brushed an errant curl from her cheek, tucking it behind the tiny shell of her ear.

Needing her to be the one to speak first, as she had yet to reply verbally, he waited. 'Twasn't as awkward as he thought it might be, the waiting.

Finally, she drew in a deep breath and slowly exhaled. "I do."

"Do what?"

She frowned, then sighed. "I forgive you, Seamus."

"Ah, if ye're back to saying me name, then ye must forgive me."

"You hurt me."

He groaned. "I would never hurt ye like that. Ye need to believe me. 'Twas the—"

"Wound fever. Calliope and Melinda both mentioned their experiences with their husbands saying and doing things totally out of character when they were injured."

"Then ye know 'twasn't what I wanted at all to send ye away." Her eyes darkened to the deep, bluish purple of a midsummer night as he stroked her cheek. When she leaned into his hand, he pulled her against the breadth of his chest, marveling at how right it felt to be holding her like this. *God in Heaven!* How much time had he wasted believing the lovely lass in his arms held any amount of affection for Garahan?

Too many days wasted…too many nights. When they could have been wed by now and spending them locked in one another's arms.

"Seamus?"

He kissed a path from beneath her ear along the line of her jaw before answering, "Aye?"

"I'm sorry that I wasn't able to speak to you that day you came to see me."

"Are ye now?"

"I just said I was." He soothed her temper with a mind-numbing kiss. "Is that all?"

She sighed and kissed him back. "I should not have avoided you for so long."

"True."

"Can you find it in your heart to forgive me?"

He wrapped her in his arms and held her to his heart—surely she could hear the way his pounded. He was unable to speak for the wealth of emotion exploding inside of him.

Finally, he managed, "Aye, lass, though ye have no need to ask for forgiveness. Ye've done nothing more than grant me the time to come to me senses and to ask more than one person what happened when I woke from that fever."

The knock on the open door had him breaking the kiss to glance over his shoulder. "It seems we've been left alone for too long, lass."

She blinked, and it was pure pleasure to watch her cheeks pinken with embarrassment as his words sank in. She tried to hide her face, but he eased back and once more tilted her chin so he could gaze into her eyes. "Ye have nothing to be embarrassed about. I need to ask ye a question."

Mary Kate bit her lip and waited.

"Will ye marry me, lass?"

"I will."

"Right now?"

She stared at him for a moment before answering, "I'd have to change my gown."

Flaherty roared with laughter. "Faith, I knew ye were the woman for me the moment I plucked ye out of the duke's carriage." Turning toward the doorway, he should not have been surprised to find Garahan and O'Malley standing there with grins plastered on their faces. "We're to be married, lads."

Garahan frowned at him. "'Tis about time ye got over yer tearing rage and realized the lass only has eyes for yerself."

Flaherty hesitated, then decided to say what was on his mind and in his heart. "But her smiles—"

"Are a gift she graces each and every one of us with every day, Flaherty," Michael said. "Accept it, and be grateful for it."

His cousins' words filled him to bursting before knocking him on the back of his head until he understood the sense of them. "'Tis grateful I shall be for the rest of me life." He pressed a kiss to her forehead and twined their fingers together. "If tonight's too soon to marry me, we can wed tomorrow."

"A wonderful idea, Flaherty!" Viscount Chattsworth boomed from where he, too, now stood in the doorway.

"Thank ye, yer lordship. I'd best be going, then. I'll need to speak to his lordship about having one of the lads cover me shift."

Chattsworth walked into the sitting room and smiled. "Congratulations."

Lady Calliope joined them a few moments later, hugging Mary Kate first, and then Flaherty. "You two will be so happy. I cannot wait until the vicar marries you. If you wait for a few moments, Flaherty, I need to send a note to Aurelia."

"Of course, yer ladyship. I'll wait for ye—besides, there are some scones left."

O'Malley snorted with laughter and the others joined in. His heart full, Flaherty stared down at the woman by his side and knew he would always be grateful to the Lord for granting his prayers.

CHAPTER TEN

MARY KATE COULD not feel the top of her head. She had so much she wanted to say to Flaherty—questions to ask—but each and every last thought in her brainbox just melted away when he kissed her. Every bit of her, between her nose and her toes, positively tingled when his lips molded to hers, coaxing her to acquiesce to whatever he'd said.

While they waited for her ladyship to pen a note to Lady Aurelia, she listened as Flaherty spoke of the changes that would have to be made after they wed. She understood all that he said and agreed—up until he mentioned her leaving Lady Calliope's employ.

"No."

Flaherty's hand froze with a lemon scone a fraction of a hair from his distractingly sculpted lips. "What did ye say, lass?"

"I said no. Is it a word you haven't ever heard before, Flaherty?"

"Ye cannot think to continue to work for Lady Calliope and be married and living with me at Lippincott Manor, lass. I do not see how it would be possible."

She fisted her hands in her lap as her mood plummeted. Elation was quickly replaced by irritation. Would the rest of their lives be like this, whenever she said no? "I cannot leave her ladyship. She depends on me."

"She'll get used to your replacement, lass."

Mary Kate rose from her seat and walked to the door. Hand to the doorknob, she was surprised when a large hand appeared on the door in front of her face, holding it shut.

"Did yer ma not raise ye any better than to walk away from a conversation without a by yer leave?"

She spun around and glared at him. "Did your mum let you have your way all of your life?"

"Lass, ye have to understand—"

"You are the one who needs to understand," she countered.

"'Twould be difficult enough the traveling back and forth with someone to guard ye," Flaherty told her. "And ye aren't going to be spending the night in any other bed than mine once we're wed."

Lord, was the man deliberately trying to provoke her temper? "What if I do not *wish* to spend every night in your bed?"

He was silent for long enough that she worried she had pushed him too far, too quickly. "Is that how ye were raised? With yer ma and da sleeping in separate rooms?"

"Of course not. What ever gave you that idea?"

"Yer comment. And for that matter, why would ye not want to spend every night in me bed if we're wed? 'Tis what husbands and wives do."

"Before I worked for Lady Kittrick, I was employed by another member of the *ton*, and I can tell you that neither the lord nor the lady of the house shared a bedchamber. There were a number of 'guests' that spent the night. But the master and mistress never spent it together."

"I'll not spend the rest of me life wondering where me wife is sleeping!"

Did he just insinuate that she would sleep with someone else when married to him? Aghast at the implication, Mary Kate did what one of the footman taught her to do after a guest of Lady Kittrick's cornered her: she kicked Flaherty in the shins and shoved against his shoulders. Momentarily shocked, he released his hold on the door. She opened it and raced down the hallway. She was hurt and so angry, she could not see straight!

Mary Kate was halfway up the servants' staircase when she heard heavy footsteps close behind her. She lifted her skirts higher to avoid tripping, and made it to the top step, only to be hauled back against an all-too-familiar, rock-hard chest. "Let me go!"

Flaherty spun her around, demanding, "Are ye daft? Did ye fall down recently and land on yer hard head?"

Incensed that he would ask such a question, she struggled against his hold, but it was no use—he was stronger. "Donovans never give up! Never give in!"

Instead of temper, she heard his deep snort of laughter. "God, ye're the only woman for me. Yer hair matches yer temper, and that's no lie. I expected ye'd be pitting yer will against me own— and look forward to it—but not quite so quickly, and not over sharing me bed. Why does me not wanting to wonder what bed yer sleeping in anger ye? I'm the one who's angry at the thought that ye'd be sleeping in the servants' quarters here at Chattsworth instead of our bed at Lippincott Manor."

It hit her then...she had jumped to the wrong conclusion! "You weren't suggesting that I'd find *someone* else..." Her words trailed off as the idiocy of what she assumed he'd meant filled her. Flaherty would never cast aspersions on anyone's hon- or...especially hers.

He tilted back his head and stared at the ceiling for a few moments before lowering it to stare into her eyes. "*Somewhere* else...not someone else. I'd never think that of ye, lass."

"But you believed I was in love with Garahan, when all of this time I have been in love with *you*!"

His bright blue eyes narrowed, skewering her with their desire-wrapped intensity. "Have ye now?" One moment they were standing in the middle of the top step, the next he had her pinned her against the wall of the enclosed staircase. "Why would I ask yer permission—and that of the viscount, whom ye work for, and the earl, whom I work for—if I wasn't half in love with ye when I asked?"

When she did not answer, he murmured, "Yer declaration of love boggles the mind, lass. For if I'd known ye felt that way, I wouldn't have waited so long to ask for yer hand."

His mouth was a fraction away from hers when she turned her head to the side, and his kiss landed on her cheek. "It all comes back to you not trusting me."

"I could say the same for yerself."

She turned back to search his gaze for a hint of what he was really thinking. "I would not have rushed over once I heard you'd been shot, Seamus, nor would I have stayed with you once you fell unconscious with fever for nearly a sennight, if I did not love you."

"I would not have asked to court ye if I did not love ye, lass. I'm thinking what we have here is a lack of understanding and trust. We cannot expect to live the rest of our lives together if we don't have that. Can we?"

She shook her head. "What do you suggest?"

He shrugged, the movement calling attention to his broad shoulders and the impressive width of his chest. "We start over and agree to trust one another."

"I might, if you would consider my request to stay with Lady Calliope."

"Lass, can ye not see that she'd be needing ye at all hours of the day? Haven't I heard ye mention that ye spend part of the night caring for their son? How can ye do that and expect me to be lying awake, wanting ye, needing ye?"

Well, that was blunt, and had her stammering, "Are you s-s-saying that you'd want to…spend time doing…things?"

He chuckled. "Aye, lass. It has been a trial *not* thinking about it."

"Well, how long could it possibly take to consummate our marriage? Furthermore, how often would ye expect to—" She felt her face flame as her throat tightened with emotion.

"Can ye not say the words, lass? Making love is what we'd be doing. As often as possible."

"I see," she rasped. "But Lady Calliope needs me."

"I need ye too, lass. Why don't we speak to Lady Calliope and ask if she'd be willing to have ye as her lady's maid during the day, but ye'd be home in time to have yer evening meal with me."

Mary Kate stared up into the deep blue of Seamus's eyes. The stark need swirling inside of her was reflected back at her. He wanted this to work and had made a viable suggestion. She would be foolish not to consider it. "If Lady Calliope agrees, would you be willing to allow me to stay the night, when needed? Under special circumstances?"

"Such as?"

"If little William is ill. He trusts me, and it may take some time for him to become used to someone else caring for him in the middle of the night."

"Does he wake up that often in the night?"

She paused to think about it. "No, not now that he isn't teething."

"Well then, I can agree to special circumstances, lass." He leaned in close, his intentions clear by the desire swirling in his eyes. "Kiss me back, Mary Kate." His lips commanded a response from her, and she willingly gave it with all of the pent-up desire and emotion that had been simmering beneath her surface calm. She did love this irritating man, and did not want to think of spending her life without him.

"We'd best be going back down to the sitting room before the viscount sends one of me cousins searching for me and banishes me from Chattsworth…right before he has me dragged back to Lippincott Manor!"

She leaned against Seamus's strength, reveling in the fact that he had been thinking of her as often as she had been thinking of him. If only she had come to her senses and realized that her thoughtlessness regarding Garahan's rescuing her had damaged two relationships: the one she had with Melinda, and the one with Seamus.

The door at the base of the stairs opened and O'Malley filled the doorway. "For feck's sake, Flaherty! Can ye not wait until tomorrow to lock lips with yer bride-to-be? Think of Mary Kate's reputation!"

"We had a misunderstanding," Flaherty grumbled. "And watch yer language around me bride. No bloody cursing!"

"She's not yer bride yet," O'Malley reminded him.

"Well, she will be by this time tomorrow."

"Only if ye don't feck it up."

"Shut yer gob, O'Malley."

His cousin chuckled. "Her ladyship is waiting for the two of ye in the sitting room. Don't be worrying her."

Flaherty laced his fingers with Mary Kate's once more and gave a slight tug, urging her to follow him. "We'd best be ready to apologize to her ladyship, lass."

"Yes, of course."

"Ye can go first."

Lady Calliope did look worried when they arrived in the sitting room. "There you are. Where did you two go off to?"

Mary Kate did not want her ladyship to think ill of her. It was best to tell her the truth. "I misunderstood something Flaherty said and let my temper get the better of me. I stormed off and was nearly at the top of the servants' staircase when he caught up to me."

"The lass thought I said something that impugned her honor." He frowned and added, "As if I would."

Lady Calliope's expression was one of disbelief. Before she could respond, Flaherty continued, "Faith, 'tis the same reaction I had. Why would the lass think I'd do anything like that? But the fact that she reacted that way was the reason I chased after her." He sighed when he confessed, "'Tis her red head."

The viscountess slowly smiled. "She does have a bit of a temper, doesn't she?"

Mary Kate wasn't sure if the subject of her having a bit of a temper would be in her favor when she and Flaherty asked their question of her future position within Chattsworth Manor's staff. Best not put it off any longer. "Lady Calliope, Seamus and I did smooth things out between us, but we still have an issue that may prevent me from marrying him."

The viscountess frowned. "I cannot think of anything that would."

"He wants me to leave my position," Mary Kate explained.

"Oh… Oh! I never thought of that." Meeting Mary Kate's gaze and then Flaherty's, Lady Calliope admitted, "I honestly do not know what I would do without you, Mary Kate."

"I had an idea, if ye don't mind me making a suggestion," Flaherty said.

"Not at all," the viscountess replied. "What is it?"

"Mary Kate would of course be living with me over at Lippincott Manor, as the earl—and His Grace—depend upon me as part of his guard."

"Without question," Lady Calliope replied.

"One of us could drop Mary Kate off here in the morning—after we share our first meal of the day together. And I could return and fetch her before the evening meal."

The viscountess did not answer right away, and Mary Kate wondered if she would refuse. Worry had her head feeling light again. She wished she could control her riotous emotions.

"MacReady mentioned the vicar has been trying to find a position for one of the young women in the village," Calliope said. "But he hasn't found one yet."

"Does she have any experience as a lady's maid?" Mary Kate did not want her ladyship to have to train someone all over again. Especially when she remembered how tired Lady Calliope had been as of late. "If she could come here for part of my shift, I would be happy to show her all that I have been doing for you."

The viscountess nodded. "A sound idea. I am quite sure William will agree to that suggestion. Far be it from either one of us to come between the two of you. Where would I be without you and Flaherty in our lives? Who knows what would have happened the day of the carriage incident or, for that matter, the morning of the duel!"

Mary Kate rushed to Calliope's side and hugged her. Calliope smiled and hugged her back. "I want you and Flaherty to be as happy as William and I are."

"Thank ye, yer ladyship. I plan to do me best to make her happy." Flaherty's smile belied the wicked glint in his eyes. Just when Mary Kate wondered what he was thinking, he added, "But I'm thinking ye'd want me to wait until we're wed before I do."

Calliope's cheeks flushed with embarrassment at his suggestion. "I believe that would be best." She picked the sealed note up off the table and handed it to him. "Please deliver this to Aurelia. And Flaherty?"

"Aye, yer ladyship?"

"Trust, compromise, and a willingness to listen are key in forming the foundation of your marriage."

"'Tis what the lass and I were discussing before O'Malley interrupted."

"We shall see you tomorrow before the evening meal," the viscountess said. "I have outlined my plans in my note to Aurelia. We'll have the vicar marry you here, as this is where the bride-to-be is currently living. William will give her away."

"As long as we are wed on the morrow, yer ladyship, the place matters not to me."

The viscountess beamed at him. "Wonderful. Until tomorrow, then, Flaherty."

He walked toward Mary Kate and took her hand. Lifting it to his lips, he brushed a kiss to the back of it. "Until tomorrow, lass."

Mary Kate sighed, promising, "Tomorrow."

CHAPTER ELEVEN

MONROE SET DOWN the horse's front hoof and patted the animal's flank. Exhaustion was settling across his shoulders like a heavy yoke. He packed up the tools of his trade in the leather satchel he used traveling from estate to estate, and shops in the village.

Parks, his friend, a stable hand at the inn, paused to speak with him. "Just heard that the viscountess's lady's maid will be marrying Flaherty tomorrow."

Monroe's blood chilled in his veins. "What did you say?"

"Mary Kate Donovan is going to marry Flaherty tomorrow. A new maid will be taking on half of Mary Kate's duties, as she'll be splitting her time between Lippincott Manor and Chattsworth Manor."

"Over my dead body!"

Parks grinned. "What do you plan to do about it?"

"I cannot kill the guard outright, but I could tear his heart out emotionally."

"How? If she's marrying him tomorrow?" Park demanded.

"By helping her see the error in her judgment tonight."

"You plan to kidnap her." It was not a question.

"Aye, if she will not come with me willingly. But I know she has feelings for me. She cannot have been gracing me with her warm and suggestive smiles for the last few months because she likes watching me shoe the viscount's horses."

"I know a number of the serving maids working at the inn like to pass the time watching you. Overheard a few of them commenting on your intense concentration and the obvious strength of your arms."

Monroe's eyes gleamed. "I have been gracious enough to give more than one of those winsome servants a tumble in the stables."

Parks snorted with laughter. "Not a one of them has complained that I've heard."

"And you would have, as you were standing guard to ensure that we were not disturbed. Have I thanked you for that lately, Parks?"

"You have not. I believe you owe me an ale or two."

"Done. After tonight's mission to secure Mary Kate's affections, do not wander toward that Irish heathen."

The men shook on it, and Parks returned to his duties in the stables, leaving Monroe to pack the rest of his tools and load them into his wagon. He had one more stop to make before he could return to his small cottage on the outskirts of town. Then he would empty his wagon and spread it with fresh hay, the quilt from his bed, a few strips of linen—that he reserved for bandages—and rope. The linen to use as a gag, and the rope to bind Mary Kate's hands and feet. No use taking chances with her mercurial temper.

He planned to set the fire in her free, after he'd whisked her away from the viscount's estate. There was a heavily wooded area west of the village—he'd already set up a temporary shelter there in anticipation of the day that he convinced Mary Kate to run away with him. Time to make use of that lean-to.

Monroe was smiling as he placed his foot on the hub of the wagon wheel and hoisted himself onto the seat. He would bed the woman tonight, and finally get her out of his system!

Visions of the night ahead of him had the farrier whistling as he drove to his last stop for the day. A short while later, he was packing his wagon and riding toward home. He had just enough time to wash his face and hands—the rest could wait until later. He was not finished exerting himself physically for the day.

CHAPTER TWELVE

G ARAHAN WAS ON his last patrol to the village for the day. Given the late hour, it was not quite as busy when he rode up to the inn in the village. One of the stable hands, Parks, looked up and watched him entering the innyard. Was it Garahan's imagination, or did Parks flinch? He didn't trust the man. Past experience taught him to trust his gut, and his gut wanted him to grab the man by his collar and shake him. But as one of the duke's guard, he did not have the luxury of giving in to every gut instinct when it involved a bit of violence. Pity—he would have enjoyed watching the man's face turn red and then apoplectic purple. *Ah well, a man cannot always have what he wants.*

As he rode past Parks, one of the younger stable lads rushed toward Garahan. He reined in his horse and dismounted. "Whoa, lad, slow down."

The boy looked over his shoulder and, seeing Parks, lost every ounce of color in his face. Moving farther away from Parks, he tugged on Flaherty's hand. "You've got to save her, Garahan!"

Immediately alert, Garahan scanned the busy yard, but did not note anything out of the ordinary. "Who, lad?"

The boy leaned close and whispered, "Miss Mary Kate."

Garahan's gut clenched. Flaherty was going to marry the lass tomorrow. After all his cousin had suffered through, he would see to it that Flaherty married the woman who had stolen his heart.

Urging the boy closer, he led his horse toward the trough and let him drink, then asked, "What do you know?"

"The farrier plans to take her away…tonight!"

"Where did ye hear this?"

"Half an hour ago. I was working in the tack room, sorting the reins—they don't always get put away when we're busy—and I overheard Parks and Monroe talking."

When the boy paused, Garahan urged him, "Ye have no fear of reprisal. I'll see to it that both men are dealt with swiftly and decisively. Ye'll not come to harm."

"I'm worried about Miss Mary Kate. She's always been kind to me, when others haven't been."

"She's a fine woman, lad. We can agree on that. Now tell me, did ye hear any specifics?"

The lad nodded. "Monroe has a place west of here. He…he plans to take her there tonight. I could tell by how they sounded that it didn't matter if she wanted to go with him or not."

"She won't go willingly," Garahan predicted. "She's marrying me cousin Flaherty."

"You won't let any harm come to her?"

"Ye have me word."

"You'll rescue her, like you did that time in London?"

"Nay, lad. Flaherty will rescue her like he did when the duke's carriage slid on ice and landed on its side."

The boy's mouth dropped open. "I forgot about that. Flaherty and O'Malley knew how to right the carriage. All of us working for the innkeeper were impressed."

"Me brothers and me cousins are wise beyond their years."

"Do you promise Flaherty will rescue her in time?"

"Ye have me word. 'Tisn't wise to question a man's word…'tis akin to questioning his honor, lad."

"I didn't mean to, but I'm worried. The farrier isn't what he seems. He treats us one way in front of witnesses and cuffs us on the back of the head or across the face as soon as we're alone with him in the stables."

Garahan curled his free hand into a tight fist and slowly re-laxed it. "I'll see to it that he learns the error of his ways. He won't be treating yerself and the other lads as if ye were chattel any longer."

Wide gray eyes, filled with trust, met Garahan's gaze. "You'd better hurry."

Garahan snorted to cover his laughter at the lad's cheeky demand. He watched as the lad raced off to answer the hostler's call and frowned. No one had the right to treat those hardwork-ing boys poorly. He'd speak to the hostler and then the innkeeper. If either of them knew what was happening and did nothing to stop it, he'd involve the viscount and the earl—even the duke if he had to!

His horse had finished drinking and turned its head as if to urge Garahan into action. "Right ye are, laddie." He swung into the saddle, and though the urge to gallop was great, he kept his horse to a fast walk until he reached the last building in the village. He bent over his horse's neck and called, "Ride like the wind, laddie!"

His horse reacted as if he scented a mare in heat, galloping toward Lippincott Manor.

FLAHERTY WAS PATROLLING the perimeter when Garahan rode at a breakneck pace toward the back of the building. He immediately gave the signal, a short, sharp whistle, that would alert the rest of the guard.

Sean bolted out of the rear entrance. "Is it the viscount?"

Dermott rounded the building from his station on the roof. "Is the viscountess in trouble again?"

Garahan locked gazes with Flaherty. "Monroe plans to kidnap Mary Kate—tonight!"

"And ye came here instead of going after the bleeding bugger to stop him?" Flaherty could not believe his cousin did not take immediate action on his own. "Why—"

"'Tis *yer* job to rescue yer bride-to-be. I know where he plans to take her."

Every fiber of Flaherty's being jolted as his brain shut off his emotions. The farrier would pay a steep price for taking Mary Kate! "Tell me when and where."

Garahan's eyes were dark with banked anger. "One of the stable lads at the inn has been watching Monroe for me."

Flaherty was about to ask why, when it hit him that his cousin had been wise to do so. The farrier had made it well known that he had his eye on Mary Kate—though the blackguard didn't start spouting off about it until after Flaherty and Mary Kate were officially courting.

Flaherty had been too blinded by jealousy at the time to think straight… Thank goodness Garahan had been able to. Neither of them had stopped the planned kidnapping—yet. Mary Kate could be harmed because of his lack of clear thinking! The very idea sliced him to the bone.

He had to clear his throat to speak past the lump of emotion constricting it. "Thank ye, James."

"Ye'd have done the same for me. Monroe has had his mind set on Mary Kate from the beginning. I'm told he's built a shelter to the west of the village. There's a path leading to it. 'Tis in the thickest section of woods—too thick to navigate on horseback. Ye'll have to dismount and lead yer horse."

"I know the path well," Flaherty said. "Though I haven't followed it for more than half a mile. 'Tis the area to the east and south of the village where most of our troubles have come from in the form of sharpshooters and those sneaking in bent on launching an attack on us under the cover of darkness."

Dermott frowned. "We cannot let Lady Aurelia know. She'll either send word to Lady Calliope or ride off to collect the viscountess on her way to find Mary Kate."

Sean waved at the stable master. "Saddle one of the geldings for Flaherty." The man ducked into the stables and returned leading one of the geldings. "Ride back to Chattsworth, Garahan," Sean said. "Alert the viscount to the possible trouble."

"'Twas me plan," Garahan replied. "Though I'll try to keep it from Lady Calliope. The last thing we need is either of their ladyships riding to the rescue. They've done it before when their husbands were in trouble."

Flaherty distinctly remembered both occasions and murmured, "God help us."

Sean nodded to Flaherty. "Go! You need to get to Chattsworth before Monroe."

Flaherty did not need to be told twice. He was already silently reciting the list of Mary Kate's duties and the hours she performed them. When he'd asked her half a dozen months ago, he had no idea it would be imperative that he have the information to save her from God knew what the farrier planned for her.

He bent low over the animal's neck and encouraged the horse to ride full out. Hoofbeats thundered beneath him as they flew down the road toward Chattsworth Manor. He prayed as he rode, "Lord, don't let the bleeding bugger get his hands on *mo chroí!*"

And Mary Kate *was* the other half of his heart.

He covered the ground in record time, causing a hue and cry as he reined in his mount by the stables and whistled. Michael O'Malley ran toward him from the outbuilding, where Flaherty knew the duke's guard stored their weapons and ammunition, in their previous sleeping quarters. Before O'Malley could speak, Flaherty shouted, "Where's Mary Kate?"

"At this hour, she'll be walking in the gardens by the stone wall by the edge of the forest."

Flaherty jumped off his gelding and raced toward the gardens and the fieldstone wall separating the viscount's gardens from the dirt path, which led into the thickly wooded portion of his property. "Mary Kate!"

Dread filled him when she did not answer right away. Had

she been abducted already? Did the blackguard have his dirty paws on his woman? He called her name again—no reply.

By the time he'd leapt over half a dozen herb plants and dodged too many thorny rosebushes, he made it to the wall, but there was still no sign of the lass. Where could she be? How long had she been gone? He needed answers…now!

He banged the heel of his hand against his forehead three times before grinding out, "Think, Flaherty!"

His brain engaged and he glanced down at the cinder path, noticing that it had been disturbed. Two sets of footprints, and right there—a sign of a scuffle. Then there was only one set of footprints moving along the wall toward the gate…large footprints!

"I'll kill him!"

Michael O'Malley joined him. "Ye won't, and we both know it. Ye'd never break yer word to His Grace."

For a heartbeat, Flaherty wished that he had no honor and he could break his word. Then a noxious taste filled his mouth and he knew that he'd best stop thinking such dangerous thoughts. He was one of the duke's men, and he would never do anything to cause His Grace to lose faith in his abilities or his word. "Ye're right. I wouldn't. Do ye see the footprints?"

Michael saw them when Flaherty pointed them out. "Looks like he used the gate, but I'm thinking ye should climb the wall and see if you can see if he continued walking along the outside of the wall or if he went deep into the woods."

Flaherty was having trouble speaking. Worry tangled words around until he was afraid to speak, fearing unintelligible sounds would come out of his mouth. He acknowledged Michael's suggestion and scaled the wall. Standing atop it, he easily spotted the big footprints—which followed the dirt path on the other side of the wall, heading past the outbuildings and stables all the way to a small road that intersected with the road leading to the village.

He climbed down off the wall. "He must have a wagon

stowed between here and the road to town."

"If I were planning an abduction, I'd have a wagon—and rope enough to bind me prisoner," Michael told him.

Flaherty sprinted toward his horse. "We've got to find Mary Kate, laddie. Are ye ready to help me?"

The horse lifted his head and whinnied loudly.

"I'll take that as a yes. Let's ride!"

CHAPTER THIRTEEN

MARY KATE REFUSED to show fear. Incensed that the high-handed farrier thought she'd go willingly, she kept a tight lock on her emotions. And the fact that he'd surprised her and tied her up...! She wanted to rail at him, but needed to gauge his reactions first. Until she could honestly believe she knew how he'd react, she could imagine punching him with her fists! Then she'd pull his hair, kick him in the shins, and jab her knee to the weakest part of him. If she kneed him hard enough, it may put him off from whatever he intended to do. She would not be taken against her will—she was saving herself for Seamus!

Her mind's eye immediately brought up the image of the tall, broad-shouldered, deep-chested Irishman. Sapphire eyes that could by turns sear you with anger...or set you on fire with the depths of the desire she sensed he held in check. Mary Kate was fairly certain that he had been holding back for months. Why hadn't he asked for her hand in marriage a fortnight after they were courting? Was it something she did or said? And then it occurred to her—she'd constantly talked about Garahan! She had been so foolish to focus on the day that changed the course of her life, rather than the day that Flaherty had captured her heart. She should have spoken more about *that* day.

The wagon lurched to a stop, cutting off her train of thought. She knew better than to struggle with the ropes binding her wrists, or the gag he'd tied around her face. Mary Kate had already promised the dolt that Flaherty would find him and beat him within an inch of his life. Remembering the hint of fear in Monroe's eyes fed her confidence that Flaherty would come for her. She had managed to evade the gag until she told Monroe that she would never have spoken to the farrier in the first place, if not for the fact that he was taking care of her ladyship's favorite mare.

She realized too late that taunting the farrier with the fact that she loved Seamus Flaherty and planned to marry him must have pushed the man too far. The tight gag tasted vile and smelled worse. It took all of her composure to remain calm and not let her stomach react to the stench of it. The man must have used the linen to wipe the sweat from his brow before using it to keep her quiet—the gag was still damp.

Glancing at their surroundings, she was surprised to see a makeshift lean-to between two oak trees. She could not tell from this distance if he'd used oilcloth or a tarpaulin for a roof, but the hastily stacked logs for the sides of the building were uneven. It did not appear as if he meant to stay for any length of time. She hoped the walls would not lean in to the point where they would collapse. At least the makeshift roof was tied to tree branches on either side of the lean-to. It should hold. Hopefully, the rain that threatened earlier would hold off until Flaherty rescued her.

Then a sobering thought hit her—had she been discovered missing yet? Mary Kate said a silent prayer that he would rescue her tonight. Tomorrow may be too late. Heaven help her, she did not want to think of what could possibly happen overnight being held against her will by the odious…make that *odiferous* farrier.

Mary Kate had been around Flaherty many times when he'd worked up a sweat performing his duties, but his scent was never malodorous. She rather liked his healthy scent—a combination of man, with a hint of horse, and honest sweat. Concentrating on the blue-eyed, auburn-haired giant, she willed him to find her—soon!

Monroe's punishing grip on her upper arms brought her

sharply back to the present. It hurt. Glaring at him only made the blackguard smile. "I like my women full of fire."

She'd like to roast him over an open firepit! Better yet, she'd like to bury him in a deep pit up to his neck. No, that would not be right. Donovans believed in an eye for an eye. She'd truss him up and gag him, like he'd done to her...and leave him in the woods.

"Whatever you are thinking, I'm all for it!"

The man had little to no brains if he thought she was entertaining any thoughts but those that would cause him as much pain as he was inflicting upon her! Deciding to ignore him and pretend as if his hold weren't bruising her to the bone, she turned away from him.

"You'll look at me when I am talking to you!"

She silently refused—how could she do otherwise when he'd gagged her?

He shook her until her head and neck ached, and she wondered if he had damaged her brainbox. She closed her eyes for a moment to gather her courage before slowly turning to look at him. She would not quail in front of her enemy. Monroe had become her enemy the moment he'd tossed her over his shoulder, carried her through the gate, and heaved her into the bed of his wagon. He'd knocked the wind out of her when she landed on his shoulder. She'd been momentarily stunned, unable to move, let alone draw in a breath. Otherwise, he'd never have managed to gag her or tie her up!

Mary Kate wasn't stunned now, but a hint of fear slithered up her spine. She did not know him well enough to guess what he was thinking with more than half a chance that she would be correct. Drawing on her reserves of strength, she ignored the emotions clawing inside of her, and prayed for strength and the chance to escape. But first she needed to somehow convince her unwanted suitor that she'd consider changing her mind about him. Anything to get him to untie her—or at least remove the disgusting gag.

"I thought you'd be pleased to spend some time alone with me."

Digging deep to hide her reaction to his statement, she dared to look away, hoping he wouldn't bruise her arms further. But he must have decided she was trying to get his attention, because his next words shocked her. "Ah, so you are embarrassed because you *do* want to be alone with me."

Lord, save me from this arrogant, odious man! She knew she had to meet his gaze and was horrified to see the lustful intent in his dark eyes. It was clear to her that she would be fighting tooth and nail to preserve her virtue.

Hurry, Flaherty!

CHAPTER FOURTEEN

FLAHERTY FOUND THE path Garahan had mentioned and dismounted, urging his horse to follow with a tug on his bridle. "'Tisn't much further, laddie. We have to find the lass, and when we do, I may need yer help with a well-placed hoof or two."

The animal lifted his head as if he agreed.

"I knew I could count on ye. Garahan said he'd give me a head start before he entered the path behind us."

The woods thinned out just ahead of him, and he spotted the lean-to the stable lad had heard Monroe and Parks discussing. It was poorly made. If the stacks of logs were any indication, a good stiff kick to the bottom log would bring the stacked walls down. He'd remember that as a last-ditch option.

Flaherty placed his hands on either side of his gelding's face. "Ye need to keep quiet as the mouse that shares yer stall in the earl's stables." The animal gave a soft snort. "Good lad." He led him over to a stand of fir trees and raised his hand, palm out—a sign he'd used before with the horse to stay. Confident that the animal would, Flaherty crept to the other side of the trees, where he had a clear view of the doorway.

No door. 'Twould save time. He wouldn't have to break it down to get to Mary Kate.

The sound of a scuffle and muffled shriek had him moving

closer. The need to burst through the opening had him by the *bollocks*, but he knew one wrong move could mean the lass might be injured. He had to listen carefully to assess the situation before diving through the opening headfirst.

"You'll thank me when I'm through with you," a deep voice promised.

Flaherty's blood shot straight to boiling. He tilted his head back, roared the Flaherty battle cry, and launched himself through the doorway. He grabbed Monroe by his hair and yanked him away from Mary Kate. "Touch her again and die!"

The farrier tried to loosen the Irishman's hold on him but couldn't. "Bloody hell!"

Flaherty's eyes locked on the lass, then he scanned her for injuries, from the top of Mary Kate's head to the toes of her half boots. "Are ye hurt?"

She shook her head, and relief speared through him.

"You couldn't have waited for another ten minutes. I'd have gotten what I wanted by then."

The man he'd yanked away from the lass had just made his last mistake.

Flaherty saw red! He spun his prisoner around, planted his meaty fist in the man's face, and knocked him off his feet. The sound of the man's nose breaking was music to Flaherty's ears. The satisfaction of watching the man bleed took the razor-sharp edge off his anger. While the farrier howled in pain, Flaherty stepped over him, extending his hand to Mary Kate. Hers felt so fragile in his. The need to protect and defend her threatened his ability to control his anger. Despite the riot of emotions swirling inside of him, he gently pulled her into his arms.

When she trembled, he sought to distract her. "Ye didn't answer me question, lass." She huffed against his chest until he eased his hold on her. Drawing her back, he noticed the gag around her mouth. "Forgive me, lass. Let me untie that."

Her exhale was followed by the sound of her gagging. Flaherty quickly spun her away from him. "Easy now—let it out if ye need to. No shame in giving in to the urge to cast up yer accounts."

She shuddered but didn't throw up. Wavering on her feet as he untied her hands, she reached for him once she was free. But he shook his head. "Hold that thought for a moment while I tie up this bugger with the rope he used on ye."

The fiery-haired lass complied. When he'd tied the farrier's hands behind his back, he drew her to him again. "Now then, I believe ye were standing here."

She smiled and wrapped her arms around his waist, burying her head in his chest. "I prayed you'd come for me, Seamus."

Hoping to prick her conscience to distract her, he murmured, "And here I thought ye'd be praying for Garahan to rescue ye."

Mary Kate tilted her head back until her eyes locked on his. Her expression was a mix of exasperation and temper. He didn't mind the latter, but worried a bit about the former.

"I take it ye *weren't* waiting for Garahan, then."

"I was not, and I am embarrassed that I had unknowingly hurt Melinda by harping on Garahan's saving me for the longest time. He may have been there when I was cast out of Lady Kittrick's town house, but you were the one to pull Lady Calliope and me out of harm's way when the carriage tipped over."

"That I was, lass…with a bit of help from Michael." He bowed his head until his forehead was resting against hers. "Did ye sort things out with Melinda, then?"

"After the viscountess pointed out that I'd hurt Melinda's feelings, I apologized to her ladyship for causing strife in her home. Then she told me I needed to apologize to Melinda— which I did, and to you for refusing to see you the other day. If you've forgotten, I can apologize to you again."

"Well now, it would seem that ye've taken care of the situation without me interference and did the right thing. Ye'll not regret it. Me cousin's a bit hardheaded, but there's no man I'd rather have at me back than James Garahan." He had to press his lips to hers in a tender kiss of promise. He winked at her, hoping to see her smile. Flaherty knew she would be all right if she smiled.

"I was in the garden," she whispered.

"I have on good authority that ye spend a good bit of yer free time there. Having been raised on a small farm back home, I understand the need to be amongst the green and growing things. Ma always said weeding her vegetable and herb patch soothed her soul."

"Seamus?"

The expectant look in her eyes had him hoping she'd tell him that she loved him and was grateful for his rescue. He could not wait to hear her say the words. "Aye?"

"Could we please leave?"

Close enough. He swept her into his arms and stepped through the doorway.

"Did you walk here?"

He snickered. "Not hardly—'tis more than a few miles from either the viscount's estate or the earl's." Flaherty whistled, and his horse walked toward them from the stand of fir trees. "I'll set ye on the lad's back. Can ye manage to stay on me horse while I deposit the blackguard in the back of his wagon?"

"Of course."

She sounded a bit miffed, but she'd earned the right to that emotion after what she'd been through—and nearly suffered—at the hands of the man he wanted to beat senseless. "I'll be right back."

He collected the farrier, dragging him outside. "I'd carry yer sorry arse, but I'm not wanting yer blood all over the back of me frockcoat. I've already ruined me spare coat when I was shot."

Wisely, Monroe lifted his gaze to nod before he dropped his head to stare at his feet. "Up ye go." Flaherty hoisted the man into the wagon, satisfied when he groaned.

The sound of someone approaching had Flaherty moving to stand in front of his horse and Mary Kate. "Don't worry, lass, I'll protect ye."

The feel of her small hand resting on his shoulder was a balm to his soul. "I know you will."

Garahan burst through the foliage. "Well now, it appears if ye didn't need me help after all."

"As a matter of fact, I'd be beholden to ye if ye'd drive me prisoner to the village. I need to take Mary Kate to Chattsworth."

"I'm thinking the viscount—and the earl—will be wanting a word with Monroe before we take him to the constable," Garahan said. "I'll follow along behind ye. By now the earl and Lady Aurelia should be waiting with the viscount and Lady Calliope for us to return with Mary Kate."

Flaherty reluctantly agreed. "'Tis true, their ladyships will be worried about ye, lass. We can send one of the stable lads or footmen to fetch the constable and have him meet us at the viscount's estate."

"Now ye're talking sense, cousin. Lead on."

Flaherty mounted behind Mary Kate and gently pulled her onto his lap. "Rest yer head on me shoulder, lass."

She relaxed against him and his heart rejoiced. The woman he loved was safe and in his arms. What more could possibly go wrong?

CHAPTER FIFTEEN

PARKS WAS WAITING at the designated spot—just as he'd promised Monroe. Anxious to have the job over and done with, he waited to hear hoofbeats approaching his hiding spot halfway up a tree. He scanned the road and the area around him while he thought over their lucrative deal. Even if Monroe did not manage to follow through with his plan to deflower Mary Kate Donovan—which didn't weigh on his conscience at all—the farrier had paid Parks half of his fee beforehand. His end of the bargain was to lie in wait and fire a warning shot guaranteed to spook Flaherty's horse to rear up and throw him. Parks grinned, imagining the laughable sight of the Irishman being unseated and tossed through the air like the clump of dirt he was.

Half an hour later, Parks cocked his head to one side and grunted. "About time." He lifted his rifle and used the sight to line up his shot. Aiming for the road—one foot in front of Flaherty's horse—he fired.

FLAHERTY TIGHTENED HIS grip on the reins and thanked God that he'd had the lass in front of him on the horse and not behind. "Easy, laddie. 'Tis just some *eedjit* poaching at this hour of the night." With the gelding under control, he brushed his lips to Mary Kate's temple. "Crisis averted, lass. Not to worry."

A heartbeat later, another shot struck the ground right in front of the animal's front hooves. Flaherty held on as he tried to calm his horse, keeping one arm firmly around Mary Kate.

Her gasp of terror arrowed through him as he felt the horse's front hooves leaving the ground. The gelding was strong, but with the combined weight of two people and someone firing shots so close to this hooves, the animal lifted up and gave a massive shake of his body, tossing Flaherty and Mary Kate off his back.

On alert, Flaherty shot to his feet as the third shot came from the same direction, grazing his cheek. He dove toward Mary Kate, who was lying in a heap at the edge of the road, and slapped a hand to the wound. Blood oozed through his fingers, but he didn't give it more than a moment's notice. He had to check the lass for injuries, but he needed to get her out of the line of fire from the sharpshooter trying to kill them.

"I'm going to lift ye, lass, and pray to God that I don't injure ye further." He gathered her to his heart, and her moan of pain sliced through his resolve. "Hang on, lass!" Like a man possessed, he ran toward the safety of the trees on the opposite side of the road.

Laying her on the ground, he quickly checked for obvious signs of a broken bone—none. But her sharply indrawn breath when he tried to rotate her ankle hinted of a sprain or torn ligaments. Having had both, as well as a broken bone or two, he knew it would already be swelling.

Mary Kate bit her lip, cutting off another moan of pain, as she opened her eyes and gasped, "You're bleeding."

"Aye." She patted his side, distracting him. "What are ye doing?"

"Where's your cravat? You always have a spare or two in your pockets."

He sat back on his heels, relieved that she was aware enough to be concerned about something other than her ankle. He fished one out of his frockcoat pocket and handed it to her. "Why aren't ye flinging yerself into me arms to protect ye from whoever is shooting at us?"

She blinked. "How would that help our situation?"

He snorted. God he loved this woman!

Mary Kate leaned toward him and placed the folded-up cravat against his bloody cheek. He clamped his jaw down against the discomfort. "Ye're a brave woman, wife of mine."

"We aren't married yet, Flaherty."

"A while ago, ye were calling me Seamus. Are ye vexed with me, lass?"

She shook her head. "I get cranky whenever I'm thrown from a horse and twist my ankle."

He held his chuckle inside to remark, "Ah, so 'tis me horse ye're vexed with."

"And whoever shot at us. Do you think he's waiting for us to show ourselves?"

"Could be. Though he'll be in for a surprise in a few minutes when Garahan comes galloping up the road. He'll have heard the rifle shots by now, as he wasn't far behind us. All we need to do is wait a few minutes. I need ye to stay here, under the cover of these trees, while I wait for him. Will ye promise me that ye won't move?"

"I could help."

"'Tisn't up for discussion, lass. I need yer word." When she still did not answer, he added, "I can wait all day, but I'd rather stand at the ready to warn Garahan about the sharpshooter in the trees on the other side of the road."

She reached for his hand and gripped it hard. "I promise, Seamus."

"There's a lass. I'll be right back. Wait right here." When she frowned at him, he added, "Ye already promised."

"Yes, I'll wait right on this spot."

He hauled her close and kissed her. With a quick prayer that the Lord would watch over the headstrong lass, he slid from their hiding spot without a sound. Flaherty fully expected her to try to follow him on her injured ankle—but hoped she wouldn't.

Scanning the area, he found a spot where the trees thinned, giving him an unobstructed view of the road. He saw the wagon with a horse tied behind it and gave a short, sharp whistle, then flattened himself on the ground.

A warning shot skimmed close enough to the top of his head to part his hair! An answering shot sounded close, and he knew Garahan had taken advantage of the shooter's mistake—his cousin had gotten a bead on the man and returned fire.

The sweet sound of agony had Flaherty smiling as he rose to his feet and stepped through the trees to greet his cousin. "Right on time. While ye collect our second prisoner—Parks, I'm thinking—I'll go fetch the lass. She's sprained her ankle."

Garahan frowned. "Hard to do while riding double on a horse."

Flaherty's heart started to pound as he remembered that moment suspended in time when he'd felt the gelding rising on his hind legs and knew they would get thrown. "Bloody bugger shot the ground in front of us, and then a second shot right by me horse's front hooves!"

Garahan clenched his jaw before relaxing it enough to say, "I'll be a moment."

Flaherty did not bother to watch his cousin cross the road— the injured shooter's shouts were enough to let him know the other man had been hit. Mayhap he had only been dislodged from his perch—either way, he was making enough noise to hint at an injury that prevented him from escaping.

Flaherty snorted as he made his way over to where he'd left the lass. She wasn't there! He bellowed her name and paused to listen… Silence.

His heart began to pound and sweat broke out on the back of his neck as he searched the ground for signs of a struggle, but surely he would have heard something, wouldn't he? If not him, then his horse, whom he just noticed was no longer there.

"*Mary Kate!*"

"Ye sound like a wounded bull, Flaherty."

"Dermott?"

"Aye, who else were ye expecting to show up and watch yer back?"

Flaherty scrubbed a hand over his face and noticed he was still bleeding—he'd thought it stopped. Pulling the cravat out of his pocket a second time, he refolded it so a drier part was on the outside. He pressed it on his face as his cousin walked toward him leading two horses—Flaherty's with Mary Kate on its back, and Dermott. "I was expecting Garahan, as he was to bring the prisoner and his wagon to Chattsworth."

"His lordship and Lady Aurelia are waiting for ye at Chattsworth."

Flaherty acknowledged Dermott's comment with a nod and walked over to his horse. Reaching for Mary Kate's hand, he pitched his voice low and said, "Ye should know that I never admit to faults in front of witnesses—especially one of me brothers or cousins."

"Faults?" Dermott asked.

Flaherty growled at his cousin, but never let his eyes stray from the lass. "When ye weren't where I left ye, fear nearly ripped me heart out of me chest."

"Do you have a spare cravat, Dermott?" Mary Kate asked. "I think Seamus needs a dry one." Dermott handed it to her, and she gently placed it on his cheek. "Hold it on tight now, Seamus. We need to stop the bleeding."

He grunted. When he did as she bade him, she whispered, "I didn't think you were afraid of anything."

"Well, now ye know."

"'Tis good to know that ye have two flaws, cousin."

Flaherty turned to glare at Dermott. "One flaw."

"Well now, I'm thinking 'tis two. Ye're jealous of any man who pays attention to yer pretty bride-to-be, and ye have a tearing fear that someone will take her from ye."

He could not think of anything to counter his cousin's words.

"Am I wrong?"

Flaherty sighed. "Nay, but I'll ask ye to keep it to yerself."

"For a time," Dermott agreed. "Let's get ye back to Chattsworth Manor. I'm thinking yer pretty face'll need a stitch or two to keep ye from bleeding all over yer spare coat."

"How do ye know it's me spare?"

Dermott grinned. "We all received two frockcoats—yer other one was ruined when ye were shot. Ye haven't forgotten that, have ye?"

"No chance of that," Flaherty quipped as he mounted one-handed, settling on his horse's back. He pulled Mary Kate onto his lap and sighed. With her in his arms and two prisoners ready to be carted off for questioning by the viscount and the earl, all was right with his world… *For now.*

After he and the lass were wed, his life would be nearly perfect. He could not wait to marry her.

CHAPTER SIXTEEN

"Quit moving, Flaherty!"

"I'm sitting on the fecking chair, aren't I?"

MacReady, the viscount's right-hand man, grumbled, "Stop talking! I can't sew the wound closed if you keep moving your mouth."

Mary Kate shot to her feet to defend her fiancé, and immediately sucked in a breath as pain seared through her injured ankle.

Flaherty heard and growled, "Sit!"

She felt her cheeks warm as her temper ignited. "I shall stand if I wish to. And may I remind you, *Mr.* Flaherty, I do not have to listen to you until we are married."

"There's where ye'd be wrong, lass." MacReady grumbled under his breath and tugged on the thread he was using to close the wound. Flaherty flinched. "Finish it, MacReady!"

Garahan chuckled. "He'd have finished a quarter of an hour ago if ye'd just kept yer *gob* shut. It's taken him twice as long to bind together the puny groove that sharpshooter carved into the side of yer face."

Mary Kate had yet to sit back down when she heard Flaherty draw in a deep breath and just knew he was prepared to blast Garahan. She touched his arm, surprised when his gaze shifted to hers.

"As I was saying, lass, ye're hurt, and I know from experience that yer twisted ankle is swollen. Ye should be elevating it on a pillow, as MacReady recommended. Why is it that ye haven't heeded his warnings and instructions when he went to the trouble to check the bone to ensure 'tisn't broken? The man has enough to do without tending to our injuries out of the goodness of his heart only to be ignored."

When she did not respond, he asked, "If ye don't intend to heed MacReady's instructions, why should I?"

Botheration! Flaherty was right, but Mary Kate was not quite ready to admit it. She tried to appeal to his sense of duty instead. "Seamus, please let MacReady stitch your wound closed. Their lordships are waiting to speak to you."

She hated the fact that she could not keep the worry from her voice. Flaherty had enough to worry about, and he did not need to take on her worries as well, especially since he was already concerned about her sprained ankle. But his latest wound was far from insignificant. From her point of view—which was too close to Seamus for comfort—she had a distinct feeling that the pistol ball that grazed his face would not slow the Irishman down one bit.

MacReady's needle pierced Flaherty's face again and again as the boiled thread drew the edges of the wound together. How many more times could he be shot before it slowed him down? It had been three times in the last few weeks! She shuddered, thinking that the next pistol ball might be his last…

"'Tis a paltry wound," Flaherty grumbled. "And MacReady's taking forever to close it."

"If ye'd close yer mouth," Dermott said, "I'm thinking the man would be able to finish the last few stitches quickly."

Frustrated with Flaherty, but unable to voice that frustration because she knew the man had to be in pain, she tried again. "Seamus, please?"

There was no way that he would refuse her when she asked him so sweetly. Could he? While she worried over the thought, MacReady tied off the threads. "Done!"

Flaherty grunted. "About fecking time."

"I heard that!" the Scotsman replied.

"I meant ye to." Flaherty got to his feet, reached out a hand to her, and frowned. "Ye're looking tired, lass. Instead of sitting with yer foot elevated, I'm thinking ye need to lie down."

"It's the middle of the day! Why on earth would I need to lie down?"

"Did ye hit yer head when we were tossed off me horse?"

Mary Kate nearly bit off the tip of her tongue to keep quiet. Anything she said would no doubt rile the man she would be marrying in a few hours' time. Were all men so difficult to get along with when they wanted their way? And how was it that a man's mind concentrated on one thing, when a woman's concentrated on something completely different? She may never know the answer.

"I did not land on my head," Mary Kate said.

Flaherty's gaze rested on her for a moment before he asked, "Then why do ye look as if ye were out all night scouring the stables?"

Mary Kate fought to keep her irritation under wraps. She owed it to the poor man. Flaherty had been grazed across the cheek not two hours earlier. Any closer and…

She shoved that thought aside and thanked MacReady. "The bandage around my ankle is snug enough that the pain is at a minimum." Needing to prove that she wasn't as badly hurt as Flaherty thought, she put more weight on it and retained her balance. Patience was called for. "One of my duties is to ensure her ladyship's horses are bedded down for the night. I take my duties very seriously."

"I'm thinking 'tis the stable master's duty ye've just described—and ye know it. Yer job is to say goodnight to her horses."

She fought to keep her expression bland, though it was not easy. "Do you have any other personal criticisms, Flaherty?"

"Facts are not criticisms, though if and when I have need to criticize ye, lass, it will be to keep ye safe from harm. And when I do, ye'll not be needing to ask. Ye'll know."

Mary Kate wondered why she felt the need to contradict everything Flaherty said or did. Examining her feelings, it hit her that she hadn't always done so. She respected him and his position within the duke's guard. Truth be told, it had started after he ordered her to leave.

She had accepted his apology, and it was time for her to let go of the hurt feelings she held tight to her breast. It was time to fully forgive him. He truly did not recall anything that he said or did while fevered. And another thought plagued her—it would not be well done of her to challenge him in front of others. It could undermine his authority and encourage others to do the same. From now on, if there was an important point that they disagreed on, she would speak to him about it privately.

Heaven only knew how often that would be happening. Flaherty questioned her more than she was used to. In order to keep the status quo, she would have to bite her tongue until she and Flaherty grew more accustomed to how each other thought and acted upon those thoughts. Her allegiance had been to Lady Calliope and Lord William. Once she and Flaherty wed, would he be competing for that top spot? Mary Kate could not imagine that he would want to feel as if he were in a tug-of-war with Lady Calliope for Mary Kate's attention. It would put her smack in the middle, with her husband on one end and Lady Calliope on the other, vying for her undivided attention. That would only add to the messy broth already in the pot of her life!

"Flaherty!" The earl strode into the kitchen and paused. Mary Kate sensed that he was assessing Flaherty's health. The earl's swift nod in Flaherty's direction was the only indication that he'd found him fit for duty. "I see you've gained another scar in service to my brother. Be assured, I shall inform him of your latest injury."

If Mary Kate had not been watching the man she were to marry so closely, she would have missed the flash of concern in the depths of his deep blue eyes as he shot to his feet to stand before the earl. But she had been keeping close watch and had seen it. Was Seamus worried that the duke would remove him from duty for being shot three times inside of a few weeks?

She had heard whispers of the duke's *new* guard that was divided into groups that scoured the bowels and dregs of London's stews, while others were stationed in and around the Dark Walk. Still others were assigned near the docks. All of the duke's newest London recruits kept up with the latest rumblings in the underworld, gathering pertinent information relating to the duke and his extended family from all levels of society. Enemies had seemed to crawl out of the woodwork when His Grace successfully restored his family's reputation and filled their empty coffers. His elder brother's mismanagement and lack of respect for the title had nearly destroyed what their father, the fourth duke, had accomplished before he died.

Mary Kate had heard more than one rumor that the fifth duke, the current duke's eldest brother, had been on the road to perdition for some years. Many had hoped to lead the sixth duke down that same road—all the while continuing to fill their pockets with the coin they planned to fleece from the dukedom. The sixth duke was a man of high integrity and principles who had no intention of gambling or spending his nights with lightskirts or actresses. Anticipated coin had been lost, forcing those who thought to gain it to try other avenues to discredit the newly minted duke—ruin via rumor, innuendo, scandalbroth, and lies.

She shifted closer to Flaherty's side, balancing more of her weight on her good ankle. Though she longed for a sign that he was not angry with her, she would never interrupt him when the earl was speaking to him. She stood silent for a few minutes more, relieved when he placed a hand at her waist and kept it there. Did he need the physical contact as much as she did? A bond had been formed months ago...the first time he kissed her. Then he'd kept proving that he cared for her. Deeply. She marveled at his strength and concentration—even after being shot in the face.

"I don't think ye should bother His Grace with the scratch on me face, yer lordship. Only required a stitch or two, and MacReady has taken care of the task."

"Eleven," Mary Kate corrected him. "I counted."

"Far from a scratch, wouldn't you agree, Lippincott?" The viscount stepped into the room, took one look at Flaherty, and shook his head. "Are you trying to outdo your cousins? I believe there is now a three-way tie for the worst injury incurred in the line of duty between yourself, Sean, and Darby. I'm not sure which one of you has suffered more while protecting the duke."

"Truth be told, yer lordship, not one of us was protecting the duke at the time," Flaherty reminded him. "I was shot protecting Dermott's wife while stationed at Lippincott Manor. Sean was injured walking out of the rear entrance to the duke's town house on Grosvenor Square. Darby was jumped from behind on the streets of London."

"All while seeing to your duties to my brother," the earl said.

"Aye, but—"

"No use arguing with Lippincott," the viscount said. "Now then, any problems with your balance or your vision?"

"None, your lordship."

"Excellent." Chattsworth turned toward Mary Kate and asked, "How is your ankle? Should you not be sitting with your foot on a pillow?"

"Aye, yer lordship," Flaherty grumbled. "That she should."

Mary Kate frowned at him, but it seemed to have no effect on the man. "I really don't think—"

He startled the breath out of her when he scooped her into his arms. "We've had this discussion before, lass. 'Tis obvious to some of us that ye don't think before ye act." Turning to the earl and the viscount, he said, "With yer permission, I'd like to take me bride-to-be to her bedchamber so she can rest with her foot elevated."

"I do not think that wise, William," Lady Calliope replied, entering the kitchen with Lady Aurelia hot on her heels. "Aurelia and I leave you alone for half an hour and you're ready to let Flaherty carry Mary Kate to her bedchamber without a chaperone?"

"Not well done of you, Flaherty." Lady Aurelia was not smiling.

He was used to her smiles, not her frowns. "The lass is being difficult."

Frustration twined with fear of the unknown as Mary Kate wondered what it would be like for Flaherty to carry her to her room—or their room, once they were wed. She needed to ask if he were still planning on marrying her later tonight, but had to clarify a salient point first. "And you *weren't* being difficult, making MacReady wait for you to stop talking so he could finish closing your injury?"

"It seems you both have been giving poor MacReady fits," Calliope said.

"But I—"

Chattsworth glared at Flaherty. "Would not think of gainsaying my wife."

"I wouldn't dream of it."

"Then please carry Mary Kate to the room at the end of the hallway," Calliope instructed him. "You know we keep a cot in that room and have set it up just like the duke's London town house and Wyndmere Hall in the Lake District."

"We have done the same at Lippincott Manor," Aurelia added. "Keeping a ready supply of healing herbs, tinctures, and stacks of linens to care for the numerous wounds all of you seem to acquire while protecting our families is a must."

"We learned just how important from our time at Wyndmere Hall," Calliope added, "thanks to Constance and Merriweather, the duke's cook and housekeeper there."

"I'll walk with Flaherty," Garahan said, "to make sure he doesn't drop Mary Kate."

The very idea had a giggle slipping out before Mary Kate could cover her mouth with her hands, which earned another frown from her intended.

"Too late," he murmured close to her ear. "I heard that."

"Follow me, Seamus," Garahan said. "I just refilled me flask."

"Did ye now. Well then, lead the way, and I'll gladly relieve ye of a sip or two."

Giving in to the warmth radiating from Flaherty's body, Mary Kate realized she was tired from her ordeal. She sighed and laid her cheek against his heart.

He brushed a kiss to her temple. "There's a lass. Let me take care of ye."

"But you're hurt, too."

"Why don't we agree to argue after we're wed?"

Garahan opened the door to the room at the end of the hall. "With all that's happened, do ye still plan to marry tonight?"

"No," Mary Kate replied.

"Aye," Flaherty said at the same time.

Garahan snorted. "I'll speak to their lordships to see if either one has sent word to the vicar. Then again, the village gossip chain is usually rife with news, so mayhap we should ask Mrs. Romney what she's heard."

"Would ye want to wait to marry if ye were in me shoes?"

"I *have* been in yer shoes, and ye know I didn't wait. Melinda needed the protection of me name."

"Well then, I expect ye to back me up when I suggest that to the earl."

"And the viscount," Garahan added.

"Aye, and the viscount."

"What about their ladyships?" Mary Kate asked.

"I'm sure they'll be stopping in to check on you in a few minutes. Neither one would want to leave ye alone with me or Garahan for long—let alone both of us at the same time."

"How right you are," Lady Aurelia agreed as she entered the room with Calliope right behind her. "Now, what's all this talk about marrying tonight?"

"Their lordships agreed earlier," Flaherty reminded them.

"All things considered—" Lady Calliope began, only to be interrupted by Flaherty.

"Begging yer pardon, yer ladyship, but given all that's happened, I think the protection of me name would guarantee no one else would dare try to abduct Mary Kate."

Lady Aurelia nodded. "He has a good point."

Mary Kate sat up. "Does anyone want to know what I think?"

Flaherty got down on one knee beside the cot and brought her hand to his lips. "Don't ye want to marry me, lass?"

Undone by the hint of worry in his voice, she sighed and watched as he lifted her hand to his lips a second time. Only this time, his lips lingered, and she felt herself falling deeper under the spell of the handsome man who'd by turns irritated and captivated her. She gave a gentle tug on his hand, and he leaned closer. When their lips were a breath apart, she whispered, "Yes, I do want to marry you, Seamus."

Mary Kate poured everything she felt—and hoped for—into her kiss. Seamus took control and passion erupted between them. Her head spun, and her heart pounded. Lord, the man could kiss!

"I believe I'll send for the vicar."

Mary Kate was not certain if the earl or the viscount made that remark, not that it mattered. What did was the man who held her as if she were precious.

"Thank ye, yer lordship."

"I'll stay behind as chaperone." Aurelia's voice sounded distant, though in truth it was hard for Mary Kate to hear anything over the buzzing in her head.

Flaherty nibbled at her lips. "No need to stay on my account, yer ladyship."

Garahan laid a hand on Flaherty's shoulder. "Time to get cleaned up, me boy-o."

"There's plenty of time," Flaherty replied.

Garahan tightened his grip, and Flaherty rose to his feet.

"Think of yer bride-to-be," Garahan said. "Sure and she'll be wanting to soak in a hot tub."

"Why don't you ask the footmen to carry in the copper tub from the storeroom, Garahan?" Lady Calliope said. "Flaherty, please speak to Mrs. Romney about the hot water to fill it. When you two have taken care of that, one of you can ask Hargrave or MacReady to see to it a bath is filled for Flaherty."

"I haven't anything clean to change into," Flaherty told them.

"We came prepared and have brought O'Malley's spare uniform for you." Aurelia made a shooing motion, then asked the men, "Well? What are you waiting for?"

Flaherty was smiling when he lowered his lips to Mary Kate's one last time. "I'll be back and am looking forward to more than one kiss, lass."

Hand to her breast, heart in her eyes, Mary Kate could only nod.

CHAPTER SEVENTEEN

F LAHERTY SANK INTO the tub and groaned as the hot water
eased the worst of the ache between his shoulder blades.
He'd landed hard and had a sneaking suspicion the lass had, too.
Not that Mary Kate would admit it. She was too stubborn and
strong-minded for her own good. His match down to the bone.

Garahan knocked on the door and walked into the guards'
former quarters. "Nothing's changed in here since I left it the day
I married Melinda. Don't worry that ye'll have to bring the lass
back here tonight to sleep."

"I don't work for the viscount," Flaherty scoffed. "I'll be
bringing her to stay at the guards' quarters at Lippincott Manor."

His cousin nodded. "True, though more than likely, the earl
will be gifting ye with a cottage. He and the viscount have done
so for all of us so far."

"There are no guarantees in life, ye know that, James."

"Well now, I cannot argue with that. Rest assured, Seamus,
no one will be forgetting ye—ye're the Duke's Champion!"

"Some champion I turned out to be, shot three times in less
than six weeks!

Garahan's gaze narrowed on Flaherty. "Stop feeling sorry for
yerself. There's not one of us that hasn't been clubbed over the
head, slashed, or shot."

"Aye, but I'm the only one so far who's had three lead balls dug out of his hide!"

"Only two were extracted from yer sorry hide," Garahan reminded him. "The third one left an impressive groove in yer face. Ye'll have another scar to boast about."

Flaherty had no ready comeback. Staring at the rapidly cooling water, he didn't want to admit to his cousin what really worried him…that the lass would take a look at his disfigured face, turn tail, and run.

Garahan pulled his flask out of his pocket. "Thought ye might need another sip or two of the Irish."

Grateful beyond words, Flaherty held out his hand.

His cousin chuckled and handed him the flask. "Are ye worried about tonight?"

Flaherty choked on the whisky he was swallowing. "Are ye thinking I need advice from a married man?"

Garahan snatched the flask back and took a swig. "Ye don't, but yer bride-to-be may be a bit hesitant about the marriage bed. Have ye forgotten what nearly happened to her tonight at the hands of that blackguard?"

Flaherty had to admit, his cousin had a point. "To be honest, I was thinking I'd need to use me manly charms to sweep her off her feet so she didn't stare at me face too long. She'd be helpless to resist me—just like all the others."

"I wouldn't advise mentioning that fact to yer bride, unless ye're thinking of sleeping alone tonight." Garahan waited a moment before he added, "As fer yer sorry mug, Mary Kate is not faint of heart, and I cannot see her tossing ye back for a tiny scar."

"She counted the stitches, James."

"Aye. Did ye notice she was trying to hide the fact that she flinched each time MacReady's needle pierced yer flesh?"

"Nay." Flaherty motioned for Garahan to hand him the flask, took a sip, and gave it back. "Thanks. That's enough for me. I need a clear head if what ye're suggesting turns out to be the case. I'm thinking it won't be—the lass is stronger than ye know."

"Even the strongest women need reassurance now and

again," Garahan said. "At least yer wife wasn't abused. When I think of me wife's cousin taking a switch to her back…"

Flaherty watched anguish contort his cousin's face. Garahan shook his head, and the neutral expression he showed the world was in place once more.

"James, I—"

"I've resigned meself to not beating the man to a bloody pulp. I was given leave to level a blow or two—no more. I'd never ignore an order from His Grace."

Flaherty motioned for Garahan to hand him the drying cloth. "But ye dream of it, don't ye?"

"Aye." Garahan scrubbed his hands over his face. "Hurry it up—the vicar should be arriving any time now."

"Close the door behind ye!"

Alone, Flaherty ignored the twinge across his upper back, dried off, and dressed. He didn't bother to glance in the looking glass. He knew his face was a sight—black and blue where the lead ball bruised the flesh that it had left behind. 'Twould be a rainbow of color over the next few days. He'd never particularly cared about stitches and bruises before, but for the lass's sake, he was caring now. He didn't want to frighten her tomorrow morning when they woke together for the first time in his bed. Lord willing, they'd have exhausted themselves making love before they fell asleep. Though he insisted to Garahan that she would not be, and though Flaherty would wish it otherwise, her first sight of his face—with the dark threads and bruised skin around the wound—might scare her.

The idea that she would be afraid of him bothered Flaherty, until he resigned himself to the fact that he had to see for himself just how bad his face looked. He flinched as he studied his reflection. "I'll see if I can have the lass stand on me good side for the vow taking." He nodded to his reflection. "Well then, 'tis time to get it done. Next time I see me ugly mug, I'll be a married man." He grinned, and his reflection grinned back at him. "A happily married man who will have wed and bedded his wife."

The thought of it had him whistling as he made his way to the manor house.

His life was about to change for the better.

MARY KATE COULDN'T seem to catch her breath. The whirlwind of activity that surrounded her once she'd dried off from the bath made her head spin. She sat obligingly in front of the looking glass while Lady Aurelia's maid fussed with her hair. "I usually just bundle it up, fasten a few pins in to hold it off my shoulders and my face. I don't need anything fancier than that."

Aurelia disagreed. "Nonsense. Let Jenny pin it up and pull a few tendrils free near your temples and the nape of your neck, and a curl or two that will dangle in front of your eyes."

Mary Kate frowned. "How will I see where I'm going?"

"We'll help you," Calliope volunteered.

Aurelia smiled. "Once you are standing beside Flaherty, he will not be able to resist reaching out to brush a wisp of hair out of your eyes."

Mary Kate was confused. "Why would I want him to do that?"

"You want him to notice everything about you. He'll be seeing you differently when you are saying your vows. Before tonight, you were the woman he was courting. After the vicar marries you, you'll be his wife, and Lord willing, the mother of his children. You want him to treasure you."

Calliope sighed. "He already does, Aurelia. Did you not see how he looks at Mary Kate whenever he enters the room?"

Aurelia nodded. "Besotted."

"I mean no disrespect to either of your ladyships," Mary Kate murmured, "but I think you both have attics to let."

The two women dissolved into laughter. The sound lifted a bit of the worry from Mary Kate's shoulders. "What if I hesitate when he's ready to seal our vows? What if I laugh? What if I cry?"

Lady Calliope motioned for Aurelia's maid to step back. "You look beautiful, and you will not cry. You may laugh, but warn him ahead of time that you are prone to laughter when you are nervous."

"Oh dear! I do laugh when I'm nervous, don't I?"

"Yes," Calliope agreed. "Remember, forewarned is forearmed. He'll be expecting you to be nervous after you warn him, and will expect your laughter, and not take it as a slur against his manliness."

Mary Kate digested that thought. "That would not do, would it?"

Aurelia shook her head. "Is there anything else that has you concerned? We did answer the few questions you had, but please do not be afraid to ask. And do not worry—we will never betray your trust or speak of what we discuss here tonight."

"Thank you, your ladyships. You have been so kind and have answered most of my questions. There is just one more thing I have been wondering—something I overheard one of the Lady Kittrick's scullery maids boasting about."

"This sounds intriguing," Lady Aurelia said.

"What did she say?" Lady Calliope asked.

"She said the young man she was...er...with—Oh, never mind!"

"Come now," Aurelia urged. "You know you can trust us. Just ask."

"Is it possible for a man to, um... How can I put this without sounding like a complete hoyden?" Mary Kate blew out a breath, and in one garbled word, asked, *"Canamanrisetotheoccasionmore thanonceanight?"*

Aurelia answered first. "Absolutely!"

Calliope blushed. "More than twice, actually."

Mary Kate swallowed past the lump in her throat. "Isn't it too painful the first time to...you know?"

"Make love," Calliope murmured. "What happens between a

man and a woman within the sanctity of marriage is called making love. If I'm right, and Flaherty is the man I believe him to be, the pain will be fleeting."

"Trust him to ready you to accept him."

Mary Kate frowned again as she felt the heat rise to her cheeks. "I have no idea what you are talking about."

Aurelia sighed. "Blush all you want, but do listen. Your husband will no doubt be far larger than you envision when you see him unclothed for the first time. Trust me when I tell you that you may worry that there is no possibility that he will—for lack of better explanation—*fit*. Trust him when he tells you he needs to stretch you to ensure that he will."

Calliope turned a darker shade of pink with embarrassment. Aurelia nodded to emphasize that she knew what she was speaking about. Mary Kate had lost the ability to speak altogether.

"Well then, I do believe you have succinctly answered Mary Kate's question, Aurelia." Turning to Mary Kate, Calliope said, "Trust me when I say that Flaherty loves you—"

"And you love him," Aurelia interrupted. "Trust him with your body—"

"As well as your heart."

Mary Kate's eyes welled with tears at the way their ladyships eased the worst of her worries, and a tiny bit of the fear that she would do something wrong later tonight. "I never imagined that I would have someone willing to talk to me so honestly about what to expect in the marriage bed. I will always remember your frankness and kindness, your ladyships. From the bottom of my heart, thank you."

Calliope and Aurelia hugged her. "Now then, turn around one more time," Aurelia said. When Mary Kate complied, she clapped her hands together. "Doesn't she look beautiful, Calliope?"

"Beautiful," Calliope agreed. "The three-quarter sleeves hide the bruises."

Mary Kate grimaced. "I had forgotten about them. Will it

bother Flaherty?"

"Yes, but he will be doing his best to soothe your worries tonight."

The knock on the bedchamber door, and the announcement that the vicar had arrived and Flaherty was waiting, had their ladyships responding, "We'll be right down."

Tugging on Mary Kate to get her moving, they walked out of the room and down the stairs.

At the bottom of the steps, the viscount was waiting. He offered his arm, tucking her close to his side as he escorted her to the sitting room. "You look lovely, Mary Kate. We'd best hurry. When I left, Flaherty was wearing a hole in the sitting room carpet waiting for you."

THE NEXT HALF an hour passed in a blur. Mary Kate was fairly certain Flaherty said his vows, and that she managed to repeat hers. She came vibrantly to life when his lips met hers. Every part of her tingled from head to toe, while her husband kissed the breath right out of her.

When he ended the kiss, she blinked and stared into eyes that held myriad emotions so chaotic, she wondered how he managed to appear so calm. She was trembling inside. Was it from his kiss or the worry that somehow she'd fall short of his expectations of the coming night?

She cupped the injured side of his face and pressed her lips below his scar. Overwhelmed with the feelings rioting inside of her, she rasped, "I love you, Seamus."

His eyes blazed with passion for a heartbeat, before the heat banked to a simmering warmth. "There's the lass I love."

Garahan hugged his wife and pressed a kiss to her temple. "The first of the Flahertys to fall."

Michael O'Malley wrapped his arm around his wife and chuckled. "Who wants to wager 'tis Rory who falls next?"

His brother Sean slipped his arm around his wife. "I'm in, but I'm placing me bet on Dillon!"

Dermott O'Malley smiled down at his wife and kissed her forehead. "Ye're both wrong—'twill be Fenton. He's the wiliest of the Flaherty brothers. Thinks he'll never get caught."

Seamus stared down at Mary Kate and brushed a lock of hair that had caught on her long, dark eyelashes. "Faith, I know that I'm a sorry sight at the moment with threads holding me cheek together, but I'm thinking I'll be able to distract ye later when we—"

She put her hand over his mouth. Seamus and his cousins roared with laughter while their wives prodded or poked them to get them to stop laughing. Instead of letting him think he'd gotten the better of her by embarrassing her in front of everyone, Mary Kate leaned close and purred, "Mayhap I'll be distracting you."

Not willing to let him have the last word, she removed her hand and nipped his bottom lip before molding her mouth—and her body—against him.

The men cheered and their wives tried to shush them, but Mary Kate's boast was turned around on her when Flaherty slid his hand to the base of her spine, urging her closer still, and slid his tongue between her lips to taste her fully.

Pinned against her husband, she was swept up in the silent promises he made to her with lips and tongue. A heartbeat later, she sagged against him when he ended the kiss.

Flaherty braced her against him for a moment, then swept her into his arms. "Thank ye all for a fine wedding. If ye'll excuse us…" He left the rest unsaid and strode out of the sitting room.

Mary Kate protested, "Seamus, we cannot just *leave*."

He chuckled. "We just did."

"But their lordships, their ladyships! Your cousins and their wives—"

"Are all well aware of what happens after a couple weds, lass," her husband rumbled. "Let them enjoy the meal they've planned for us. I'm certain Lady Calliope and Lady Aurelia will have sent a tray of food to the guest bedchamber the viscount told me was ours to use for the night. I'm expected back at Lippincott Manor tomorrow, though his lordship did say that I wasn't expected to resume my duties for three days."

"Then why do we need to leave?"

"We cannot very well share yer bed in the servants' quarters on the third floor. 'Tis too small."

She had to agree. "I had not thought of that."

Flaherty took the steps up two at a time, tightening his hold on her. "Not to worry. I did." He stopped in front of the last door on the left. "Open the door, lass."

Mary Kate turned the knob and opened the door.

He stepped over the threshold and spun around. "Lock the door."

Her hands shook, though she did as he asked.

"Now then, bride of mine, I'm thinking ye need to follow through with yer promise to distract me."

She smiled and lifted her lips to his. "Kiss me, Seamus."

CHAPTER EIGHTEEN

FLAHERTY WAS LAUGHING when he kissed his wife. God, she tasted of sass and honey. Deepening the kiss, he tasted her fully. Lost in her flavor and the curves nestled against him, he felt his control start to slip. He growled, yanked it back, and lifted his lips from hers. "Ye pack a powerful punch, lass."

His lovely bride was having trouble catching her breath. Flaherty did not mind in the least.

"I'm thinking we could eat later."

"Eat?"

He chuckled. "Did ye not notice the table set for two with the candles and flowers?"

Her mouth opened and a garbled sound emerged.

"I'll take that as a no." He did not want to let her go just yet. "If ye're that hungry..." He didn't bother to finish, because the lass wasn't looking at the food. She was staring at his mouth. Thoughts of what he could not wait to teach his sweet bride fanned the fire already burning inside of him. He clamped down on his libido, or else their joining would be over in a matter of minutes. That was not what he had in mind for their first time making love. He needed to be fully in control. There was no way he would let his overwhelming need to lay her on the bed and uncover the gift God placed in his hands take over.

Flaherty sucked in a deep breath and slowly set her on her

feet. "Well?"

She blinked. "Well what?"

"Are ye?"

"Am I what?" The dazed look in her eyes had him tightening the hold on his control until he groaned.

"Hungry."

Mary Kate stared at her feet. "Not especially." She raised her gaze to meet his and admitted, "Nervous. Anxious and a bit frightened."

"That's a bit of a list, *mo chroí*. Ye have no need to fear me, lass. I'll do me best to ease the way until ye body is ready to accept me."

Her face turned a delightful shade of rosy pink. *Better than pale and pasty.* She laughed and immediately clapped a hand over her mouth.

Eyes wide with worry stared at him, leaving him to suspect the lass laughed when she was nervous. "Well now, as I have not said anything funny, I'm thinking ye tend to laugh when yer nerves get the better of ye."

Mary Kate dropped her hand. "I have tried to break the habit, and have somewhat…but I have never been in a situation like this before."

"I should hope not."

Her blush deepened, and he almost felt sorry for her. The lass was about to have her first lesson in love, and if he played his cards right, she would be mindless with desire by the time they sealed their vows. He would soothe her tender feelings along the way, but 'twas time to put actions to his words.

"Then if I removed me frockcoat and waistcoat…" He took off his coat and shed his waistcoat, and sure enough, the lass covered her mouth again, but not before a snicker emerged.

Taking a chance that she would not turn from him in disgust when she saw he was riddled with scars from a lifetime of fighting—in particular from the last few years protecting the duke and his family—he removed his cravat and shirt.

She wasn't laughing now. The lass was humming as her gaze dropped from his eyes, to his chin, to his chest. As it trailed across his abdomen, lingering at his waist, he could not resist asking, "See something ye like?"

Her eyes shot up to meet his. "Forgive me. I've never… Well, you see… The thing of it is…"

He chuckled. "Ye've never seen a man without a shirt before and are overwhelmed by the sight of me broad and manly chest?"

She nodded.

"Not even yer da, if he was working outside in the heat of the day?"

She cleared her throat. "No."

"Haven't ye wondered what I looked like beneath me coat?"

Mary Kate shook her head.

"It hasn't escaped me notice that ye've measured the width of me shoulders and breadth of me chest with yer eyes, lass."

She gulped, and he strove not to laugh. Lord the lass was a delight! "Never wondered what I looked like in me shirtsleeves and waistcoat?"

She bit her bottom lip, and he fought to keep his ironclad control firmly in place. "Ye have parts of me going hard as a rock when he bite yer lip like that, lass."

She frowned. "Parts of you?"

He drew her against him, felt her tremble, and wondered how quickly he could convince her to remove her gown. Her soft gasp had him repeating his vow to go slowly. He wasn't a rutting beast! The lass had been through a traumatic experience earlier, and then thrown off his horse. She could have a cracked rib and not even know it.

His head battled against his body's need. *Slow down! Treat her as if she were made of fine bone china.* "As ye aren't hungry, why don't ye let me help ye undress?"

"Now?"

"Aye, lass. Now."

"Wouldn't you rather wait until later?"

He frowned. "How much later?" She mumbled beneath her breath, and he snorted with laughter. "No. I do not want to wait until next week."

Mary Kate glared at him. "You weren't supposed to hear that."

"Then ye should not have said it aloud."

"I don't know if I'm ready. I keep thinking of…"

When her voice trailed off, he knew that she was thinking of the bloody farrier's abducting her. He needed to distract her to ease her worry. "Why don't we compromise?"

"Yes, please!"

He slowly smiled. "I'll remove yer gown—as it doesn't seem fair that ye get to ogle me standing here in just me trousers, socks, and boots—and ye can leave yer chemise on. We'll share a meal and have a glass or two of wine—or brandy if ye wish."

She wrinkled her nose. "I'd rather have whisky."

"Would ye now? I happen to have a flask in me waistcoat pocket."

Mary Kate got a bit of her grit back and mimicked his accent. "Do ye now?"

He laughed and hugged her close to his heart. "Faith, I love ye, lass. In truth, I cannot wait to make ye mine, but I'll go as slow as I'm able and tell ye when I'm about to burst with need so I don't ruin the bed linens."

Her eyes were wide as saucers. "I don't think it's necessary for you to shred the bed linens—"

He could not contain his laughter. When she smacked him in the shoulder, he swallowed the rest of it. "Ye have no idea what I'm talking about, do ye?"

She narrowed her eyes at him. "Whatever gave you that idea?"

"Ye're a sassy bit of goods, Mary Kate Donovan."

Her frown softened into a smile. "Mary Kate *Flaherty*."

"Aye, bride of mine. I'm after making ye me wife, and need to ask, do ye know what happens in the marriage bed?"

"Of course."

"But ye didn't get me meaning when I said I'd ruin the bed linens."

"Obviously."

"Do ye know what a man's seed is?"

Her face flamed. "Yes."

"Do you know how it's planted?"

This time she covered her face with her hands. "Yes!"

He fought not to smile as he gently removed her hands so he could see her expression. "Well, there's more of it than ye might think, when a man's blood is hot and his seed is ready to be planted."

She groaned.

"As I was saying, if it's ready to be planted and not in his wife's warm, soft passage, what do ye think happens when it erupts out of his shaft?"

This time, Mary Kate ducked her head and moaned. "Could we please cease talking about this?"

It was exactly what he hoped for. "Aye. Why don't we eat later? And since ye already know the mechanics of the act, why don't I show ye the how yer body will weep for mine? Ye'll feel ready to burst with need by the time I've caressed each and every bit of ye that is just waiting to learn me tender touch."

She licked her lips, and he held on to his control by a thread. "Let me help ye off with yer gown." His voice sounded hoarse, but at least he was still able to speak.

His bride turned her back to him so he could undo her buttons. That done, he turned her back around, needing to see the expression on her face when he slowly removed her gown. He tossed the garment on the chair by the bed and turned back, but paused. "Ah, lass, yer poor arms. Let me soothe the hurt he caused ye." Gently, reverently, he kissed where rough hands had been wrapped around her upper arms, leaving dark bruises behind. When she went pliant at his tender touch, he pulled her close and plundered her mouth with lips and tongue, mimicking how he planned to plunder her soft depths once he'd stretched her to the point where her body would welcome his with as little pain as possible.

They were both gasping for breath when he ended the kiss and lifted her into his arms and onto the bed. He joined her on the bed, lying beside her. She was trembling, but he knew just where to lightly touch to ease her worry. Gazing at the bounty of the beauty he'd married, he rasped, "Trust me, lass."

THE DEPTH OF his voice reverberated through to her spine as his lips whispered kisses along her collarbone. She could not answer, couldn't speak. A low moan wrapped around them, until she realized *she* was the one who moaned.

Seamus's lips increased their pressure as he kissed his way back to the base of her throat. His tongue dipped into the hollow. "Ye taste of lilac and roses. May I taste ye elsewhere, lass?"

She had no idea where exactly *elsewhere* would encompass, but the sensations his lips, teeth, and tongue evoked had her moaning one moment and gasping the next.

His callused hands stroked from her shoulders to her wrists and back before slipping beneath her arms. He slid the tips of his fingers along her curves, nudging the fullness of her breasts.

She drew in a breath and held it while his hand tested the weight of one breast and then the other. The fabric of her chemise added to the sensation of his huge hands cupping her. Slowly, her eyes closed, as the heat from his hands warmed wherever he stroked.

"If ye need me to stop, ye need to say the word, lass."

She couldn't think, let alone speak. His feather-soft caresses opened a whole new world of sensation as her body responded to the magic of his touch.

"God, ye're beautiful." His lips nipped below her ear before he nuzzled her there, pausing to draw in a deep breath.

Was he inhaling her scent, or trying to slow down the pace? She wanted to ask, but he traced the same path along her curves with his lips, licking and nibbling her sensitized breasts through her dampened chemise. Unable to control what was happening to her, she arched up and moaned his name.

"That's the way, lass. Imagine how it would feel if there wasn't a garment between us. Me tongue would be able to sample yer flavor, while me lips would gently kiss, then draw ye in and suckle ye."

She opened her eyes and stared into the dark sapphire depths of the gaze holding her captive. "Help me take it off."

He stripped it off her and groaned. "God in Heaven, yer beauty takes me breath away. Let me unlock yer passion."

"Yes, please."

His head dipped, and his mouth settled on her breast, and she would later swear she saw stars as his tongue toyed with her nipple, setting off a series of explosive reactions inside of her. The heat of him, the weight of him, added to the ministrations of his mouth…his tongue…his teeth, tying her in knots, as tension built in her core.

As if he sensed what was happening inside of her, he pressed his hard length against the apex of her thighs, sending her spiraling until she screamed his name and flew into oblivion.

She snapped back to awareness when his weight lifted off her. "No! Don't leave."

He choked out a laugh. "I'll never be leaving ye, Mary Kate." He removed his boots and socks, then shucked his trousers.

The heavy length and breadth of him should have been frightening, but she'd felt the pressure of him and it had sent her spinning out of control. Needing to feel that connection and heady elation again, she lifted her hand, beckoning him. "Am I ready for you yet?"

He closed his eyes and groaned. "Not yet. Are ye willing to let me stretch ye?"

She nodded, and he settled on the bed once more, caressing her everywhere at once, until her breath caught and she felt the tension building inside of her again. "Don't be afraid of me touch, lass." He slid his hand from her breast to her belly and lower still, finding her soft, damp, and wanting. "Yer body knows what it wants."

"Does it?"

He dipped a finger inside and growled as he slowly urged her to relax and accept his touch, gently stretching her while plumbing her depths with first one finger, then two. When he added a third finger, she felt herself pulse around him as she came apart once more. She was still gasping when he removed his fingers and poised above her, his shaft nudging her entrance. "Ye're as ready as ye'll be. Take me inside ye, lass."

She lifted her hips, offering herself. He started off slowly, gradually sliding in further, sinking deeper, until he pressed against her maidenhead.

"Look at me." When she did, he warned her, "I'm sorry to be causing ye pain, but there's no other way. It will ease, and when it does, ye'll feel more than pain. When ye do, tell me, and I'll take ye to Heaven."

She hesitated, and he murmured, "Trust me."

"I do."

He lowered his mouth to hers, kissing her slowly at first, matching the pace he'd already set making love to her. His next kiss stole her breath, and he plunged into her, filling her to the hilt. He didn't move his body, but rained kisses all over her face and neck as her ragged breathing finally slowed. He tenderly kissed her. "There's a lass—it'll be easing now. Tell me when ye're ready."

A heartbeat later, the sensations she felt earlier, when he was finding places she had not known existed, returned. She was still sore, but the whispered promise of Heaven pulled at her as his kisses drugged her. "I'm ready."

With a shout of elation, he withdrew and plunged into her carefully, yet with a determination that had her sliding her hands from the mattress around his waist and lower…to cup his buttocks. The taut muscles tensed beneath her fingers. "God, lass, I cannot hold out much longer."

She had no idea what he was waiting for, because in her heart she sensed that Heaven was one forceful stroke away. She called his name, and he plunged into her one last time, pouring his seed inside her as she fell apart in his arms.

She must have drifted to sleep, because she woke to his fingertips tracing the line of one eyebrow and then the other. "Seamus?"

"Aye, wife."

"Not your bride?"

His deep, rumbling laugh had her slowly smiling, waiting for him to answer. "Nay, me wife, and Lord willing, in nine months the mother of me son or daughter."

Tears welled up and spilled over. A babe? So soon?

He kissed her tears away, worry creasing his brow. "Don't ye want children?"

She nodded. "I just didn't think it would happen the first time we made love."

"Well now, 'tis because ye married an Irishman. Ye'd best be knowing that we're a fertile lot. Who knows, when I make love to ye again in the morning, we could end up with two babes in nine months instead of just one."

She laughed. "Now I know you are making fun of me."

"An Irishman never jokes about babes, lass. Family is the glue. As da to our brood, I'll be the head of our family. As their ma, ye'll be the heart." He stared at her until she worried that he may have found her wanting.

"Was I all right?"

He swooped down and kissed her soundly. "Faith, ye nearly killed me, lass."

She slowly smiled. "You were all right, too."

He pinched her. "Minx! God, how I love ye."

She pinched him back. *Hard.* He was laughing when she confessed, "I love you too."

Chapter Nineteen

"I CANNOT BELIEVE his lordship's generosity." Flaherty had been on hand to help move furniture into each one of the cottages the earl had had built and furnished for the married men in the duke's guard stationed at Lippincott Manor. But he had not thought to marry so soon, if at all, and therefore did not expect such a grand gift. Nor did he imagine that Mary Kate would have felt as he had while she twisted him up in knots and ran circles around him. She smiled and chatted with him, the same as she did every other person she came into contact with, but *he* was the man she loved.

Sometime during the first few days of their marriage, he realized it was not just men that she bestowed with her sunshine smiles, but women and children, too. No matter their station in life, she generously treated them with the warmth he'd come to understand was an intrinsic part of the wife he had come to cherish.

"He would never give a gift to the rest of us and slight ye, Flaherty." He grunted, and Dermott chuckled. "Ye haven't gotten used to the fact that yer heart and yer guts are tied up in knots wondering when yer shift will be over and how soon ye can talk yer sweet wife into—"

"Ye'll want to stop there," Flaherty warned, "else I'd be obliged to club ye in the mouth for saying such things about me wife."

Dermott grinned. "Mary Kate made a beautiful bride. Ye're a lucky man, Seamus."

"And well I know it, but…" He paused. "I thought I would have had the time to question the farrier and his accomplice before they were carted off to the constable's gaol."

"Ye were otherwise occupied at the time. Trust that he was questioned at length by both the viscount and the earl."

His cousin meant well, but Flaherty needed to look in Mary Kate's abductor's face and watch while the arrogant expression faded to fear while Flaherty described in detail how he was going to break every one of the man's fingers before hobbling him. What he really wanted to do was either skin the man or geld him, but he didn't think the duke would be forgiving him for either of those two minor crimes. After all, the man had thought to take what the lass—*his wife*—was not willing to give the bloody, buggering bastard!

"Ye'd best calm down, Flaherty, else ye'll be scaring Lady Aurelia and the little master with yer frowns."

He immediately ran a hand through his hair and tamped down his anger. "Ye're right. Thanks for the warning." Flaherty nodded and strode off to man his post on the rooftop, where he'd scan the perimeter of the huge park that ended at the tree line. It was impossible to see into the deep, thickly wooded area that surrounded the earl's property, protecting it from prying eyes.

Flaherty had an hour to go before the shift change, where he would take over the patrol that led into the village and back. The quiet unnerved him—usually there was birdsong, and a deer or two that wandered onto the open meadow that stretched to the trees. Alerted that something was off, he walked along the front of the building, studying the area surrounding the earl's home. Was something amiss? Was trouble headed their way?

He'd just finished his scan of the perimeter when a man on horseback galloped up the long drive. His rifle was trained on the man. When the rider drew closer, Flaherty recognized him as one of the stable hands that worked at the inn in the village and let out a short, sharp whistle.

"Dismount and state yer business."

"She's gone!" the younger man said as he did as Flaherty bade. The look of desperation in his eyes had Flaherty's blood turning cold.

"Who's gone?" Sean called out, approaching from the south side of the building.

"Ainsley?" Dermott shook his head. "Are ye mad thundering up to the earl's home like that? Her ladyship and the little master are out in the gardens—ye nearly scared the life out of them."

Flaherty lowered his rifle and descended the ladder. "Where are they?"

Dermott frowned. "I sent them inside. Finch took them into the kitchen—plenty of sharp weapons within reach there."

"Who's missing?" Flaherty asked.

Ainsley's Adam's apple bobbed up and down before he could speak. "Your wife, Flaherty."

The world stood still for a heartbeat, while a buzzing sounded in Flaherty's brain. Then it began to move again as he understood that his wife was missing. "How do ye know, and why isn't it one of Chattsworth's men or one of me cousins to deliver the news?"

"The innkeeper told me to ride straight here and give you the news."

Something was off. Flaherty saw Ainsley's look of fear shift to calculation. But he blinked, and the stable hand was back to looking fearful again. Did the lad worry that Flaherty would take his anger out on the messenger? Well, he had been known to do so a time or two, but that was before. He was a married man now and had a wife to think of before reacting.

"Get it said," Sean ordered the stable hand.

"Your wife stopped for tea at the inn with the vicar's wife. She was apparently summoned to the kitchen and never came back."

Flaherty knew the man was lying. "Why in the bloody hell

would me wife be in the village when she's needed at Chattsworth Manor?" He glanced at Sean and then Dermott. With a slight nod, he advanced on Ainsley.

"She was with the vicar's wife—"

Keeping the emotions rioting inside of him contained, Flaherty stated, "The vicar's wife is visiting with her sister in London and won't be back for a sennight."

Ainsley backed up a step and bumped into Sean. He turned around and slammed into Dermott. When he spun back, Flaherty grabbed him by the shoulder and squeezed until Ainsley cried out, realizing he was surrounded by the men of the duke's guard. "Ye'll tell me the truth, or so help me, I'll gut ye where ye stand and feed yer gizzards to the crows!"

The stable hand's eyes narrowed. "You don't have a knife on me."

Flaherty grabbed hold of the man's abdomen and dug his fingers deep. "I don't need one."

"Wasn't that a sight to behold that time Flaherty faced one of the lads from Kerry who'd been bent on terrorizing the young Macy twins?" Sean said.

"Aye," Dermott agreed. "Left the lad doubled over, bruised and groaning, later swearing that Flaherty had a hold of his innards and tried to rip them out through his belly!"

Flaherty was tired of waiting while his cousins baited Ainsley. He let go of the man's stomach and grabbed hold of his throat, lifting him a foot in the air. "Tell me now!"

"Hulkner is riding out to Chattsworth Manor right now to lure her away."

"What in the bloody hell for?"

Ainsley gasped, and Sean ordered Flaherty, "Let him go, Seamus."

He did so reluctantly. "Where is she?"

"I don't—"

"The next words better be a location, or they'll be yer last words on this earth."

Sean grabbed hold of the stable hand and shook him until the man answered, "The abandoned barn on Squire Dean's land."

Flaherty was halfway to the stables when the earl rode toward him on his stallion. Lippincott dismounted and handed the reins to him. "Go! I'll send someone to Chattsworth Manor to verify that Mary Kate is missing."

Ainsley urged Flaherty, "If you ride hard, you should catch Parks before he leaves."

"Leaves? Where in the bloody hell is he planning to take my wife?"

"The Borderlands."

Flaherty rode like the devil was nipping at his heels. Fear in his heart that he wouldn't reach the abandoned barn in time nearly took hold before his calm warrior's control slipped into place with a click. "Hang on, lass. I'm coming for ye!"

Leaning low, he whispered in the stallion's ear of their urgent mission with the promise of sweet hay, carrots, and a cup of oats as a reward. The burst of speed from the animal soothed the worst of Flaherty's fears. Questions hammered in his brain as he rode toward the village, then through it toward Squire Dean's estate on the other side. But he had to ignore them, or else the worry that he would not reach his wife in time would eat him alive!

"MRS. FLAHERTY! MRS. Flaherty! Your husband had an accident. He's asking for you!"

Mary Kate ran from the kitchen garden toward the stables and the man riding toward her. She thought she recognized him as one of the men working at the inn, but in her panic and worry that Seamus was hurt badly, she let it go. Her husband needed her, and she would move Heaven and earth to get to him.

"Where is he?"

"On the other side of the village! You have to come quickly."

"Take me to him!" Without waiting to tell anyone where she was going or why, Mary Kate reached for the man's hand and let him pull her up onto the horse behind him. "What happened?"

The man grunted and kicked the horse into a gallop.

It was either hold on or fall off. She wrapped her arms around the man, praying that Seamus was not injured severely.

Please, Lord, let him be all right.

✦━━━◇━━━✦

CHAPTER TWENTY

FLAHERTY'S HEART POUNDED in time with the stallion's thundering hooves tearing up the road leading to the squire's home. The distant baying of hounds had him wondering if the squire knew Flaherty's wife was missing and that she had been taken to his land. Judging from the call of the hounds, he quickly realized it was feeding time at the squire's kennels—they weren't being gathered to go off on a hunt.

The din of hungry hounds clamoring to be fed covered the sound of his approach.

Flaherty whistled to get the man's attention. Squire Dean glanced over his shoulder. "Flaherty, to what do I owe this visit?"

"Is there an abandoned barn on your property?"

The squire scratched behind the ear of the hound leaning against his legs. "Why?"

"I'll explain later. There's no time! Where is it?"

Picking up on the urgency, the squire gave him directions. The blasted barn was a quarter of a mile away! Flaherty was off like a shot, covering the ground easily on the earl's prized horse. He saw the dilapidated building ahead of him in the distance, and pulled back on the reins. "Easy, laddie, ye made good time. I won't forget the promised treat." He slid off the horse and tied him to a nearby tree a good distance away from the barn. "Wait here."

Approaching the building slowly, he searched the area surrounding it first. No sign of life. The roof was nearly caved in, and the doors and windows were missing. He walked up to the doorway, leaned in, and called out, "Mary Kate? Are ye in there?"

The silence was deafening. A frisson of worry slithered through his gut. "I'm here to set ye free, lass." He entered the building and was struck on the back of the head. He fought against the blinding pain, but could not hold out against the devastating blow. The last thing he heard was deep voices whispering.

"WHAT IN THE bloody hell am I supposed to do with him? He weighs a ton!"

"Grab his legs, Leeds, and lift his shoulders."

The two men worked in tandem, carrying Flaherty into the barn. "Make sure the knots are tight, Samuelson. Monroe won't pay us if he escapes."

"What about the woman?"

"Hulkner will be delivering her shortly. Help me tie his feet together."

Finally, the men were satisfied that they'd secured the duke's man to the best of their ability. "You don't think he'll escape, do you?" Samuelson asked.

Leeds snickered. "Nay. There's every chance that he won't rouse before the smoke or the fire get him."

"I'm not so sure about setting the barn on fire...or letting a pretty woman like Mary Kate die that way," Samuelson rasped. "We could tell Monroe that they both perished in the fire and keep the woman for ourselves."

His partner in crime seemed to think about it, but then they heard hooves fast approaching. "That'll be Hulkner. Let's go grab the woman and tie her up."

They walked out of the barn in time to see Hulkner help Flaherty's wife off the horse—and strike her on the back of the head.

Samuelson shook his head. "It'll be a blessing that she'll be unconscious when the fire takes her."

The trio worked together in silence. Hulkner tied Mary Kate up and left her propped up next to Flaherty on the dirt floor of the barn, leaning against an empty water trough. Leeds and Samuelson gathered the dried hay by the armful and placed piles of it strategically around the inside of the barn. Next came the stacks of twigs they'd gathered ahead of time. They placed the thin bits of branches in and around the hay, ensuring that once the fire caught, the straw and twigs would ignite quickly, and the fire would engulf the barn, burning everything inside of it— Flaherty and his wife included.

Leeds stood back to watch while Hulkner removed the flint from his pocket and struck it until it sparked.

Samuelson glanced at the still form of the couple one last time. "Are you sure we can't take her with us?"

Hulkner growled, "If you don't want the promised coin…"

"Never mind. Light it!" Leeds said.

"Hands up, ye sorry sons of bitches!"

The men took off in three different directions. Garahan nabbed the man about to toss the flaming handful of dried straw onto the stacks surrounding Flaherty and his wife, and used the man's chest to smother the flames. Ignoring the screams, he yanked the blackguard's hands behind his back. After tying them together, he hauled the man out of the barn and tossed him on the ground next to the constable.

The constable's men captured the other two would-be murderers, bound their hands behind their backs, and dragged them toward the constable as Garahan raced back inside.

He knelt beside Flaherty, shook him, and yelled, "Wake up!" The answering groan was music to Garahan's ears as he sliced through Flaherty's ropes. "We've got to save Mary Kate!"

Flaherty blinked, frowned, and shot to his feet, swaying from side to side before he was able to stand still. "What the feck happened, and why do I smell smoke?"

Garahan ignored the question and sliced Mary Kate's ropes, then tucked his knife back in his boot.

He reached for her, but Flaherty elbowed him out of the way. "I've got her." Everything clicked into place as Flaherty's mind cleared. "Someone hit me head."

"Knocked ye both out," Garahan added. "Hurry! I don't trust this barn not to blow over in a stiff wind, or… Bloody hell! Do I smell smoke?"

Flaherty grunted. "I asked ye first."

They noticed the flames licking the bottom of the far wall at the same time. "Move it, boy-o." Garahan shoved Flaherty in front of him. "Get her out of here. Now!"

They ran toward the front of the barn as the back wall caved in.

"Duck!" Garahan yelled, then grabbed hold of Flaherty's arm, yanking him out of the way as a section of roof fell where they had been standing.

Flaherty curled his body around his wife, praying that she wouldn't wake until they were free of the burning building, cursing the size of the barn as they sprinted toward the doorway. He heard an ominous creak behind him, and dug deep to sprint through the opening. Garahan never let go as they cleared the building.

The post and beam construction gave way. The barn collapsed as fire claimed the building.

Ignoring the searing pain at the base of his skull, Flaherty staggered farther from what was left of the barn. The squire arrived on horseback, followed by a handful of his servants in a wagon loaded with ropes, shovels, pickaxes, and buckets. Orders were shouted, and the men were soon shoveling up the dirt surrounding the barn and tossing it onto the flames. Another wagonload of men arrived from the village and formed a bucket brigade using the water from the well.

Garahan walked toward Flaherty and Mary Kate with a small bucket. He knelt beside them, untied his cravat, and dunked it in the water. He handed it to Flaherty. "She's strong. Ye'll see."

Flaherty gently bathed her face, searching for cuts from the splintered wood that had exploded when one of the beams crashed behind them. Relief filled him when he only uncovered abrasions.

"Seamus?"

The lass's smoke-roughened voice was the sweetest sound he'd ever heard. "There's a lass. How's yer head, *mo ghrá?*"

Garahan rinsed the cravat and handed it back to Flaherty. "Do ye remember what happened?"

She turned to her husband. "You were in an accident. Hurt. Calling for me."

He glanced at Garahan and then back. "Nay. I'm fine, lass."

"But he told me—"

"Who told ye?" Flaherty asked.

Garahan frowned, then nodded to the trio of men bound and leaning against a boulder. "Which one was it?"

"The one wailing. Did he fall in the fire?"

"I wouldn't be knowing, lass," Garahan replied.

"I should have realized the depth of the farrier's obsession with ye, *mo chroí.* He wasn't through with his plans for ye."

Mary Kate frowned. "I thought he was cooling his heels in the constable's gaol while waiting to be transported to London."

"'Twas the plan, but his accomplices had instructions to lure ye away from Chattsworth."

She placed her hand on his arm. "While you were lured away from Lippincott Manor?"

Flaherty clenched his jaw before relaxing it enough to answer, "Aye, his plan nearly worked, but Garahan arrived to save the day."

"Ye would have rescued yer wife if ye hadn't been clubbed on the back of the head, Seamus."

"That I would." He gently brushed a thin smear of soot that he'd missed off Mary Kate's face, then pressed his lips to her forehead. "If Garahan hadn't arrived when he did—"

"But he did," she said. "Thank you for saving us, James."

"I'd be saying 'twas me pleasure, but I hate to lie. I had to rouse this *eedjit* and cut his ropes off, then we had to free yerself. We were doing a fine job of it until we smelled the smoke and realized the barn was on fire."

"How could you not know?" Mary Kate asked.

"We were otherwise occupied," Flaherty grumbled, then kissed her to keep her from asking any other questions.

"You two wait here, while I have a word with Squire Dean. Ah," Garahan said, pointing toward the road leading to the barn. "The constable looks like he's ready to be taking these three blackguards into custody to join Monroe. I'll be sure and tell him if I hadn't arrived when I did, the buggers would have succeeded in murdering the both of ye!"

Flaherty watched his cousin stalk toward the constable, soothed by his anger. "Garahan's partial to ye, but he loves me like a brother."

Mary Kate agreed. "And you feel the same way about him."

"Faith, ye aren't wrong. 'Tis the sainted O'Malleys that fall last in line, behind me brothers, James, and the rest of the Garahans." He felt a nudge on his shoulder, glanced over it, and chuckled. "Well now, here's his lordship's stallion come to remind me that I still haven't fed him the promised treats."

"The squire may be willing to take care of that for you. After all, the earl and the viscount take excellent care of the villagers."

"That they do."

"Seamus?"

"Aye, love?"

"Garahan's timing is impeccable."

Flaherty grudgingly agreed.

"But I wouldn't race off with someone I did not know for Garahan. I would only do that for the man I love."

Flaherty pulled her onto his lap and held her to his heart. "Ye could have died."

"It would not have been your fault."

"Promise me ye won't go haring off with the next man who claims that I've been injured."

She narrowed her eyes and lifted her chin. "I cannot."

"Well, ye can be sure that I won't be calling for ye if I'm hurt. It won't be that I don't want ye near me, lass. 'Tis a precaution that we must take so ye don't run headlong into danger."

She cupped his cheek, staring at the threads that closed the gouge in his cheek. Finally, she rasped, "I cannot take the chance that you really do need me. Isn't there some way to ensure that the message would be from you—or one of your cousins, if you are incapacitated and cannot speak?"

Flaherty fell silent, thinking about it until the lass pressed her lips below his stitches, kissing a path to the corner of his mouth, where she nibbled his bottom lip until he grumbled, "Ye're playing with fire, lass." As if he realized what he just said, he closed his eyes and groaned. "Forgive me, I—"

"I know what kind of fire I'm playing with, husband. And it is not your fault that we were both lured to this abandoned barn, knocked unconscious, and left on a makeshift funeral pyre." Placing her hands on either side of his face, she whispered his name.

Unable to deny his wife, Flaherty lowered his mouth and took possession of hers with a drugging kiss that left no doubt what he wanted to do—*needed* to do. But now was not the time, nor the place. "Later, love."

Linking her arms around his neck, she pulled him even closer and kissed him as if it were their last kiss before the world ended. He felt the depth of her love. Their hearts were linked. The fear was a living, breathing thing: they'd nearly died! He longed to make love to the lass. Right here. Right now. But as he'd realized a few moments ago, now was not the time, nor the place. *Later.*

He captured her lips in a kiss of promise. "I'll give serious thought to yer request, lass. I won't want ye to worry needlessly about me while I'm on duty. We'll figure out a signal, mayhap a word or two, when either of us is in danger. Rest here for a moment, while I see if I can speak to the squire about the earl's stallion."

He shifted her off his lap, cupped the back of her head, and pressed a kiss to her forehead. He felt her wince. "God in Heaven, lass. I forgot ye were knocked unconscious too. Let me have a look at yer head. Mine aches at the base of me skull. Where does yers hurt?"

"The back of my head…in the middle of it."

He used the tips of his fingers to palpate the area. He froze when he felt the warm, wet evidence that it was more than a bump. "Ye're bleeding, lass. Don't move."

He whistled, and Garahan sprinted over. "What's wrong?"

"The lass's head's bleeding. Stay with her while I fetch more water?"

"Hand me the bucket. I'll fetch it for ye. Check the lass's eyes."

"Look at me, Mary Kate."

She squinted up at Flaherty, but when he asked, she opened her eyes wide and stared into his.

"Close them now and count to ten." When she did as he asked, he urged. "Open yer eyes, lass." He watched closely, pleased that her pupils seemed to be the same size.

Garahan placed the bucket next to Flaherty. "I used me spare cravats to tie up the prisoners."

Flaherty untied the one around his neck. "I still have one left." He dipped it into the water and squeezed the excess water out of it. "This may pain ye, but try to hold still." He bathed the wound, pleased to note that it wasn't as deep as he'd thought.

"She'll need a stitch or two, else it'll bleed all over her neck," Garahan said. "Ye wouldn't want that, now would ye, Mary Kate?"

She sucked in a breath when Flaherty wiped away the rest of the blood. "I'm sorry, lass, but I've got to clean out any dirt."

"I know. I'm not crying—"

"The blackguard Hulkner is," Garahan informed them. "He's

the one who lit the rag and started the fire."

Mary Kate looked over at the bound men. "Why is he crying?"

Garahan grinned. "Well now, he was the one holding a flaming rag, now wasn't he?" Before either Mary Kate or Flaherty could answer, he added, "And I had to douse the flames, now didn't I?"

"Yes, of course," Mary Kate agreed. "But what does that have to do with his weeping?"

He shrugged. "I may have used his chest to put out the flames."

Mary Kate covered her mouth with her hands to hide her gasp.

"Did ye want me to let him toss it on the kindling he'd placed around yerself and Seamus?"

"Of course not," she said. "If it were me, I would have tried to stomp the flames out."

"'Tis easy to speculate what ye would have done in an urgent situation when ye haven't been placed in it. Besides, I could not, because it would have taken too much time. Judging by the girth of his belly, I figured he had enough mass to smother the flames."

Flaherty snorted, then cleared his throat. He did not want to upset his wife by laughing at her naiveté. "We'd best stop in the village and have the physician take a look at ye, lass."

She put her hand on his elbow, drawing his attention. "MacReady did an excellent job stitching you up. Since Lady Calliope and I arrived at Chattsworth Manor, he has had to use his skill with a needle more than once. A tenant farmer sliced his hand on his sharpened scythe, and one of the stable lads backed into a pitchfork—though MacReady did complain the entire time he sewed the gash closed on the poor young man's backside. Then there was—"

"Fine, lass," Flaherty interrupted. "Ye've convinced me to take ye to MacReady." He rinsed out the cravat one more time, folded it up, and pressed it against the wound. "This will have to do until I can get ye back to Chattsworth Manor."

"A dry bit of linen would be better." Mary Kate lifted the hem of her gown, ripped a strip off the bottom of her chemise, and handed it to her husband. "Use this."

"I'll be sure and have a new chemise made for ye, lass." He wadded it up and asked her to hold it on the back of her head. When she did, he sighed. "Ye're hurt, and I cannot ask ye to hold on to me and this wad of fabric on yer head while we ride back to Chattsworth Manor."

She frowned and, without being asked, ripped off another strip and handed it to him. "Here."

Flaherty bit the inside of his cheek to keep from chuckling. When he'd tied the knot, securing the bandage, he pressed a kiss to her cheek. "Ye've got grit, lass."

"Ye'll need it, as ye're married to Flaherty." Garahan held out a hand to help Mary Kate to her feet. "Ye may need to sweet-talk the earl's horse into waiting a bit longer for his treat—mayhap add in a thorough brushing. The viscount's stallion loves a good rubdown, and I'm thinking the earl's would, too."

"A brilliant idea." Flaherty walked over to the animal and crooned, "We've an injured lass to deliver to Chattsworth Manor. 'Tis me wife, and I know ye're partial to her. I'll have the viscount's stable master rub ye down and brush ye till yer coat shines, while ye enjoy fresh hay, two cups of oats, and three carrots."

The horse lifted his head and gave a trumpeting call.

"Well now." Garahan snickered. "That sounded like an aye to me. I'll meet ye at Chattsworth Manor."

Flaherty nodded and lifted Mary Kate onto the horse. He mounted behind her and pulled her onto his lap. "Swing yer legs off to the side, lass, and lean on me. Close yer eyes. That's the way. We'll be at Chattsworth before ye know it."

"I love you, Seamus."

"Faith, I depend upon it, lass."

CHAPTER TWENTY-ONE

FLAHERTY RODE UP to the stables, trying to wrap his head around the fact that the blasted, blackhearted farrier had more than one plan to abscond with Mary Kate. For the love of God, she was a married woman—his *wife*!

Michael O'Malley walked over. "Hand her down to me. I'll try not to wake her."

Because of the fire and their close call with death, Mary Kate seemed fragile to Flaherty. Instead of leaping out of the saddle with the lass in his arms, as he'd done before, he nodded. "Have a care—she was knocked unconscious and needs tending."

Michael stared at the bandage around her head. "'Tis starting to bleed through." He looked at Flaherty. "Ye used her chemise?"

Flaherty shook his head and handed the stallion off to the stable master. "'Twas her idea. So was bypassing the physician in the village so that MacReady could sew her hard head back together."

When Michael started walking toward the rear entrance to the building, Flaherty called out, "Give me back me wife!"

Michael grinned. "Didn't think ye'd mind if I carried yer hardheaded wife into the house."

Flaherty held on to his temper. But his failure to protect his wife, anticipating that the farrier had connections and would continue to try to kidnap her, even after he'd been captured, had his head pounding—and not where he'd been hit! That they'd had such a close call in that burning barn had him frantic to get her alone and satisfy his worry that she had been injured elsewhere. He needed to touch her, feel the connection of their bodies locked together as they made passionate love to remind him that they were alive—he had not lost the love of his life.

Michael paused at the back door and sighed. "There's no pleasure riling ye when ye're not responding in kind." Without another word, he carefully shifted Mary Kate in his arms and handed her back to Flaherty. "MacReady should be having his tea right about now, and having a chat with Mrs. Romney."

Flaherty nodded. "Thank ye."

Michael opened the door. "Ye'll let me know how Mary Kate fares?"

"Aye." The door closed behind Flaherty, and a sliver of worry settled in the vicinity of his heart. The lass hadn't roused when he handed her off to Michael. Was it more than exhaustion that had her so still in his arms? Her breathing wasn't shallow; 'twas normal. Her coloring was a bit mottled because of the soot that he had not been able to completely wash off her face without the aid of soap and a soak in hot water.

He nodded to the footman stationed in the hallway leading to the kitchen. "Is MacReady in the kitchen?"

The footman frowned. "What happened?"

"Where. Is. MacReady?"

His tone got through to the younger man. "In the kitchen."

Flaherty did not bother to thank the man—he'd worry about manners later. Right now, his wife needed MacReady to close her wound.

He burst into the kitchen. Mrs. Romney gasped and jumped up to fill a large bowl with hot water from the pot on the stove. Then she filled a smaller one, handing both to MacReady, who stared at the woman in Flaherty's arms and asked, "What happened?"

"You can both wash up in the alcove, where I leave the pitcher full, or in the room at the end of the hallway." Mrs. Romney eyed Flaherty. "You still have her blood on your hands."

He glanced down and fought not to react. He'd had plenty of practice over the years, but the fact that the blood was Mary Kate's brought it too close to home, hitting him in the heart. "I was more concerned with washing the gash at the back of me wife's head to see how bad it was."

"Forgive me, Flaherty. It's just such a shock to see her in such a state."

"She's sleeping now, but was fully conscious when we left Squire Dean's barn burning."

"And what were the two of you doing on the squire's property—near a burning barn, no less?" MacReady asked.

"Long story." Flaherty didn't bother to say another word as he retraced his steps to the room where the healing herbs, tinctures, and linens were kept. He laid his wife on the cot and brushed a lock of hair out of her eyes. "Mary Kate? Can ye hear me, lass?"

She mumbled something unintelligible.

"What did ye say?"

His wife blew out a breath and slowly opened her eyes. "I was having a wonderful dream until you called my name."

"What were ye dreaming about?"

"I turned my head to smile at you, and I tripped and hit my head. It still aches." She lifted her hand to touch her head, but he grabbed hold of her hand and kissed the back of it.

"Don't be touching it just yet. MacReady's right behind me with the hot water. We've both got to wash our hands before tending to ye."

Mary Kate sighed. "I do remember asking you to bring me here." She looked at MacReady. "Thank you."

"I haven't done anything yet," he said.

"But I trust you, and know that you will take good care of me like you did Seamus…and the others."

"Now then, lass, lie still while I wash up."

"Can you tell me what happened?" MacReady asked her.

"A strange man galloped up to the stables and said Flaherty had had an accident and was hurt, calling for me."

"Oldest trick in the book," MacReady grumbled. "Then what happened?"

"We arrived at Squire Dean's property…and that's all I remember."

"Blackguard must have hit you hard enough that you don't recall." He elbowed Flaherty aside and washed his hands. "Now then, help your wife sit up, so I can unwrap the bandage." They worked quickly together. MacReady murmured, "Hmmm…the cut isn't very long, but it's deeper than I'd like. I may need to snip a bit of the hair around the gash, but you've got plenty to spare." He parted her hair and mumbled, "Flaherty, hold this hank of her hair away from the wound. Aye, like that. Be still, Mary Kate— I'm only snipping a bit. It won't show at all when you scoop your hair up on top of your head."

Flaherty cleared his throat, and MacReady nodded as if to silently assure him that Mary Kate would be fine.

"Now, if you can hold this other bit of her hair away from the wound, I'll clean it out and thread the needle. Mrs. Romney keeps them handy and dumped them in a bowl of just-boiled water for me. I won't have you fretting—or threatening me with dire circumstances—if I don't take every precaution with your wife."

"Thank you for taking care of me," Mary Kate said. "I didn't want to go the physician in the village."

"I don't blame you. You've seen me tend to others, and have helped me a time or two when I've patched up more than one of the viscount's people."

"You were meticulous taking care of Seamus."

"A scar will only enhance his looks. You'll have to keep an eye on the innkeeper's daughter—she's had her eye on Flaherty since his first patrol into the village. Now that he looks more roguish, she'll be after him."

"Don't be putting false worry in her mind, MacReady!" Flaherty interjected. "No woman's followed me since that one time when Michael and I escorted Lady Calliope and Mary Kate here from Wyndmere Hall, and ye know it."

MacReady harumphed. "I heard that young woman still casts her lures at you every chance she gets."

"Oh, does she?" Mary Kate asked.

"Be still!" MacReady ordered her.

"Forgive me, but you should not speak of inflammatory topics, or make such suggestions, when you have a needle and thread in your hands, especially when you are casting aspersions on my husband's character."

"I'm only speaking the truth, not telling tales. It's not my business if the man only has eyes for you and doesn't notice when another woman is trying to catch his attention."

"I'm saying no one has tried." Flaherty wanted to punch the man, but couldn't, not while MacReady hadn't tied off the last knot yet.

"So you *have* noticed when women flirt with you, Seamus," Mary Kate said.

"Ah, lass, ye're the only woman I have noticed since I pulled ye from the carriage. 'Tis easy to ignore the others."

"But you barely spoke to me for the longest time," she reminded him. "Why would you ignore the others when you were ignoring me?"

"And what would ye have had me do, when ye kept spouting off about Garahan?"

She sighed. "You are absolutely right. I don't blame you, but I am glad to hear that you ignored the other women."

"Finished! Kiss your wife so you two can settle your nerves. She'll be fine and so will you." When neither Flaherty nor Mary Kate moved, MacReady added, "Kiss her already!"

"Don't mind if I do." Flaherty gently drew her close, pressed his lips, gently, reverently, to her supple mouth, and groaned. "Lass, ye'll be the death of me. How does yer head feel?"

"How does yours?"

"What's this?" MacReady demanded. "Did you get knocked in the head, too?"

"I'm not bleeding."

"And you have a hard head," MacReady replied, placing his tools on the tray and leaving it on the table beneath the hanging cabinet. "I'll take care of clearing this away after I wash up. The both of you look as if you could use a hot bath." He sniffed the air and added, "And a change of clothes. You smell of smoke."

Flaherty was about to launch into the tale of what happened when MacReady raised his hand. "Why don't you wait until you're both clean and have changed your clothes? Then Mrs. Romney can ply you with tea and scones, and his lordship and Lady Calliope can hear the full tale."

"That we can do. Would ye mind sending one of the footmen in with a tub, and have someone bring a change of clothes for us? I can tend to me wife."

MacReady stood in the doorway, frowning. "You'll not be doing what I know you want to be doing until she's had a chance to rest. Tomorrow at the earliest. Neither one of you should exert yourselves with a fresh head wound."

"Hasn't been a problem for me before," Flaherty mumbled.

"Oh?" Mary Kate sounded annoyed.

"I did not live like a monk before I met ye, lass." He threw his hands up in the air. "I'll apologize to ye both if ye send the bath, the hot water, and clean clothes." MacReady opened his mouth to speak, and Flaherty groaned again. "Ye have me word to keep me hands to meself while me wife bathes."

Mary Kate's face reddened, and MacReady grunted before stomping into the hallway.

"I thought he'd never leave."

"Thank you agreeing to wait until after I soak in a hot tub and scrub off the scent of burning wood."

"Me pleasure, lass."

She leaned close and pressed her lips to his. "I won't mind if you want to make love to me tonight, but I'd rather be clean first."

"Good thing I only promised to keep me hands to meself while ye bathed."

Mary Kate smiled. "I need another kiss, Seamus."

"Anywhere in particular?"

Her soft laughter eased the tightest knot of worry tangling in his gut. She tilted her head to one side and pointed to the spot beneath her ear. "You could start right here."

Flaherty bent to kiss her neck as MacReady strode back into the room. "For the love of God, man. Can you not wait until later?"

Mary Kate put her arms around Flaherty's neck and pulled him closer. "He might be able to, but I can't."

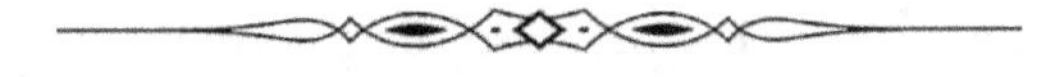

CHAPTER TWENTY-TWO

FLAHERTY SCOWLED AT MacReady when Cook walked into the room and ordered them out. "Ye didn't have to send Mrs. Romney in to help me wife with her bath."

The curmudgeonly Scot glared at him, then grinned as they walked toward the rear door. "Hah! It wasn't that long ago that I was a man in my prime like yourself. You'd have forgotten all about your promise the moment the door was closed and you were alone with your wife and that piping-hot bath."

Flaherty closed his eyes and moaned. "Now ye've done it. I'd just managed to get that particular image of me wife out of me head…and ye've placed it right back front and center in my brain!"

MacReady chuckled. "I always believed that your love for Mary Kate was strong. She deserves to be loved for who she is by someone who will protect, cherish, and love her. I know that you are that man."

Humbled by the older man's words, Flaherty thanked him. "I know ye understand how close the both of us came to dying earlier. What would be a more natural way of celebrating that we did *not* die?"

"Raising a fine glass of good Scotch whisky?"

Flaherty grunted. "Hah! Ye mean a glass of fine Irish whiskey."

"I do not."

"Ah, but ye should, as the Irish distill it best."

"And any Scotsman worth his salt knows that it's the aging in a proper wooden cask that is the secret to the finest Scottish whisky."

"Are ye planning to continue arguing with me, MacReady?"

"I enjoy a good argument."

Flaherty snorted. "Are ye sure you don't have a bit of Irish blood in ye?"

MacReady shook his head. "Go take a bath and wash the soot, blood and sweat off you. The viscount asked you to come to the sitting room when you are finished."

Flaherty nodded and retreated to the outbuilding, where he knew a hip tub was waiting for him. A short while later, he was once again walking toward the sitting room.

"Ah, Flaherty." The viscount walked toward him. "Your wife will be along in another moment—she and Calliope were deep in conversation when I went to collect them."

"As they are not here yet, there's something I need to speak with ye about...Monroe."

"MacReady filled me in a bit on the situation. What I do not understand is what the man hoped to accomplish by abducting your wife."

"The man has no honor—why would the fact that Mary Kate and I exchanged vows and made promises to one another matter to him?"

"A salient point that occurred to me too, but not the first one. I was thinking about the money he apparently promised to Parks and the others to aid him in the deed. A farrier normally would not have that amount of ready coin. Where do you think he got it from?"

"Underhandedly, no doubt. As I said, the man has no honor. He could have robbed someone for all we know."

The viscount slowly inclined his head. "The vicar recently reported that money from the poor box went missing."

"How long ago?"

"A fortnight."

"But the vicar has been supporting the poorer families in the village, and no one mentioned that they had to go without. Where else would he get the funds if not from the coin in the poor box?"

Chattsworth cleared his throat. "The vicar came to me explaining what happened, and I made a separate contribution to the church."

Flaherty's gut clenched. "What type of man steals from the church?"

MacReady shrugged. "The same man who tries to steal another man's wife."

"Darling, there you are. Sorry we are late." Lady Calliope swept into the room, her arm linked with Mary Kate's. "I do hope this won't take long—Mary Kate needs to lie down."

Flaherty was on his feet and reaching for his wife by the time the viscountess finished speaking. "There ye are, lass." He stared into her blue-violet eyes, relieved that the size and shape of her pupils seemed to be normal. "Yer eyes are clear. Is yer head paining ye?"

She sighed. "A bit, but I'm not quite sure if it's from whoever hit me, or the stitches."

"Both, I'd imagine," MacReady replied. "Speaking from past experience."

"Ye're right about that," Flaherty had to admit. "Having suffered from more than one knock on the head, and stiches, I'd have to agree."

"Well then, as we do not wish to tire Mary Kate out," Calliope began, "why don't we let her tell us what happened to her first?"

Chattsworth agreed. "Excellent idea, my dear."

Mary Kate shared her story of the stranger seeking her out, and the urgency he expressed, and the bone-deep fear she felt knowing her husband was gravely injured.

Flaherty wanted to punch something—but now wasn't the time. "I'd like a chance to wring the man's neck for lying to ye, lass, but I'll have to wait until I have a chance to speak to the prisoners. They're at the constable's cooling their heels behind bars."

"What made you ride to Squire Dean's, Flaherty?" the viscount asked.

It was Flaherty's turn to explain how the stable hand from the inn arrived at Lippincott Manor with the news that Mary Kate had been taken. The viscount did not blink when Flaherty described how he'd had an inkling that the man knew more than he was telling, and that he'd had to convince the stable hand to tell him where his wife had been taken.

"And that's how you both ended up in Squire Dean's abandoned barn—then it was set on fire."

"Aye, but we had no idea because we were both unconscious," Flaherty told them. "Thanks to Garahan, we're both alive to tell of it."

"Ye'd do the same for me, Seamus." Garahan entered the sitting room. "What did I miss?"

"Mary Kate and me retelling the sequence of events," Flaherty grumbled.

"I already heard enough to put the pieces together before we left the squire's place. Are ye ready to hear what I know?"

Chattsworth and the others listened as the last pieces of the puzzle fell into place. When Garahan finished, he turned to the viscount. "So ye see, the farrier had put his plans into place the moment he settled in the village and spied Mary Kate for the first time. He had no idea she was spoken for at the time."

"Did he bother to ask anyone of his numerous customers?" The viscount's voice was hard.

"Not that came to light. Although the young lads working in the inn's stables were quick to tell their side of the story when pressed about delivering messages and spying for Monroe." Garahan shook his head before continuing, "I heard something that cannot be true, but as one of the duke's guard, I need to ask the question, yer lordship."

Chattsworth inclined his head. "What do you need to clarify?"

"The vicar hasn't spoken of it, but I heard a rumor that the poor box has been robbed," Garahan said. "Is it true?"

"I'm afraid it is. The vicar did not want to worry the villagers on the outside chance that it was someone who was in greater need than he or she let on. It isn't always easy to accept help when you are in need."

"Aye," Flaherty said. "Pride gets in the way."

"Only if one lets it," Chattsworth reminded him.

"Noted, yer lordship." Flaherty needed to speak to the constable and question the prisoners. "Yer lordship, may I leave Mary Kate here under yer protection?"

"Of course." Chattsworth stared at him for a moment before asking, "Where are you headed?"

"Into the village."

"Ah, to question the prisoners further. Noted and understood. I expect a full report from the constable and yourself. I'm certain the earl does, too."

"Don't be forgetting His Grace," Garahan added.

"He is the reason the earl and I need to know everything. That way we can succinctly add the facts to our report to His Grace."

Mary Kate reached for Flaherty's hand. "Do you have to leave now?"

"Aye, *mo chroí*. I won't be more than a few hours. Depends on how long it takes to convince the blackguards to spill their guts."

"Do ye need me to accompany ye?" Garahan asked.

Flaherty shook his head. "I'd rather ye stayed behind to protect me wife along with the others."

"Done."

Flaherty kissed his wife's forehead and rose from his seat. "I'll be collecting a kiss from ye later, lass—otherwise I wouldn't be able to concentrate on the task before me. Stay inside."

"I guess I'll have to wait," Mary Kate murmured.

"Aye, lass. I'll make it worth yer while." His wife turned a delicate shade of rose, and he drank in the beautiful sight. "I'm a lucky man, Mary Kate."

"Hurry back, Seamus."

"I'll do me best, lass."

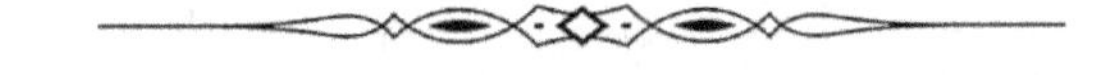

CHAPTER TWENTY-THREE

NOW THAT MARY Kate was safely ensconced within the walls of Chattsworth Manor, Flaherty was ready to get to the bottom of whatever the bloody hell had happened that the buggering farrier thought he could get away with stealing the lass from him.

He wanted to pound his fists into the man until he was nothing but a bloody pulp, but knew the duke would not be a party to it. His Grace had his rules, and every man in the duke's guard strove to follow them to the letter. Flaherty knew he could get a few solid punches in, and would have to be satisfied, as the duke would not allow much more than that.

He knew from Garahan's tale of what happened when Tremayne and Emmett O'Malley accompanied him to the tavern where Garahan's wife had been working before they wed. Garahan told him the earl had been very clear that the three of them were each allowed one blow—one man at a time—and no more, believing it would be in the spirit of what his brother the duke would have approved of. Not many men were of the same fighting caliber as Garahan, Tremayne, and O'Malley—therefore, one punch each.

Which was part of the reason Flaherty needed to go alone. He did not need anyone counting the number of times he punched the bloody blackguard who thought to take Mary Kate from him. He planned to send a message to anyone else who thought to steal her. He'd pledged to love and honor the lass, promised her he'd give her babes to love.

His breath caught in his lungs—*God in Heaven!* Was she carrying his babe even now?

He tossed the reins of his gelding to the stable master. "I'll be right back." Sprinting to the rear entrance, he called her name as he entered the building. "Lass, where are ye?"

She rushed out of the kitchen. "What's happened? What's wrong?"

"I'm needing a private word with ye. 'Twill only take a moment."

"Of course."

He led her far enough from the kitchen so as not to be heard, then dipped his head low to quietly ask, "Lass, have ye been feeling weak or nauseated in the mornings?"

"I think you would have noticed, wouldn't you?"

"Sure and I would hope so. But it takes quite a bit of concentration for me to shift me thoughts from me delectable wife to me duty once I'm out of our bed." He cleared his throat to add, "I may not have noticed."

Her cheeks pinkened again, and he just had to brush his lips against hers in a whisper-soft kiss. "After all ye've been through today, with yer head injury and being in all that smoke from the fire—God help me, I cannot even begin to imagine it, yet have to confess the thought that just hit me, lass."

"Whatever is on your mind, don't let it worry you so. Just tell me."

He grabbed hold of her hands and pulled her into his embrace, hugging her to his heart. As she slipped her arms around his waist, he murmured, "Lass, ye're a strong woman, but if ye're carrying me child, the trauma today may be too much for yerself and the babe."

She grew still in his arms. "I hadn't thought it possible to conceive so soon after being wed."

"Ah, lass, did ye already forget what I told ye about we Flahertys being a virile bunch?"

"No, but I did think you were exaggerating."

Her sweet smile felt like a hug, and he hated to burst her bubble of happiness, but needed her to understand what still might happen. "Lass, did ye hear what I said?"

"Yes, you are warning me that I may be carrying our babe, only to lose it because of what happened."

"Ye were knocked unconscious, and we barely escaped the fire." She nodded against his chest, but didn't let go of him. Flaherty rested his chin on the top of her head. "I'm needing to warn Lady Calliope and Mrs. Romney so one of them will be with ye while I'm gone. Send for me at once if ye experience any cramping."

Again she was silent. He eased back from her and, with the tip of his finger, tilted her chin so he could see her eyes. "I'll have yer word, wife."

A tear escaped before she gathered her composure around her like an invisible cloak of strength. "You have it. For our babe's sake…if there is one."

He kissed her with barely controlled passion. "Do ye have any idea how much I love ye, lass? If I didn't have to gather the information for His Grace—"

"Why can't Garahan go in your place?" she rasped.

"Ye're me wife. 'Tis me place to avenge ye, and me place to question the prisoners. Garahan went when it involved his wife. Trust me, lass. I'll be asking God to watch over ye and our babe until I return."

"But what if I'm not—"

He grinned. "When I return, I'll be tending to me duty to ensure you will be, come morning."

"You say the most outrageous things."

"Aye, and by the high color on yer cheeks, ye don't really mind. Do ye, *mo ghrá*?" He kissed her again, deeply, lingeringly, before reluctantly letting her go. "I'll just have a quick word with

Mrs. Romney and ask her to speak to Lady Calliope. If I wasn't pressed for time—and worried that the prisoner transport from London would arrive before I get to speak to the blackguards—I'd be telling Lady Calliope meself."

Mary Kate lifted to her toes, flung her arms around his neck, and kissed him boldly, setting off a fire inside of him. He'd come to expect it, as it happened every time their lips met.

"Lass…"

Just as quickly, she released him. He brushed a lock of hair out of her eyes and called out Mrs. Romney's name. The older woman rushed out of the kitchen. "What's wrong?"

"Mary Kate needs either yerself or Lady Calliope to stick close to her until I return."

"Do you fear that her head injury is more severe than we realized?" the cook asked.

"Nay, 'tis something of a more delicate nature that I'm worried about."

Without being told, Mrs. Romney nodded. "Of course. I don't know why I did not think of that myself. I'll make sure Mary Kate rests with her feet up. We'll keep a close eye on her and send for you should it become necessary."

"Thank ye, Mrs. Romney. I'd only just thought of it meself and didn't want the lass to be suffering alone should the worst happen."

"Mary Kate will not be alone, and we shall all pray that nothing happens."

Flaherty surprised the cook by kissing her cheek. "Thank ye."

He drew his wife in his arms for one last kiss and then strode down the hallway. Duty called. He had a group of prisoners to question, and a wife to return to. Flaherty did not plan on wasting any more time.

The stable lad handed him the reins, and Flaherty quickly mounted his horse. "I'll be with the constable."

As he rode to the village, his thoughts were on his wife. Her smile was imprinted on his brain and branded on his heart. "Lord,

I know it's too soon to know for certain, but I've got this gut feeling. Please watch over me wife and our babe. Thank ye, Lord."

Feeling better having prayed, he arrived at the constable's building ready to wring every last bit of information out of the men. He was not above using force if need be, though he'd prefer to save it for when he questioned the farrier.

He entered the building and was greeted by the constable. "Ah, Flaherty, I've been waiting for you. I understand from Garahan that you will be questioning the prisoners, in particular Monroe."

"Aye, thank ye. Oh, and I'll be questioning Monroe about another matter altogether as well."

The constable frowned. "Pertaining to the kidnapping and other charges?"

"Aye. In particular, the matter of how he came to be in possession of the large amount of coin he promised to pay Parks and the other henchmen."

"This is the first I'm hearing about the coin. As constable, I need to know how he came into the money as well. I have recently been made aware of a recent rash of coin mysteriously disappearing from a few of the villagers. At first some thought they had miscounted, and others blamed their wives or husbands for not paying close enough attention to their household accounts. Still others blamed it on the pixies and faeries, though I'll never question that. The fae will do what the fae will do, and take what they feel is their fair share."

"I could not agree with ye more. Ma has been known to say the same. 'Tis interesting what ye've been told. I have it on good authority there is another party who has reported missing coin." Before the constable could question him, which would delay his getting back to his wife, Flaherty said, "Now then, why don't I start questioning the henchmen and work my way up to Monroe?"

"Right this way."

Flaherty followed the constable down the hallway to the back of the building, where two cells had been erected with thick bars fashioned by the blacksmith, a formidable giant with a talent for forging iron. "I see ye have the farrier in a cell by himself."

"Aye," the constable said. "I thought to divide the men equally between the two cells, but the minute I closed the door, they went for Monroe's throat."

Flaherty stared at the farrier. "Pity you did not let them finish the job. I would have left them alone with him a bit longer."

"Would you like to speak to each man individually?"

He thought about it, and the time that would take, and decided against it. "I need to return to me wife, so I'll be speaking to this group first, and then Monroe."

"Shall I remove the farrier?"

"No need." Flaherty glared at Monroe. "He knows what I'll be asking him, and best prepare himself to answer me— honestly." He walked to the cell door and deliberately took his time looking at one man at a time, meeting their gazes, studying them, exerting his will over them before speaking. "Me name's Flaherty and 'twas me wife ye nabbed. If we were home in Ireland, it would be within me rights to kill ye without fear of repercussion."

One man wavered on his feet, and another sat down hard on the floor of the cell.

"But we're in England," Flaherty continued, "so I won't be able to avenge me wife the way she deserves. Instead, I'm asking ye a two-pronged question: why did ye do it, and was it worth it?"

By the time he was through gathering his answers, he felt sorry for one man, who had six children to feed and had just buried their mother a fortnight ago. The others were hardened criminals, in his opinion, and deserved whatever a judge sentenced them to.

He walked over to the other cell. "Monroe."

The man met his glare with his own.

"Why did ye steal from the poor box?"

"What?" one of the other prisoners demanded.

"Is that where you got the coin, Monroe?" another asked.

"You could not have thought to pay us with the money the poor of the parish depend upon, could you?" the third man—the widower with the children—asked.

"Aye, I'm thinking the blackguard intended to. Why don't ye tell yer henchmen, Monroe, then ye can tell me what in the bloody *fecking* hell ye were thinking to steal me wife!"

The farrier's face paled in the face of Flaherty's anger, but he did not answer. Instead of asking him a second time, Flaherty decided to take the viscount up on his suggestion of three solid punches to the sorry excuse for a man. "Constable, if ye wouldn't mind opening the cell now, I'll be needing a *private* word with Monroe."

The farrier glanced from the constable, who was fitting the key into the lock, to Flaherty, who stood with no expression on his face. He hoped the man *shited* himself—then again, he wouldn't want to have to deal with stepping around a mess like that. He'd have to settle for the look of abject terror on the man's face. Flaherty's reputation obviously preceded him.

The cell swung open and the farrier took a step back. No matter—Flaherty had a long reach and delivered a solid right cross before the man knew what hit him. He followed with a jab and an uppercut that lifted the man off his feet and onto the floor of the cell.

Flaherty walked over and placed his foot on the man's chest. "Ye're lucky I work for the duke, and he is against his men taking a life, otherwise ye'd already be dead."

The man's eyes glazed over a moment before they rolled up in his head.

With a grunt, Flaherty pushed off the man's chest and stalked out of the cell. "If he has anything to add to his confession, I'd be obliged if ye send word to me at Chattsworth or Lippincott Manor."

"It would be my pleasure, Flaherty."

"Thank ye, constable."

"I'll let the vicar and the others know that they are about to regain the coin they thought they lost, plus a donation from their former farrier."

"Ye're a good man, constable. I'll let the viscount and the earl know."

Finished with his duty, not having overstepped—well, except for the pleasure of standing on the man's chest—he untied his horse, vaulted into the saddle, and rode back to Chattsworth Manor.

All was quiet when he handed over the reins to the stable lad. "Anything happen while I was gone?"

"Not that I know of."

Flaherty strode toward the rear entrance, picking up speed until he was flat-out running. He yanked open the door and plowed right into one of the footmen. "Where is she?"

The footman was shaking his head and appeared dazed, having knocked heads with Flaherty.

"Me wife. Where is she?"

"In the kitchen."

"What is she doing on her feet?" Without waiting for an answer, he called, "Mary Kate!"

"Seamus?" She was flushed from being near the hot stove. Tendrils of her fiery hair framed her face.

"What are ye doing on yer feet?"

"Helping."

"Ye're to be resting."

"I got bored."

"I don't give a fecking damn if ye were bored. When I give an order—"

Mary Kate placed a hand to the middle of his chest. "No man orders me around."

"Except yer husband."

"I take orders from no man."

"Ah, lass, there's where ye'd be wrong." He scooped his wife into his arms, spun around, and stalked to the end of the hallway toward the servants' staircase. He nodded to the footman he'd knocked into. The man opened the door and closed it behind them.

Flaherty didn't say a word to the lass until they were standing outside the guest bedchamber that the viscount had permanently assigned to him when he married Mary Kate, knowing there would be times when he would need to stay overnight at Chattsworth Manor with her. "Open the door, lass."

The delightful, feisty woman crossed her arms beneath her ample breasts, calling his attention to them.

He chuckled. "Please?"

"Humph." But the lass opened the door.

He closed it with his foot. "Lock it, if ye would, lass." When she did, he sighed. "God, how I love ye, Mary Kate." He placed her gently in the middle of the bed and started to undress her. "I believe I made a promise to ye, lass, that I intend to be keeping. Best resign yerself to the fact that we'll be making love until the break of dawn."

Her eyes positively glowed. "Nothing happened while you were gone. I'm fine."

"I could not agree more. Ye have always looked more than fine to me." When she was naked on the bed, he began to undress himself. "Now then, we'd best make sure ye're ready to receive me, lass."

He covered her body with his, and she wrapped her legs around his waist. Plundering her mouth with urgent kisses, he discovered what he needed to know. "If ye were any more ready, ye'd kill me."

"Make love to me, Seamus."

"Me pleasure, wife."

<hr>

CHAPTER TWENTY-FOUR

MARY KATE WOKE when her husband slipped his arms from around her and got out of bed. Seamus had been true to his word and made love to her all night long. Even when she didn't think she had the strength, he convinced her with his lips and teeth and tongue that she was stronger than she knew.

She heard the water pouring into the wash bowl and knew he was washing before getting dressed. It would be a miracle if she could even walk over to the washstand today!

Dear Lord, how could she explain her malady to Lady Calliope? She would die of embarrassment! Then she remembered those first few months after Calliope and the viscount had been living at Chattsworth and smiled. Things that she'd thought odd became crystal clear now. Calliope had been exhausted from spending nights in her husband's arms, not some other odd, unexplained condition. Mrs. Romney must have known what was going on, but never said anything. Smart woman. It wouldn't do to have anyone making comments about the viscountess and her husband when it was plain to see they were head over heels in love with one another.

"Are ye thinking to spend the day with sheets pulled over yer head, then, lass?"

Mary Kate slowly lowered the covers. "I'm not sure I can walk."

His lightning-fast grin irritated her. He did not feel sorry for her—he was proud as a whitewashed pig! "Well now, ye'd best stay in bed. I'll know right where to find ye when I take me midday break."

"You aren't thinking to go back to Lippincott Manor without me, are you?"

"Do ye work at Lippincott Manor?"

"Well, no, but—"

"Do I work here?"

"No, but—"

"Then I shall explain to her ladyship that ye're recovering from yer ordeal yesterday and I recommended ye stay in bed."

Mary Kate frowned at her husband. "She'll know why I cannot get up, won't she?"

Flaherty's bark of laughter irritated her as much as his grin had. "As a happily married woman, me guess would be that she will."

"Then you have to help me get up." She tossed the covers aside and swung her legs over the side of the bed. Not waiting for Seamus, she got out of bed on legs that wobbled.

Before she could ask for help, her husband lifted her off her feet and into his arms. "Lass, I truly did not mean to take the starch out of yer legs."

"But you knew it could happen," she accused him.

He fought not to smile, and she wondered why she'd ever thought that she loved him. Just when she was about to ask him that very same question, he kissed her and every other thought just slipped right out of her head.

"I love ye, lass. It might be best if ye rest today. You never know, ye could be carrying me babe."

Her mouth gaped open until she saw the devilish look in his deep blue eyes. "You're going to say that every time we make love, aren't you?"

"Why not? The chances of ye being with child grow exponentially every time we make love, lass. Let me know when ye start to feel queasy of a morning."

"Mayhap I won't."

"Won't what, feel queasy or tell me?"

She narrowed her eyes at him. Instead of the reaction she anticipated, he pinched her chin until she glared at him. When his lips covered hers and his mouth worked its magic until she was mindless once again, she sighed and leaned into his kiss.

He was dressed and standing by the door before her head cleared.

"You cannot keep kissing me to distract me to get your way, husband."

"Aye, wife, I can. I shall speak with her ladyship on yer behalf."

"I'd rather you did not."

"Well, if ye can walk from the bed to the door, I'll let her know ye're delayed instead of staying in bed today."

With a will of iron, Mary Kate stood once more. This time she concentrated, locking her knees so they did not wobble, and slowly walked over to her husband, put her hands on her hips, and frowned at him. "Please apologize to her ladyship, and tell her that I shall be down shortly."

"I love ye, lass." He cupped her face in his hand and gently, reverently molded his mouth to hers. "Do not overdo today. Although I'm thinking her ladyship would not expect that of ye, given all that has transpired since yesterday."

"I love you too."

"Faith, I know ye do." He was halfway out the door when he stopped, turned around, and drew her into his embrace for one more lusty kiss. "That'll have to hold me until tonight."

Mary Kate was still staring at the closed door ten minutes later when she felt a chill and realized she'd been standing with one hand to her heart and the other on the door—without a stitch of clothing on! She shook her head at the incongruity of the situation. She had never done anything out of the ordinary all of her life...until she met Seamus Flaherty. Meeting him had been the undoing of her.

Instead of fretting, she was smiling when she wobbled her way over to the washstand. It took twice as long as normal, but she managed to wash and dry herself before sitting down to regain enough strength to dress.

Finally ready for the day, she slowly made her way down the servants' staircase—it was the fastest way to reach the kitchen, and she was starving.

"There you are." Lady Calliope looked relieved to see her.

"I am sorry for being so late, your ladyship."

"Nonsense," the viscountess said, walking over to study her face. "Pale, but all things considered, not unexpected. I should have reminded you to rest today. The very last thing I would want is you collapsing from breathing in too much smoke, or from the blow to the back of your head."

Linking her arm with Mary Kate's, Calliope bit her lip, then said, "Had Flaherty not swept you off your feet and up the stairs, I would have had a chance to mention it."

Mary Kate felt a flush sweep up from her toes to her forehead. Mortified, she had no idea how to reply.

Fortunately, the viscountess took pity on her. "Forgive me for teasing you, but I do so love seeing you happily married to Flaherty. The two of you were meant to be together."

"I could never quite decide if he cared for me, or was irritated with me."

Mary Kate's confession surprised a laugh out of Lady Calliope. "Do you know, when I first met William, we were sitting beside one another at Aurelia and Edward's wedding and started talking. It seemed as if we'd been friends forever, and I thought I sensed he was interested in more than friendship...until he learned that I was a poor relation. He was quite cool after that, leaving me to wonder if I had wanted him to be interested in more than he was. Until that fateful day he burst out of the duke's upstairs study and collided with me."

"Had I not been booted out of my former position, I would

not have ended up at Wyndmere Hall and therefore would not have accompanied you here to Chattsworth Manor. We have had some life-changing events happen, haven't we, your ladyship?"

The viscountess softly smiled. "And most of those moments we were protected by the duke's men—and so was my William during that duel."

"I'll not have it, Calliope!"

The two women spun around at the viscount's raised voice. Calliope released Mary Kate's arm and walked over to her husband, frowning. "What on earth—"

"I do not give a bloody damn whose duel you think to interfere in this time, wife. You are not leaving Chattsworth Manor!"

"Do lower your voice, William. I was speaking of the past. Besides, neither Aurelia nor I have had any false rumors lodged against us—or recorded in White's betting book—since the last duel."

"It was your honor that I was prepared to avenge, my love." The viscount drew her against his side. "I was set to duel with Chellenham right after Lord Coddington bested the man."

"You never had the chance," Calliope whispered. "Chellenham cheated and was going to shoot Aurelia's uncle in the back. Instead you leapt in the way and took the lead ball meant for him."

While Mary Kate watched, the viscount tenderly brushed away his wife's silent tears. "And I would do it again to protect your dearest friend's uncle—the man who took you in after discovering your relatives all but forced you into a menial position without taking care of you. My only regret is that Chellenham was unable to meet me on the dueling field."

Mary Kate slowly slipped into the hallway, but heard Calliope's reply. "He thought he could best a man his own age and experience, but I think he sensed you were younger and would have had quicker reflexes. He knew you would defeat him. I truly believe that is why he turned on the count of fifteen paces instead of twenty."

Watching the couple had Mary Kate examining her relationship with Flaherty. They had been through harrowing times together too, while he had been protecting her ladyship, and by default herself as Calliope's lady's maid. But he never treated her as if she were a maid—he treated her as if she had as much value as the viscountess.

All of the duke's men had. Which led her to wonder if it was because of the overall head of the extended family. The Duke of Wyndmere took his cue from his duchess, who treated servants as if they more than mattered. His brother Earl Lippincott and their distant cousins, Viscount Chattsworth and Baron Summerfield, treated their staff in the same manner.

They relied on one another to keep their estates running smoothly, extending their care and concern to not only their staff, but to the tenant farmers and their families, plus the villagers who depended upon the largesse of the families.

It was some moments before Mary Kate realized she had been lost in thought long enough that Mrs. Romney had linked arms with her, urging her back into the kitchen to sit down at the large kitchen table. "Drink up. Judging from the way Flaherty was whistling this morning, you're in need of more than a strong cup of tea. You need a good, solid meal."

Mary Kate stared at the heaping plate of eggs, sausages, fresh bread, and butter and completely forgot her embarrassment. "Thank you, Mrs. Romney. I could eat."

By the time she'd eaten every last crumb, the cook refilled her teacup and joined her. "Now then, I had not intended to interfere yesterday when Flaherty was beyond worried about you and the possibility of what could happen after you'd been injured. Today is another matter."

Confused, Mary Kate set her cup on her saucer. "It is?"

"Most men have no idea how strong a woman is. We have been carrying babes in our bellies, all the while continuing to care for our menfolk, and other babes we've already birthed, for generations. Then there's the birth itself—no man could stand up to the rigors of bearing children. Do not spend your time worrying whether or not you will miscarry a babe because of performing everyday duties. Sometimes circumstances happen that are beyond our control. But most often we women are sturdy and strong enough not to ever have that worry."

"Mum used to say it was up to the Lord, and that there are times when something isn't quite right with the babe because it simply was not meant to be."

"Your mum was a very wise woman."

Mary Kate smiled and reached for the cook's hand. "You remind me of her. Thank you for reaffirming what she told me." She sipped from her cup and frowned into it. "Do you have any advice for how to keep Flaherty from chasing me back inside once I find myself carrying his babe? I have a feeling he'll want me to rest for the whole nine months."

Mrs. Romney smiled. "You promise not to overdo, but keep up with what you have the energy for. Eat well, rest when you are tired, and never hesitate to ask for help—even if it is to run interference with your well-meaning husband."

"Thank you, Mrs. Romney." Mary Kate shot up from her seat, intending to dash off to the nursery, but a wave of dizziness assailed her, forcing her to sit back down.

"Well now," the cook said, "we'd best start out as we mean to go on, with you putting your feet up for half an hour. You can rest on the cot in the room at the end of the hallway if you do not want one of the footman to escort you to your room. Cannot have you fainting on my watch."

"It could just be exhaustion," Mary Kate reminded her.

"You are absolutely right. However, I am not willing to incur the wrath of your handsome husband if he is right." Mrs. Romney tilted her head to one side, staring at Mary Kate for a few moments before asking, "Are you?"

Mary Kate blew out a breath. "He'd probably lock me in our bedchamber."

Mrs. Romney laughed. "We'll do our best to avoid that happening. Now then, can you stand?" When she did, the cook slid her arm around Mary Kate's waist. "We'll walk slowly, no need to rush."

Mary Kate hesitated to admit that she *was* still a bit lightheaded, so she bit her lip and did as the cook bade. Walking into the room, she spied the chair and asked, "Couldn't I just sit in the chair by the cot?"

"As I have the midday meal to start preparing, I'd rather you lie down. Give your system time to absorb the meal you just ate. You'll feel better for it." Mrs. Romney helped Mary Kate lie down and drew up the blanket. "I'll send one of the maids down to check on you, but you have to promise not to get up on your own—or I'll send word to Lippincott Manor and Flaherty."

Mary Kate did not want to interrupt her husband's duties. "I promise not to get up."

"As long as we understand one another."

"We do."

"Don't fret. You're young and strong, and surrounded by people who will look after you until Flaherty returns at teatime to collect you."

"But what about her ladyship?"

"I'll speak with her myself later, as the viscount whisked her away while you were lost in thought." The cook walked over to the door. "I'm going to leave it partway open. One of the footmen will be just a few feet away—within hearing distance— so just call out if you need anything."

"Thank you."

"You're welcome. Now close your eyes!"

"Yes, Mrs. Romney."

Mary Kate had no intention of sleeping, but she did as she was told and closed her eyes, not sure how long the cook would stand in the doorway to ensure she kept them closed. Mary Kate sighed and waited. Listening.

The last thing she remembered was how warm and cozy the blanket felt and how surprisingly comfortable the cot was.

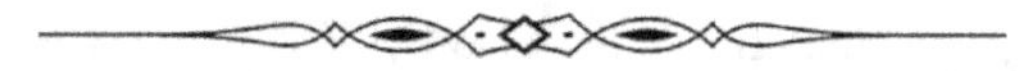

CHAPTER TWENTY-FIVE

HARGRAVE STRODE INTO the kitchen and frowned at Mrs. Romney. "Well?"

She glanced over her shoulder at the butler, sighed, and set the teacakes on the rack to cool. "Well, what?"

His expression darkened. "Are you going to summon Flaherty, or shall I?"

"The man's working. Before you ask, I have checked on Mary Kate every time I take another batch of scones or teacakes out of the oven. She's resting—something he did not think to let her do last night."

Hargrave's pained expression was comical. "Are you… Did you just suggest…" He closed his eyes and drew in a deep breath. "Flaherty will have to be told how his wife spent the morning— instead of seeing to her duties, she's been sleeping."

"Why? Her ladyship is aware, and has no issue with Mary Kate resting today. Poor woman was abducted and nearly perished in a fire! Do you begrudge the young woman a bit of rest?"

"No, but—"

"I would stop there if I were you, Hargrave."

"Knowing Flaherty, he'll be angry that we did not send word," the butler insisted.

"Did Mrs. Meadowsweet suggest that you speak to me directly when you could not convince her that someone needs to bother Flaherty before the midday meal?"

"Hargrave!" The housekeeper entered the kitchen and tapped her foot in annoyance. "I thought you planned to listen to my advice."

"I did listen, Mrs. Meadowsweet—however, if you will recall, I did not agree with your advice, hence necessitating my speaking to Mrs. Romney…whose advice I am not going to follow either."

"Good heavens," Lady Calliope said, walking into the kitchen. "I do not believe I have seen the three of you at odds since Mary Kate and I first arrived at Chattsworth. At the time neither yourselves nor Mary Kate and I knew what to expect or how to deal with one another."

The butler, housekeeper, and cook gaped at her, but did not utter a sound. Finally, she sighed, "It was a jest. I am sorry if it fell short of the mark. Do forgive me. What are you discussing in such overly loud hushed tones?"

Hargrave squared his shoulders. "Mary Kate has been sleeping for hours now. I believe Flaherty needs to know."

"He'll only wake her up to ask her why she is so tired." The viscountess mumbled, "As if he did not know."

"Precisely, and that's why there is no need to bother the man," Mrs. Romney said.

"But his temper," the butler reminded the women.

"He does not need to worry about his wife sleeping, when she is clearly exhausted," Mrs. Meadowsweet said. "Who wouldn't be after being abducted, knocked over the head, and then nearly dying inside of the squire's barn when it was set on fire?"

Calliope looked from one servant to the other and asked, "Did our new footman sound the alarm, Hargrave?" Before he could answer, she continued, "He is not used to dealing with a hot Irish temper, but he will need to become accustomed to it."

"Aye, your ladyship. Though I have to agree with the young man—Flaherty has a right to know."

"That his wife is exhausted and sleeping, or that Mrs. Romney, Mrs. Meadowsweet, two maids, and myself have been taking turns checking on her for the last few hours?" When the servant did not answer, Calliope asked, "How do you expect Flaherty to perform his duties to Earl Lippincott? The man needs to have his wits about him when he's stationed on the roof, scouting the perimeter, on patrol to the village and back, or guarding the interior. The poor man has enough on his mind."

Hargrave's face paled. "But what if he arrives, and she's still sleeping? He will demand to know why."

"The stable master has been informed that Flaherty must speak with my husband immediately upon his arrival on an urgent matter."

"I see," the butler replied.

"I thought you might. Let William handle Flaherty."

"Aye, your ladyship."

He bowed before returning to his post, and Calliope called out to him, "Hargrave?"

"Yes, your ladyship?"

"See that the new footman understands that nothing in this household escapes my notice, nor his lordship's. I trust that you do know how deeply we care for every member of our staff—especially those of you who have been in service to William's father and his grandfather."

"I shall rectify the matter immediately."

"Thank you, Hargrave. For that, and your years of loyalty, and for caring for the newest members we have welcomed to our staff." She turned and beamed at the housekeeper and cook. "Thank you too, Mrs. Meadowsweet, Mrs. Romney. William and I depend upon you all so much more than you know. So many traditions that I would not have known about would have been brushed aside, and eventually forgotten, had you three not remained with MacReady to pass on the inner workings of Chattsworth Manor to William and me."

The butler retreated, and Calliope waited until he'd quietly spoken to the footman stationed in the hallway between the rear entrance and the kitchen and returned. "Problem handled, your ladyship."

"Wonderful, Hargrave. My thanks." She waited until he'd exited the servants' side of the house before continuing the conversation. "Now that that issue has been solved and a crisis averted, I believe my little darling should be waking up from his nap. I'll be in the nursery if you need me."

FLAHERTY HAD NOT had trouble concentrating on his patrol in a long time. But this morning, halfway through his shift on the rooftop, he found his mind drifting back to the way his lovely wife had bidden him goodbye. For half a moment, he savored the image of her—rumpled from just rising from their tangled bed linens, her riot of curls curtaining her shoulders, flowing to her waist. His smile came as he remembered the vision of his wife standing gloriously naked as he kissed her goodbye. Poor darling would no doubt wake up and realize it once she was no longer plastered against him and noticed the chill.

Movement at the edge of his field of vision had him snapping to full attention. The rifle was in his hands, and the target within range, as he lined up the sights. At the last moment, he relaxed. Just a doe and her fawn, not a sharpshooter. The events from yesterday still had him on edge, expecting the worst. He needed to forget about his wife—easier said than done, when all he wanted was to see her smile as he changed shifts going from the rooftop to the perimeter patrol. Was it too much to ask that they both live and work at the same estate?

"Aye. And ye know why; the lass spelled it out for ye." Mary Kate and Calliope had developed a closeness—a crisis or near disaster would do that—most likely formed from the moment Mary Kate was assigned as her ladyship's personal maid. For the remainder of his shift on top of the roof, he forced himself to set thoughts of his wife aside. If he needed to think of her, he would allow himself to in between shifts as he moved from location to location—the perimeter to the village patrol, the patrol to interior guard duty—before he would be given leave to collect his wife.

He allowed himself a few minutes longer to think of Mary Kate, reasoning that he needed to decide if he would ask to borrow one of the carriages, or fetch her on horseback. Horseback, definitely. He could hold her in his arms for the entire ride back. Though not a long ride, just a few miles, it was far enough that he would be able to breathe in her scent, feel her curves against him, the distracting weight of her in his lap, the silky-soft, fiery tendrils that would have slipped from the hastily fashioned twist of hair she piled on top of her head daily—before she presented her back to him and asked him to please button her up.

His wife was more than just the woman who had been Lady Calliope's right hand for nearly two years now—she had become a part of the viscountess's inner circle, trusted to watch the viscount's heir. Just as Mollie and Francis had become irreplaceable to Her Grace when she was expecting the twins. Both maids had been elevated to the shared duty of lady's maid to the duchess, and then trusted to care for the duke's heir and his twin sister when they were born. Flaherty could not remember who had replaced Mollie when she married Finn O'Malley—mayhap no one. The duke and duchess had had the foresight to hire a highly regarded nanny when the twins were born, and she ended up marrying Patrick O'Malley.

For some reason, neither Lady Aurelia nor Lady Calliope had hired a nanny yet, preferring to care for their sons with the help of their lady's maids and others on their staff. Now that the lads were standing up and would be learning how to walk—and then run—Flaherty wondered if their lordships had talked their wives into hiring if not a nanny, then a governess. Not that it was any of his concern—he rather thought it was the way that all people of wealth and social standing did things.

Ye're a bloody eedjit, boy-o. *'Tisn't as if the earl or the viscount will ask yer opinion on the matter.*

With a sigh of disgust at his lack of concentration, Flaherty made it through the rest of his shifts without further distracting thoughts of his wife. Likely due in part to the fact that he'd made a game of counting how many hours it would be till he held her in his arms again. Kissed her again. Made love to her again. He clamped down hard on his desire before it became a problem.

He really should not have tired the lass out to the point of exhaustion during the night, but God help him, every time he closed his eyes, he was back in the squire's barn! Garahan was there, shaking him, demanding he wake up because the lass needed him. He remembered it all: Garahan slicing through their bonds, setting them free. Smoldering piles of dried hay and twigs bursting into flames all around them as the back wall of the barn caved in.

Shaking free of the nightmare, he'd managed to make it through the day without mishap, but not without a nagging headache.

As he strode toward the stables, Sean was walking toward him. "Ah, there ye are. I'm proud of ye for lasting through yer shifts, Flaherty. I know it was not easy, having been in yer shoes dealing with the aftermath of rescuing yer wife from a dangerous situation. Wanting to check on her every hour, but not at liberty to."

Flaherty nodded, but kept walking toward the stall, where his gelding was already saddled and waiting for him. His cousin had done this. He glanced over his shoulder. "Thank ye, Sean. If ye don't mind, I need to hurry. I'm not wanting the lass to worry if I'm late."

"It'll get easier once ye're both accustomed to a routine."

Routine? Marriage shouldn't be reduced to something one did at the same time every day, like rising in the morning and washing one's face. It should be something special—two hearts that pledged to love one another for the rest of their lives.

Building a strong foundation to raise the family he hoped to have.

Sean told him, "Go to yer wife. Mignonette and Georgiana helped Lady Aurelia with a few of the finishing touches to yer cottage. As Harry was out in the field, she sent Bart over to lay the fire."

Flaherty snorted. "Do ye know the first time I heard Michael married Harry, I thought to meself, well now, it'll never work, as Michael always swore he wanted children, and as far as I know, two men… Well, I'm sure ye know what direction me mind went in."

Sean grinned. "I think me brother enjoyed having a laugh at everyone's expense simply because his wife preferred being called Harry instead of Harriet."

"Only an O'Malley." Flaherty met Sean's intense look. "Please thank yer wife and Dermott's, Bart, and Lady Aurelia for me. I have a feeling the viscount may want to speak to me about yesterday."

"That I will." Sean walked through the stable doors with him. He nodded when Flaherty swung into the saddle before adding a warning they used to use for one another back home: "Watch out for poachers."

Flaherty was laughing as he followed the long driveway that would lead him to the road back to Mary Kate. Lord willing, she would be ready and waiting for him to arrive. He couldn't wait to see her reaction to the surprise gift from the earl and countess— their new home among a cluster of cottages built for the married men of the duke's guard and their wives.

The duke had started the tradition after Patrick O'Malley married the twins' nanny, wanting the head of his guard to have a home of his own—not far from where his duties lay, but just far enough away to be able to relax and enjoy married life.

Flaherty was honored to be included among the married O'Malleys and Garahans who had already received the gift of a cottage. Never in his wildest dreams had he envisioned working for the duke and his family, nor receiving such an extravagant, thoughtful gift. His friends back home would never believe him. Ah well, no matter. He had a beautiful wife, a lovely new cottage, and the rest of his life ahead of him.

What more could he possibly want?

CHAPTER TWENTY-SIX

FLAHERTY DISMOUNTED AS the stable master took the reins from him.

"His lordship wishes to speak to you—on an urgent matter."

He swallowed the curse and inclined his head. "Aye." Instead of heading for the side entrance to the building, which would lead him directly to the viscount's study and library, he walked to the rear entrance, closest to the kitchen, where he hoped to find his wife.

"Where are you going, Flaherty?"

Irked that the stable master would question him, as if he hadn't heard the man the first time, he didn't bother answering. He lengthened his stride and was crossing the threshold when he heard the sound of raised feminine voices coming from the kitchen. "Must be a discussion over which teacakes to serve." Chuckling to himself, he strode past the first room and came to an abrupt halt—Mary Kate was sitting up on the edge of the cot where, just yesterday, he'd held her still while MacReady stitched her head wound.

Rushing into the room, he had his arm around her as he asked, "What's happened? Were ye feeling faint? Does yer head pain ye?"

Blue-violet eyes stared into his, and he could not decide if she had been hit on the head again and was dazed, or if she was still marveling over the fact that they had indeed outwitted death and lived to see another day. "Seamus, you're here."

"Were ye expecting someone else, lass?"

Her lips lifted and the smile transformed her face from beautiful to stunning. "I'm happy to see you. Please take me home."

"That's me intention, *mo ghrá*, but the viscount wishes a word with me first on an urgent matter."

Her brow furrowed. "Then why didn't you go directly to see him?"

Flaherty bent and gently pressed his lips to hers. "Because ye're me wife and yer wellbeing is just as important to me. If the viscount doesn't understand, then I'll be giving His Grace notice that I am leaving me position within his guard."

Shock drained every ounce of color from her face. "But you cannot do that."

"Last time I checked, lass, I'm a free man and able to make me own decisions. If I choose to leave, then that's what I'll do."

"But you took a vow to the duke."

"That I did, and I have honored it every day."

"Who will take your place?"

"No doubt someone else Coventry has hired. He has been steadily gathering a group of injured former military men. Some of whom ye've met—Tremayne, Hennessey, Bayfield, and Masterson, to name a few."

Mary Kate placed her hands on either side of her husband's face and stared deeply into his eyes. Was she looking for a shadow in the depths? Would she ask him something he was not ready to discuss with her? It felt as if she were searching his mind, thinking to find the true reason he would leave the duke's guard.

Some things were more important than holding on to a good-paying position—even one where he got to work alongside his cousins, and for a man he admired, the Duke of Wyndmere. Fighting for what one believed in—the Irish had been doing that all their lives. The poor lass did not realize her worth to him. He'd finally found something more important that his position within the guard, more precious to him than his own life—his wife.

"Do ye not understand that now we are wed, ye are the reason I live and breathe, Mary Kate? Ye're me heart, me love. Haven't ye heard me calling ye *mo chroí, mo ghrá?*"

"Yes, and I thought I remembered that it meant something along those lines, but I was afraid to upset you if I asked. I didn't want you to be angry with me."

Flaherty paused for a moment as a realization occurred. People had often spoken of his temper and anger as if it were a defining part of him that was to be avoided. Was it so noticeable that others would rather steer clear of him than listen to him rail at something that irritated him? Though it would break his heart to hear her answer, he needed to ask…

"Lass, are ye afraid of me?"

"No, of course not. Why would you think that?"

As if she'd lost her mind, he very quietly reminded her, "Ye said ye didn't want me to be angry with ye."

"And I mean it. I don't like being at odds with you, although as your wife, it will be my duty to soothe your temper. I have some ideas about that."

He blew out a breath. "I am all for listening to yer ideas, and have a few of me own. But before we discuss them, I need to ask, are ye the only one who feels that way? Do I come across as having a temper to ye?"

Instead of answering him, she snorted with laughter. *Snorted!*

"'Tisn't a proper response, wife."

She laughed harder. When he growled at her, she managed to stop laughing. "Seamus, everyone knows of your temper and respects it. Of course, no one wants to get on the wrong side of it—they'd be foolish to want to do so. I'd go so far as to say your temper is a formidable weapon."

"But ye're me wife. Ye should not have to worry about saying anything that would anger me, lass."

Mary Kate sighed. "Well, that is good to know, because I am

quite sure I shall be pricking your temper for the rest of our married life. I do believe it is *my* formidable weapon."

And as quickly as that, his worry evaporated. Mary Kate had a way of making sense of his world and the things that worried him. Maybe it was because his eyes had been opened to the possibility of losing his life *and* his wife so soon after marrying her. "This must be what Emmett felt like."

"Emmett O'Malley?"

"Aye, lass. He and Michaela had only just said their vows the night before he was knifed in the back. He nearly died—actually, Tremayne and Garahan's brother insisted that he had. I'm thinking I would like to have a conversation with Emmett and listen to what he swears was a visit to Heaven, where he spoke with his da and grandda…and their first cow Siobhan. To hear Tremayne tell it, apparently there's something I never knew— cows earn their angel wings, too."

Mary Kate stared at him and shook her head. "Not that I doubt what Emmett saw and heard, but I do believe we should arrange for a day to ride into London to visit with Emmett and Michaela. Mayhap they could see to it that Tremayne and Garahan's brother would be available to speak to us as well. By the way, which brother is it, Aiden?"

"Nay, Aiden Garahan's married to Emily, and they live in a fine cottage on the grounds of Wyndmere Hall."

"Then it must be Ryan."

Flaherty shook his head. "Nay, Ryan's married to Prudence, and they live in a cottage in the Borderlands on the grounds of Summerfield Chase."

Mary Kate put her arms around Flaherty's neck and lifted on her toes, trailing kisses along the line of his jaw, distracting him. "Then it must be the brother who was injured and wears an eye patch."

"Aye, lass, 'tis Darby. He's married to Aimee and lives in Captain Coventry's building near Grosvenor Square."

"If you speak to the earl, and I speak to Lady Calliope, we

may be able to arrange the time." Before he could reply, she nipped his bottom lip, fused her mouth to his, and burrowed into his embrace. He was lost in the lush kiss they shared and did not hear footsteps approaching the room until someone cleared their throat.

"Flaherty!"

"Feck me, lass," he whispered against her lips. "I'd forgotten about the viscount."

"Bloody hell, Flaherty!"

He coughed to cover his laughter, knowing the viscount also had a temper. Flaherty kissed her temple and murmured, "Definitely should not have ignored his request." In a louder voice, he said, "Excuse me, wife. Hold that thought and yer kisses."

He loosened her hold around his neck, slid his arm around her waist, and tucked her against his side, then turned to face the viscount. "Ah, yer lordship. I was on me way to see ye."

"Apparently the words *urgent matter* were lost on you."

"They were not. Did ye forget what happened just yesterday and think there was a chance I would not check on me wife before speaking with ye?"

Affronted, Chattsworth grumbled, "Of course I remember what happened. Otherwise, we would not have let your wife spend the day sleeping. She needed to recover."

Flaherty clenched his jaw and held tight to his control. He should not let his anger have free rein in speaking to the viscount. Such an action could weigh heavily on how his brothers would be treated after he left the duke's employ. And as of this moment, that was now his plan. He fully intended to resign from His Grace's private guard. No man would ever tell him to put his wife last. He needed clarification from the duke if that was in fact what was expected of him. Depending upon the duke's reply, he would either ask to be relocated to another of His Grace's properties, or resign.

Before he could put his plan into motion, he would ensure

that the earl and his family were well protected. As of right now, he only needed to send word to Coventry to ask that a temporary replacement be sent to Lippincott Manor at once—he could also ask Gavin King of Bow Street to send one of his men. There were half a dozen or more that Flaherty could recommend off the top of his head. Men who knew the drill, and had spent time protecting the earl and his family when asked to lend their additional aid.

But first, he would put the question to the viscount. "Are ye telling me, as a member of the duke's guard, that I'm expected to put the duke and his family before me own wife's wellbeing and safety?"

"No one would expect you not to protect your wife, Flaherty."

"'Tisn't an answer, yer lordship. 'Tis an evasion. Answer me question."

The viscount glared at him. "That sounded like an order."

"Ye can take it however ye wish, yer lordship, as long as ye answer me question."

"You swore a vow to protect the duke and his family with your life."

"And by God, I have! Or did ye forget I was shot in the back twice, and more recently had a lead ball carve a groove in me cheek?"

"You took two lead balls in the back protecting Dermott's wife," Chattsworth reminded him before admitting, "Although it was after you had stopped those men from abducting Lady Aurelia."

Flaherty was incensed. Had the viscount just glossed over the fact that Dermott's wife had been in danger and deserved to be protected? Did the other men in the guard know that they were expected to put the duke and his family first—even now that they were married, with babes of their own?

He swallowed the bitter truth and turned to his wife. "We're leaving, Mary Kate."

She stiffened. "Of course. Please let her ladyship know that I shall return tomorrow."

"Nay, lass," Flaherty said. "We leave for London immediately."

Chattsworth looked shocked. "You'd walk away from your duties? What of your vow?"

"Do ye think, just because ye have a fancy title, that yer life, and those of yer wife and son, are more deserving of me protection than me own wife or me cousin's wives and babes?"

Before he said something he might regret, Flaherty swept his wife into his arms and slipped around the viscount. "Not a word, Mary Kate," he rasped.

He strode out of the rear door and stalked over to his mount. Placing the lass on the horse's back, he quickly mounted behind her and pulled her onto his lap. He met the stable master's direct look and said, "Tell Garahan I'll send word to Coventry and King. The earl and his family will not go without protection."

Flaherty tightened his hold on his wife and rode away from the stables. Neither of them spoke as his gelding picked up the pace to a fast trot and they rode along the winding drive leading to the road that would take them to London. He had contacts in the underbelly of London, as well as on the docks and in and around the Dark Walk. Part of the duke's guard's mission had been to develop even more contacts within all levels of society. He would use his cousins' and brothers' contacts as well.

No one would be able to say that Flaherty left in a temper and did not fully see to the protection of the duke's brother, and the duke's cousin, and their families. He'd given his word, and he intended to keep it—one last time. Then, and only then, would he be ready to send his resignation to His Grace.

He would no longer be the Duke's Champion.

CHAPTER TWENTY-SEVEN

T HEY HAD BEEN riding for a few miles before Mary Kate felt she had given her husband enough time to tell her what on earth he was thinking. "Are we really just going to leave? You aren't going to let me say goodbye to Lady Calliope and little William?"

When he grunted, she poked him in the side of the head to get his attention. His gaze slid to hers, and she could see hurt mixed with anger in his expression. She had her answer. "I see. Do you want to tell me what prompted your decision to leave the duke's employ?"

"Ye were there! Ye heard what the viscount expected, but I can tell ye this—if Chattsworth were in me boots, he would have checked on his wife first, too. Ye cannot tell me he would do otherwise."

She sighed. "You're right, Seamus. He loves her."

"I would never put ye second, lass, and I'm thinking none of me cousins would put their wives or babes second either. Though I'm not sure if any of them have been challenged the way the viscount challenged me right to do so."

"Emotions were high just now."

"'Tis no excuse, lass. 'Tis a slight to ye and the other men's wives and families." He was silent for a moment. "I'm thinking someone needs to speak to the duke and let him know that he has to take a hard look at the vows the sixteen of us took—and amend the rules and whatever else needs amending. The married men of his guard should not be expected to put their wives and families last. They should at least be on equal footing with the duke and his family. Don't ye see, lass? Without ye, I'd be nothing. Ye're me life now, and deserve to be first."

As they rode away from Chattsworth Manor, she was sorry not to have been able to bid Calliope goodbye, but knew that she would be sending her ladyship a heartfelt letter as soon as they stopped at one of the inns on the road to London. She would encourage Seamus to write to the duke and state his case. One thing was certain—he needed to alert his brothers. If they were as close as she'd heard they were, they may feel the need to resign as well in support of Seamus.

As that thought whirled around in her brain, she made her decision. No matter what he decided, she would write to Her Grace.

Her stomach growled. First they needed to stop for a meal. She was starving!

He snorted. "I'd best be feeding ye, and may need to see to renting a carriage. 'Tis over fifty-five miles to London, and although 'tis a pleasure to carry ye the whole way, I'm thinking 'tisn't wise for me horse to carry us double for that long."

"I remember Lady Calliope and I were constantly changing horses on our journey from Wyndmere Hall to Sussex."

"Not constantly, lass, just every twenty miles. Did ye forget Michael O'Malley and I were yer guards on the journey?"

She sighed and settled more securely in his arms. "You and Michael were the perfect distraction for the unknown that lay ahead of her ladyship and myself. Have I thanked you lately?"

"Aye, wife. Just last night."

Mary Kate sat up and brushed her lips to her husband's cheek. "I did not have a chance to tell you how I was feeling today."

His eyes met hers. "Oh, and how are ye feeling, lass?"

"Woozy."

His eyes seemed to change in hue to a lighter shade of blue. "Were ye now? Anything else I should know?"

"I did not mean to sleep all day. I only meant to close my eyes for half an hour."

He shifted his large hand to rest low on her abdomen. The warmth of his touch seared through her gown and chemise. She wondered if the imprint of his hand would appear on their babe when he or she was born.

"Well then, it's a fine thing that ye won't be working yerself to the bone for her ladyship. I've something else in mind for us now, lass. I'm hoping that ye'll not fight me on this, and know that ye'll be vexed with me for the near future, but I had to stand up for ye, lass. Ye are more important to me than me own life. No one is above ye. *No one.* We said vows before witnesses, the vicar, and the Lord. Anyone who expects a man to just toss the woman he pledged his life to aside in favor of the man who pays his wages is dicked in the nob."

Her lips twitched as she fought not to smile. "Did you say dicked?"

"Aye."

"In the nob?"

"Aye. Have ye never heard the expression before. 'Tis English."

She had to smile. "Ah, in other words, you would say *fecking eedjit.*" His snort of laughter warmed her heart. There was the man she loved. "Seamus, I love you, and I know it's hard to understand, but I do not think the duke would ever expect you to set your own wife below his. If I'm remembering the sequence of events as it was told to me, when the sixteen of you vowed to protect the duke and his wife with your lives, he was newly married to Her Grace."

"Aye. What of it?"

"But then Their Graces' twins were born, and it added to those you were expected to protect."

"The earl and countess married, and it was somewhere

around that time that the duke received letters from his two distant cousins, the viscount and the baron. Both of whom married not long after, and the sixteen of us were put on a rotation between the duke's properties, and the viscount's home, and the baron's home. What are ye getting at, lass?"

"That the duke has continued to add to those whom you were expected to protect since you vowed to do so, without asking you to include them—it was assumed you would."

"'Twas our job, lass."

"I understand that, husband, but you are missing the point. When did the duke finally decide that you no longer had to move from estate to estate to familiarize yourselves with his homes, staff, and local villagers?"

"I'm thinking it may have been around the time four of the O'Malleys had married and Garahan was about to be."

"So His Grace did think enough of the married men in his guard not to take them away from their wives while they were stationed at his other residences."

"So it would seem. As I wasn't even thinking of marrying yet, I paid it no mind."

"But now you are married, and I think it's important that you bring the matter to His Grace's attention. He needs to meet with Patrick O'Malley and discuss it. Attempts have been made on the lives of your cousins' wives as well as the duke's family. Surely he must understand that his men should not be expected to believe their wives do not matter and are last in the line of those to protect."

"When ye put it that way, lass. I'm thinking it makes sense. But the viscount—"

"Let us not talk about his lordship right now. I'm hungry."

Flaherty pressed a kiss to the top of her head and breathed deeply. "I don't know that I deserve yer love, lass, but I'm willing to fight to keep it."

"Then I expect that you will take this fight to the top and speak to His Grace."

He eased back to glare at her. "And where will ye be?"

"Right beside you, Seamus."

"Well now, we'd best see about feeding yerself and our son."

"Daughter."

He laughed. "Mayhap both. How do ye feel about twins?"

IT WAS A bit later than she'd hoped to eat when they finally were able to stop at an inn. She remembered being here more than once, traveling back and forth to the duke's town house on Grosvenor Square and Lippincott Manor and Chattsworth Manor in Sussex.

"Promise me that ye aren't planning to leave me now that I walked away from me duties to the earl."

"I promise, and it's rude of you to think that I would. I don't just love you because you are a member of the duke's guard."

"Were, lass. I left, remember?"

"You need to send a written resignation to His Grace for it to be official."

"I'd better feed ye, lass. Ye're peckish and getting grumpier."

"I'm tired and hungry, Seamus."

He nodded to the hostler at the inn, dismounted, and handed over the reins.

The older man smiled. "I thought I recognized you as one of the duke's men. Flaherty isn't it?"

"Aye. Me wife isn't used to her condition yet," Flaherty confided. "She's tired and hungry."

"Congratulations. I hadn't heard that another of the duke's men married. It's not easy on our womenfolk when they are expecting. Happened to my wife all eight times."

"Eight?" Just the idea had Mary Kate's head feeling light and her limbs unsteady.

Flaherty scooped her off the back of his horse. "I do not want ye to faint on me, lass."

"I'll send one of the lads ahead of you to ensure they have a nice spot for you in one of the rooms at the back of the inn," the hostler said. "A pot of tea and warm meal is what your wife needs."

"And rest," Flaherty added.

"Aye. I'll take care of this fine gelding for you. I realize it is still early, but given your wife's delicate condition, will you be staying the night?"

"We will."

"I'll settle him in for the night, and you can continue on your way in the morning, though if I may make a suggestion, you may want to think about renting a carriage."

Flaherty frowned. "I've been discussing that with me wife, and think we should. Thank ye."

"Mr. Flaherty, Mrs. Flaherty," the innkeeper greeted them as Seamus carried Mary Kate inside. "Welcome to our inn. It has been a while."

"Thank ye. Aye, it has."

"Glad to have you back. I understand you'll be staying the night, and that your wife needs a hot meal and pot of tea. Poor dear. Women have the hardest road in the making of a family."

Mary Kate could not hide the fact that she was embarrassed by the innkeeper's frank talk with her husband. Her face flamed, but she pretended not to notice and let Flaherty continue to do the talking. She was too tired to think, or talk, as she had done most of the talking on their way to the inn.

"I'm thinking it'll get harder before it gets easier," Flaherty mumbled.

"Follow me," the innkeeper said. "I have just the spot where you can have a bit of privacy at a table off to the side in the back room." He led them through the great room into one of the smaller rooms. Only one or two patrons were seated at the smattering of tables. The man nodded to the customers and led Flaherty and Mary Kate to a table separate from the others. "Your tea and a hot bowl of stew with dumplings will be served in just a few minutes."

"We're grateful. Thank ye."

"My pleasure."

Flaherty sat, but seemed loath to let go of Mary Kate. "Isn't it going to be hard to eat and hold me at the same time?" she asked.

His expression darkened. "I'm afraid if I let ye go, ye'll change yer mind and demand that I take ye back to Chattsworth Manor."

She cupped his face in her hand. "I won't change my mind. You are my husband, and I love you. I may not always understand the reasons you do things. I may, however, question what in the bloody hell you were thinking, but I won't gainsay you."

"Ah, Mary Kate Flaherty, ye are the only woman for me."

"I should hope so. You married me."

"That I did, lass. Now rest just a bit more in me arms. I'll set ye on yer own seat when yer meal arrives."

She soaked up some of his strength as they waited for their food to arrive. One thing was certain—it was going to be a battle to ensure that the duke heard and understood just what his men had been going through. It was high time someone pointed out to His Grace that he was ignoring the changing needs of his men as they married and started their own families. Mary Kate believed she was going to be the one to do so—with a little help from Her Grace.

CHAPTER TWENTY-EIGHT

GARAHAN GAVE A short, sharp whistle as he jumped from the ladder leading to the rooftop. Michael O'Malley came running from the other side of the building.

"Where's the threat?" Michael demanded.

"'Tis Flaherty."

"Is he late?"

Garahan scrubbed a hand over his face. "Nay, he just rode out of here with Mary Kate on his lap as if the hounds of hell were nipping at his heels."

Michael frowned. "And he didn't stop to speak with either of us."

Garahan grunted. "We'd best find out what's happened. The constable was supposed to send the prisoners on to London early this morning. Unless one of them escaped…"

He took off running to the rear entrance of the building with Michael right behind him.

"Where's his lordship?"

The footman stationed in the hallway pointed toward the kitchen. The duke's men strode toward the room, tension radiating off them as they prepared for the bad news. It had to be bad, otherwise why would Flaherty have left in such a hurry?

"Yer lordship! What's happened? Is it Mary Kate?"

"Or one of his brothers?" Michael asked.

The viscount stared at the men and shook his head. "Neither."

"Well, something's not right. Flaherty never pushes a horse to his limit like that without a reason," Garahan murmured.

"Ye might as well tell us," Michael added. "We'll be finding out from the staff otherwise, and we'd rather hear it from the source."

"He's right, yer lordship," Garahan said. "The stunned expression on yer face tells me it has to do with Mary Kate."

Finally the viscount asked, "What gives you that idea?"

"Because Flaherty would have come outside to trade punches with one of us if it had to do with himself. He'd take any kind of criticism about himself, but if anyone were to say anything that in some way maligned his wife, well then…" Garahan let his words trail off and left it to the viscount to figure out just where he'd gone wrong.

"I may have come on a bit too strong just now," the viscount admitted.

"Why did ye feel the need to?" Michael asked. "Flaherty works just as hard as the rest of us—ye know that, as he used to be stationed here."

"I left word with the stable master that I needed to speak to Flaherty on an urgent matter as soon as he arrived."

"Ye had to know that he would be stopping to check on his wife first, yer lordship," Garahan said. "They nearly died yesterday."

The viscount raked a hand through his hair until it stood on end. "Bloody hell, I know that! But I was trying to appease Calliope in her bid to keep Flaherty from getting angry."

Garahan opened his mouth to speak, but Michael held up a hand and spoke first. "'Tis part of the Flaherty clan's charm. Their tempers are mercurial, and those of us in the duke's guard use it to our advantage whenever possible. Whether it be gathering information from reluctant sources, questioning prisoners, or what have ye."

"So ye found him with his wife, and ye demanded to know why he ignored a direct order to speak with ye first. Is that it?" Garahan asked.

Chattsworth frowned, and Michael picked up the thread of the conversation. "Well then, what did he have to say in response?"

"I was too surprised by the way he spoke to me," the viscount replied. "Not deferential at all."

"Ye were questioning him as to why he stopped to see his wife first," Garahan said. "I'd be hard pressed to speak in a deferential tone to ye, if it were meself."

"Even you?" the viscount asked.

"Bloody hell! Have ye no thought to what the man and his wife went through yesterday at all? Are ye so far removed from the lower rungs of society that ye think yer life, yer wife, and yer family are all that matters?"

"By God, that's more or less what he said before he turned his back on me, swept Mary Kate into his arms, and walked out."

"Then the lass did not get to say goodbye to her ladyship. Did she?" Michael asked.

When the viscount shrugged, Michael glanced at Garahan, who held up both hands. "Don't be asking me. I was at me post on the rooftop."

Chattsworth finally rasped, "She's going to be vexed with me."

"Her ladyship will have to get in line," Garahan growled. "Because right now, I'm bloody well furious with ye, yer lordship. Has the fact that we have bled for yerself and yer family been forgotten entirely? Is it because we don't show the pain we're in as we're stitched back together, hiding the fact from ye because 'tis our sworn duty to protect ye?"

Chattsworth's blank expression spoke volumes. The man had not even considered that fact.

Michael sighed. "Have ye sent one of the footmen to Lippincott Manor to see if Flaherty was simply taking his wife home?"

"'Twas supposed to be their first night in the cottage the earl gifted to them for their wedding," Garahan added.

"I have and am waiting for the footman to return with any news from Lippincott Manor before I speak to my wife," the viscount replied.

"I'll be sending a missive to His Grace," Garahan informed the viscount. "He'll need to understand that when one of our own is mistreated after all we've done for ye—after the blood each one of us has spilled for ye—'tis a blow to us all." Unable to stand the sight of the man before him, a man he used to admire, Garahan spun on his heel and retraced his steps.

"I did not dismiss you," Chattsworth thundered.

"And ye did not hire me," Garahan shouted over his shoulder as he yanked open the rear door and stalked outside.

Michael shook his head. "There's one bit of pertinent information ye seem to have forgotten, yer lordship."

The viscount vibrated with anger, but still turned to hear what Michael had to say.

"Each one of us swore a vow before the vicar and God Himself to love, honor, and protect our wives. Our vow to the duke will never rank higher than our vow to the Lord and our wives. Think about that."

"Are you going to leave, too?" Chattsworth's voice cracked. "What about my wife and son?"

"I'm going to let Harry and Bart know that there's trouble. We will round up the tenant farmers we've been training since the attack on Harry's farm. The men will fill in for meself and Garahan. I need to speak to the earl, as I'm sure Garahan will be headed to London."

"Why London?"

"'Tis where the lot of us have infinite connections in the lower classes we were born into—those we can trust to have our backs. Ye'd best be prepared to have yer reasons for cutting out Flaherty's heart and stabbing his pride. Ye'll need to explain it to His Grace, because ye just lost the best of us when Flaherty and

Garahan left."

Michael was halfway to the door when he stopped and looked over his shoulder. "Ye'll not be left unprotected, but I'd advise ye to pack up her ladyship and yer son and seek refuge with the earl. Sean and Dermott will not likely abandon the earl and her ladyship...but as they have been training footmen and tenant farmers as well, 'tis hard to say. We Irish may not have much—or seem worthy in the eyes of those of ye in the *ton*—but we have the will to live, the strength to fight, and our pride. And if God in His infinite mercy sees fit to bestow it upon us, we have the love of good women."

CHATTSWORTH WATCHED O'MALLEY leave and felt a small, familiar hand slip into his and hold tight. "What have you done, William?"

"Made the second biggest mistake in my life."

Calliope moved to stand beside him. "What was the first?"

"The day I walked away from you immediately after saying our vows at Wyndmere Hall."

Calliope sighed. "I'd say that up until today, you seemed to have managed to correct that first mistake."

He turned and stared down into the worried face of the woman he loved. "Calliope, what if I have single-handedly dismantled the duke's private guard? His Grace will never forgive me."

"I highly doubt that you have. Those men are family— cousins and brothers. I hope it will take more than the misunderstanding that occurred here today to break up with the duke's guard. But His Grace may hold it over your head to get you to do whatever he asks for the foreseeable future, at least until the four of you figure out how to put the guard back together again."

"Four of us?"

"His Grace, Edward, Marcus, and yourself." She tugged on his arm. "Come, you have missives to write and send off immediately. With any luck, you can alert His Grace to the situation before he receives Flaherty's resignation."

Chattsworth jerked to a stop. "He would not resign, would he?"

"If he felt it was the only way to protect Mary Kate." She paused for a moment before asking, "What would you do to protect me?"

"Whatever it took."

Calliope smiled, though it was tinged with sadness. "It's a start, William. Come. You have missives to write."

The viscount didn't argue as he let his younger, and much wiser, wife lead him to his study, where he would briefly and succinctly explain what had happened in three urgent missives: one to the duke, one to the earl, and one to his cousin Marcus.

"Mayhap you should ask Mary Kate…" He cleared his throat, realizing Mary Kate was gone. "I shall ask Mrs. Meadowsweet to have one of the maids help you pack some things in a trunk—probably best to prepare to stay with Aurelia and Edward for at least a fortnight."

"Yes, dear. As soon as you are through, I shall pack little William's things—we cannot forget his favorite books—and ask MacReady to pack for you."

Chattsworth followed his wife into his study, closed the door, and pulled her into his arms. "How could I have been so thoughtless?"

She sighed as she leaned against him. "It is easy to do so when those who have been protecting us for the past few years have always been there, ready to defend us without question. They have spoiled us, and we let them. Now it is time that we prove to them that we do value them, admire them, and recognize the danger they face because of us. The danger their wives and babes have to accept as part and parcel of who these brave men are. Do not forget to tell them how grateful we are to have had them watching over us all this time."

"I will not forget." Chattsworth pressed a kiss to her temple and held her to his heart. "I do not deserve you, Calliope."

"That may be—however, you are stuck with me. No matter how thoughtless and foolish you have been today."

"Would you forgive me if you were Mary Kate?"

"I'd have to think about it. She's more than my lady's maid—she's a trusted friend. Little William trusts her, too."

"I should be horsewhipped." He pulled out a sheet of foolscap and prepared to write the first missive.

"I would not mention that too loudly around here just now, because there may be someone ready to take you up on the suggestion."

"No one would dare!" he barked.

She shook her head as someone knocked on the study door. "Come in."

"What in the bloody hell did you do, your lordship?" Mac-Ready demanded. "Garahan left, and Michael O'Malley just returned with his wife, stepson, and four of our tenant farmers to stand as guards. And where are Mary Kate and Flaherty? Mrs. Romney has tea prepared for the lot of you."

"Is that any way to speak to me?" Chattsworth demanded.

MacReady sighed. "You have so much left to learn about running the manor, your lordship. I hope whatever you said or did does not damn us all." With that, he spun on his heel and stalked out.

"Well, that went better than I thought it would," Calliope murmured. "Best hurry and write the other missives. I'll sand the one you just finished and seal it for you."

Chattsworth could only nod. His ability to think straight and speak without insulting those he depended upon had obviously been damaged sometime between last night and this morning. He'd have to figure out what happened in order to hold a conversation with Michael and the others before he tucked his family in his carriage and begged to seek refuge with the earl and his family. God help him, he'd need a miracle before he faced the earl!

Finishing the last missive, he handed it to his wife and watched her sand it and seal it. "Promise you won't leave me, Calliope."

"I made that promise before the vicar and the Lord, too, William."

Pulling her into his arms, he wondered how he was going to fix this disaster—and then he knew. "I've got it! I'll send a missive to Gavin King and tell him that Flaherty—"

"Do not even suggest that you will have him arrest Flaherty and hold him in custody so he cannot leave," Calliope warned. "Or William and I will move in with Aurelia and Edward permanently!"

Defeated, Chattsworth picked up the stack of sealed missives. "We'd best have these sent immediately."

Calliope held out her hand. "I'll give them to Hargrave and tell him they are urgent."

The viscount placed the missives in her hand. "I promise I'll think of something to fix this."

She nodded. "We'll put our heads together. With any luck, Edward and Aurelia will help us."

"Lord willing."

CHAPTER TWENTY-NINE

GOOD NEWS TRAVELS fast, bad news faster. The next morning when Mary Kate and Flaherty went down to eat breakfast, there were whispers among those already eating. Everyone stopped talking as they walked into the common room.

"Ah, Flaherty, Mrs. Flaherty," the innkeeper said. "Please have a seat and your meals will be right out. I trust you slept well."

Flaherty's gaze swept the room before he answered. "Aye. Thank ye." He pulled out Mary Kate's chair and waited for her to sit before helping her scoot it closer to the table. With a sigh, he turned and looked at another table, where an older couple sat. He met their curious looks with a nod, then did the same with every last person in the room. Once he had, he crossed his arms and grunted, "Out with it."

The older man chuckled. "I always appreciate a man who can understand the situation with just a glance. You and your wife were the topic of conversation, Flaherty, especially after two messengers changed horses and rode out of here as if their lives depended upon them delivering their urgent missives."

Flaherty reached for Mary Kate's hand and gave it a reassuring squeeze. "I sent missives to London and the Lake District. Where were the messengers earlier today headed?"

"The Lake District and the Borderlands." When Flaherty

shook his head and started to sit, the older man added, "It was wise not to wait to send your missives yesterday."

Mary Kate laughed. "My husband is a cautious man."

"Excellent. By the way, name's Horne, and this is my wife, Mary."

One by one the others in the room introduced themselves, congratulated Flaherty and Mary Kate on their recent marriage, and wished them well with whatever problems they were currently facing.

As they were finishing their meal, Horne helped his wife to her feet and walked over to stand beside Flaherty. "Watch your back, and ask the Lord for wisdom. A man can never have too much wisdom."

Flaherty thanked them and watched them leave. When they were finally alone, he chuckled. "That was surprising."

"Not really, Seamus. I do believe those of us who are not members of the *ton* outnumber those who are."

He took her hand and brought it to his lips. "I have married a wise woman. Well, what do ye think our chances are? Will the duke agree to listen to me proposal?"

"Flaherty! Where in the bloody hell are ye?"

"Garahan?"

"I knew it, Melinda!" His cousin strode into the common room with his wife's arm tucked against his side. "Didn't I tell ye the *eedjit* would not make Mary Kate travel too far yesterday?"

"I never thought otherwise, James." Patting her husband's hand before she slipped her arm free, Melinda walked over to where Mary Kate was sitting. "Do you mind if I join you for a cup of tea? It was chilly when we left our home this morning."

Flaherty motioned to one of the serving girls, who returned with a pot of tea and more teacups. As Garahan pulled out a chair for his wife, Flaherty nodded toward the back of the inn. "I need a word with ye."

"No matter what ye hear, or who comes into the inn," Garahan warned the women, "neither one of ye leave this table."

"We wouldn't think of disobeying you, James," Melinda replied.

He frowned at his wife before he kissed her. "I'm wise to yer tricks, Melinda. Ye're feeling secure and would not hesitate to leave if ye got a maggot in yer brain to do so."

"How can you speak to Melinda that way?" Mary Kate demanded. "She does not deserve your censure, when all she asked was to join me for a cup of tea."

Garahan frowned at her. "It always starts with *just* a cup of tea." He was halfway to the back of the room with Flaherty when he paused to call out, "I'm meaning what I said, Melinda."

"I love you too, James."

Garahan ignored the snicker of laughter from Flaherty and answered, "Faith, I know it."

⇶✴⇶

"WHY AREN'T YOU worried that he did not tell you he loved you?" Mary Kate asked.

"That's his way of saying he loves me when we are in public," Melinda explained. "Once you and Flaherty have been married for more than a sennight, you'll find a way to speak of your feelings without necessarily using the words, too."

"Right now, I'd settle for a way to fix this disaster I've created without trying," Mary Kate confessed. "All I did was fall asleep yesterday."

"I have never heard of such a thing causing such a disruption before, but stranger things have happened," Melinda replied. "I hope you don't mind, but James insisted that we accompany you and Flaherty."

"Where?" Mary Kate asked.

Melinda reached out and placed her hand on Mary Kate's arm. "Wherever you are going. James insists that he will watch Flaherty's back. As if only the Irish can truly protect one another's backs, because no one else would understand the trials and strife they have been through."

Tears welled up and spilled over before Mary Kate could stop them. "I know Flaherty would never have asked, but it will mean the world to him that James would offer."

"Once my darling makes up his mind, there is no stopping him," Melinda confided.

Mary Kate sighed. "Flaherty is the same way, which is why I have to come up with a way to fix this mess his pride has gotten us into. Flaherty does not know, and I'd appreciate it if you would not say anything, but I sent a missive to Her Grace."

Melinda smiled. "I have no doubt that Lady Calliope and Lady Aurelia will be doing the same, without alerting their husbands to that fact. It will be up to the wives to help mend this breech before it becomes too wide and the parties on either side of it refuse to speak to one another."

"I am so glad you have come. How was her ladyship this morning? I feel so bad that I did not have the chance to say goodbye."

"She understands, and by now she and little William, and the viscount, have probably settled in at Lippincott Manor."

"Oh?"

"Michael and Garahan spoke ahead of time. Once Garahan made up his mind to stand alongside Flaherty, he and Michael put the plan together for the viscount and his family's protection. Those on the viscount's staff who have been trained to step in when one of the duke's men are injured, and the tenant farmers who were instrumental in saving Harriet's farm when under attack, have rallied around Garahan. They will act as escort with Michael, who will insist the viscount and his family seek shelter with the earl and his family."

Mary Kate nodded. "And Michael and those from Chatts-worth Manor will stay on?"

"I believe he will—otherwise, how can he state his case for Garahan and Flaherty?"

Mary Kate hesitated before asking, "You do not believe that Sean or Dermott would leave the families without protection, do you?"

Melinda shook her head. "Trust the men in the guard to do all within their power to continue to protect the duke's family. They have been training others in the event that they are badly injured. Flaherty was just over a month ago. It is always best to be prepared."

"I have watched Michael and James training with a few of the tenant farmers and footmen—Bart, too. I never thought Flaherty would abandon his post."

Melinda sighed. "You still have not realized that he did it to protect you, not because of any other reason. Their lordships have to realize that *their* wives are not the only ones deserving of protection. We are equally deserving of protection. And that is what Flaherty is railing against, the viscount's misguided assumption that Flaherty would pretend what happened the day before had not occurred."

Needing to soothe feathers that were becoming ruffled, Mary Kate hoped to distract Melinda, saying, "Harry O'Malley's son is growing into a fine young man. Do you think he has aspirations of working alongside his stepfather in the duke's guard?"

Melinda paused to think about it. "I assumed he would have wanted to take over the family farm. He has been working alongside his mum since his father died unexpectedly."

"He's young yet and still has plenty of time to decide," Mary Kate reminded her.

"Because of O'Malley and the others working for the duke, Bart will have a chance and a choice."

Mary Kate's belly churned. "I hope that Flaherty's looking out for me hasn't taken his choice away from him."

"Family should stick together. I believe James has led the way for the others to follow and fall in line. Whether or not they will do so by leaving, or standing their ground and going head to head with the viscount, remains to be seen."

Mary Kate was more than concerned by Melinda's statement. "You don't believe the other men would disrespect the viscount, do you?"

"If he disrespected—mayhap dismissed is the better word—their wives as he did to you, yes, I believe they would. James more or less echoed what your husband said to the viscount, giving his lordship something to think about—seriously. As Garahan walked out, there is a very good chance that Michael will follow, after he sets their secondary guard in place and escorts the viscount's family to Lippincott Manor. The men are equally trained in everything except bare-knuckle fighting. No one excels at it like our husbands."

Mary Kate's worry increased. "Then Sean and Dermott may walk away from their posts as well?"

"As I said, there is a chance, but who knows? Cooler heads may prevail. Especially if Lady Aurelia has anything to say about it. Nevertheless, no one will leave unless and until the secondary guard is in place. Having the viscount and Lady Calliope already stationed at Lippincott Manor will make it that much easier for them to be protected."

Mary Kate was only marginally reassured. "Flaherty also sent word to Coventry and King, asking them to send reinforcements right away."

Melinda nodded. "That's what James and Michael were planning to do as well. Coventry will no doubt view this as the desperate situation it could turn into and immediately dispatch four of his most trusted men to Lippincott Manor. According to what James was thinking, King should be sending at least two or three men as well."

The roiling in Mary Kate's belly eased. "Flaherty mentioned that His Grace hired additional men a few months ago, when he traveled to London alone. From what he said, they are well trained and can step in at any time. The duke is wise to have so many different options to protect his family."

Melinda sighed and sipped from her teacup. "Then His Grace

should be understanding when he realizes that Flaherty was protecting you. You are Flaherty's family now, too, and as such are under the protection of the duke's guard."

Mary Kate had just taken a sip of her tea when Melinda asked, "Have you met your new brothers?"

She shrugged. "Not yet—they are all scattered between the duke and his family's properties. Rory is stationed at Wyndmere Hall, Fenton is at Penwith Tower, and Dillon is at Summerfield Chase."

"Depending on how things go, and whether or not the duke is half the man Garahan believes him to be," Melinda said, "you may have a chance to meet them before Flaherty is reassigned to a different location."

"I don't know that he'll willingly go back now that he has sent the duke his resignation."

"Did he sent it along with his explanation of what happened, including your being kidnapped, knocked unconscious, and left in the barn those blackguards set on fire?"

Mary Kate shivered. "Aye."

"I do believe the viscount is in for a shock when His Grace calls him to the carpet."

"But he wouldn't reprimand the viscount," Mary Kate said. "Would he?"

"Once Her Grace reads your missive—and Calliope's and Aurelia's—he just might. The duke has been swayed by Her Grace more than once before. It is always wise to see both sides of the story from a fresh point of view."

"Well now, Flaherty, aren't our lovely wives a sight for sore eyes? Such beauties sipping tea like the fine and brilliant ladies that they are."

Melinda and Mary Kate smiled as their husbands walked back into the room, followed by one of the serving girls with another pot of tea, a plate of scones, and another of teacakes.

"We thought to join ye for a bit of tea," Flaherty said as he approached their table. "But faith, ye know I like me sweets, lass."

Mary Kate reached for his hand. "That you do, my love. Now then, why don't you and Garahan tell us the plan? It is going to take His Grace some time to read the flurry of urgent missives while considering your resignation. Then he'll have to come up with a plan to sort out the situation."

"What other missives? I know Garahan and I sent one each."

Melinda smiled at her husband. "And you must know that their ladyships will be sending missives off to Her Grace. I did."

"You did?" Garahan shook his head. "I should have known."

"I did, too," Mary Kate confessed.

"Well now, that's grand," Garahan murmured. "Their Graces will have plenty to read and mull over. If I remember correctly, Patrick tendered his resignation a year or so back."

"But isn't he still the head of the duke's guard?" Melinda asked.

"Aye," Flaherty answered. "In the meantime, Coventry and King will be sending their men to Lippincott Manor. I left it to O'Malley and yerself, Garahan, to ensure they would be protected. I couldn't take the chance that the men we've been training were not up to the challenge. No matter how angry I am that the viscount brushed aside me need to see me wife before I spoke to the man, I would never leave them without proper protection."

"'Tis why O'Malley agreed that bundling the family up and escorting them to Lippincott Manor was the answer. By the by, I sent word to Coventry, King, and His Grace as well," Garahan said. "Me missive hinted that the rest of the O'Malleys would no doubt fall in line and back us up. It could just have easily been *their* wives that the viscount slighted."

"Sometimes people act first and think second," Melinda rasped.

Garahan gathered her close to his side. "No Irishman would."

"True enough," Flaherty agreed. His lips twitched as he added, "But there are times we Irish may *drink* first and think second."

Mary Kate scooted her chair closer to her husband and leaned against him. Safe within the circle of his arms, she sighed and closed her eyes. Whatever happened, no matter whether she had to seek work at an inn, or changing bed linens, she would do whatever was necessary to support her husband. "You're not alone, Seamus. I will abide by whatever you decide. I have your back."

He kissed her forehead. "Rest now, lass. It has been an exhausting few days."

"When is she due?" Melinda asked.

Flaherty pitched his voice low, so as not to wake his wife. "I'm thinking she's only just realized she's carrying." He studied the smile on Melinda's face and then Garahan's. "When are *ye* due?"

Melinda blushed. "Five or six months from now."

"Congratulations. Ye'll make a fine mother, lass. Although I'm not sure about himself becoming a da."

"What's that?" Garahan demanded, then grinned. "Can ye believe it, Flaherty? The two of us raising our babes of our own."

"The Lord has smiled down on us, James."

"That he has, Seamus."

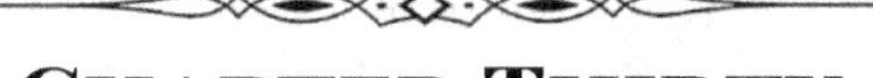

CHAPTER THIRTY

COVENTRY READ THE missive once before bolting out of his office on the second floor of his building. Pounding down the staircase, he called out, "Tremayne, Hennessey, Bayfield—stand guard! Masterson, with me!"

His men assembled quickly from their posts around the building. Masterson was the one to ask, "Bad news?"

"Aye. I need to speak to King immediately to form a plan of action."

"In regard to?" Tremayne asked.

"Flaherty."

Hennessey sighed. "Which one is it this time?"

"Seamus. He's planning to resign. Be ready for immediate instructions when I return."

"Aye, captain," Bayfield replied.

"I don't have to tell you, men—"

"We shall guard Miranda and Emma with our lives," Tremayne interrupted.

"We'll enlist Michael to guard the women inside your apartment," Hennessey added.

Relief coursed through Coventry. "Excellent. Thank you."

Masterson was moving slower than normal, which was why Coventry asked him to ride with him. "Before you ask why I did not leave you standing guard, Lieutenant Sampson recommended another fortnight before you return to strenuous duty."

"I'm fully recovered," Masterson grumbled as he and Coventry mounted their horses.

"Need I remind you how much blood you lost?"

They were already on their way, weaving in and around the slower-moving carriages. "Nothing wrong with my memory."

"Save your ire for whatever Flaherty told King."

That comment had Masterson staring at Captain Coventry. "Do you believe he only told you half of the story?"

Coventry snorted. "This is Seamus Flaherty we are speaking about."

"Will you tell me what's happened before we meet with King?"

The captain shook his head. "It would be best if you remained an impartial party and heard the news when King and I exchange the missives we've received. That way, no one can point a finger at either of us for having received more information than the other. His Grace will need all of the facts and our impartial opinions."

"Sounds like the makings of a mutiny."

"Aye, Masterson. Let us hope neither Flaherty nor myself ends up clapped in irons in the hold of one of His Grace's ships bound for America."

"JACKSON, GREEVES! MY office at once!" King bellowed.

Two of the men he reserved for protection duties regarding His Grace rushed into his office.

"Close the door."

Jackson shut the door behind him and stood with his feet spread, ready to spring into action. Greeves mirrored his stance.

King waved the folded foolscap in front of their faces. "What in the bloody hell to you know about this?"

The men exchanged a look before Jackson replied, "Depends on who it's from."

"One of the duke's men?" Greeves asked.

"Aye." King rubbed the back of his neck. "Seamus Flaherty."

"Neither of us have been in direct contact with him recently. Best just fill us in," Greeves said.

The pounding on King's door had him barking, "Go away!"

"Not bloody likely!" The doorknob turned and Coventry and Masterson walked into the room. One look at the missive clutched in King's hand had Coventry shaking his head and removing one from his waistcoat pocket. "What do you make of this?"

"First. let's compare what we've been told, then we'll see," King replied. He held out his missive to Coventry, who did the same with his. The room was silent while the two men read one another's missives.

"Flaherty's left his post and sent his formal resignation to His Grace," King muttered.

"Before doing so, he made certain that the viscount and his family, and the earl and his family, would be well protected." King slowly nodded, and Coventry continued. "They have been training footmen and tenant farmers at Chattsworth and Lippincott Manors to stand in for them—God forbid one of the duke's men became incapacitated."

King's frown was fierce when he demanded, "What of the O'Malleys? Did they remain behind at their posts?"

There was another knock on the door, which had King ready to blast whoever it was verbally. Before he could, a deep voice announced, "Urgent missive for you, King."

"Enter." He snatched the missive from the man and motioned for him to leave. He scanned the front, then met Coventry's intent stare. "It's from Garahan." King broke the wax seal and read the short note. "It appears that Garahan is standing with Flaherty in his decision to resign and will be making the trip to Wyndmere Hall to demand that the duke amend his agreement with the men in his private guard."

"You'd best not be thinking the need for more coin is behind this," Coventry growled.

King shook his head and handed the missive to Coventry to read. "Not the direction of my thoughts, but I will admit I had not expected a reasonable request from Garahan. He is as hot-tempered as Flaherty." He clasped his hands behind his back and paced. "What do you make of this, Coventry?"

The duke's London man-of-affairs was silent as he considered all they had been told. "Don't you find it odd that neither man mentioned what happened to Mary Kate to you?"

King shook his head. "Every man in the guard is close-mouthed whenever it has to do with their wives."

Coventry had to agree. "They are not always forthcoming regarding personal attacks on themselves through their wives—to me either, unless the situation is dire." The captain cleared his throat. "Given the circumstances and Flaherty's and Garahan's accounts about what happened to Flaherty and his wife, I believe the viscount owes him and Mary Kate an apology."

"We will have to proceed with caution," King murmured. "It would not be advisable for one of us to appear that we are attacking the viscount's good name."

Coventry's green eye darkened as he bit out, "Given what we have learned, I do not give a bloody damn about the viscount's good name." He rounded on King and demanded, "Do you believe that because they are Irishmen and in the duke's employ that their lives—and that of their wives and babes—do not matter?"

King locked gazes with him. "That you felt it necessary to ask shows where your sympathies lie."

Coventry glared at the esteemed Bow Street Runner. "Flaherty and Garahan—as well as the rest of the men guarding the duke—have bled for him, been clubbed over the head for him—" King raised a hand, which Coventry completely ignored. "I believe cooler heads will prevail once their wives receive a response from Her Grace."

"What do you know that I do not?" King asked.

Coventry snorted. "I married an intelligent woman who is always looking out for my welfare, especially when it involves those that I care deeply about. She knows how I feel about the sixteen men I hired on the duke's behalf. I believe His Grace and the earl feel the same way. What I do not know is where the viscount's and the baron's loyalties lie."

"I may not have married," King said, "but that does not mean I have not given my heart to someone I cared deeply about. Had circumstances been different, I would have married years ago."

Coventry stared at King for long moments before inclining his head. "Forgive me. You do understand."

"Aye. I have no doubt that Garahan's and Flaherty's wives would have immediately sent missives to Her Grace too."

"And Lady Calliope and Lady Aurelia would have done the same," Coventry said.

"Thick as thieves, those two," King agreed. "Do we wait, or go into the middle of this fiasco swinging?"

"Swinging," Jackson and Greeves said simultaneously, causing King to grin.

"Aye, that would relieve much of the tension if we had an all-out, no-holds-barred, bare-knuckle bout." Then he sighed and shook his head.

"I wouldn't mind it myself," Coventry admitted. "But as to what His Grace would prefer, I do believe that would be a round-table discussion in neutral territory."

"Wyndmere Hall?"

"Aye," Coventry replied. "Flaherty's resignation, and Garahan's, will cut His Grace deeply. The duke considers his men brothers-in-arms, and is bound to them by the blood they have shed for him and his family."

Masterson spoke up: "Her Grace will be devastated if Flaherty and Garahan resign. She is quite fond of the men and their wives. She, too, considers the men in the duke's guard, and their wives, as an extension of her family."

"Then we are agreed?" King asked. "We request Flaherty and Garahan meet with us here first, before we decide if an escort to Wyndmere Hall for a second meeting is called for."

"What if neither one is amenable to meeting with you?" Greeves asked.

King's face lost all expression. "They will have no choice."

Coventry snorted. "You aren't planning to do what I think you are. Are you?"

"I believe the best move is an offensive one. Jackson, take O'Shaughnessy. Greeves, partner with Varley. Leave at once and encourage Flaherty and Garahan to accompany you here. I believe the men will have stopped at the closest inn to where they were stationed in Sussex, given that their wives were with them."

"And if they resist," Coventry said, "remind them that Her Grace would want them to be accommodating."

Masterson smiled. "They would do anything for the duke—and Her Grace."

"Aye," King agreed. "I expect to see you back here late this evening, men, if not early in the morning. Hopefully, Garahan's and Flaherty's wives will not be a hindrance."

"From having met both Melinda and Mary Kate," Coventry said, "I believe they will do all in their power to resolve this situation without the need for either of their husbands to resign. They will come."

"Excellent," King said. "Men, you have your assignment. Get moving, as time is of the essence. All hell could break loose if word leaks out that there is trouble within the ranks of the duke's guard and the wrong parties hear of it."

"I expect to be receiving an urgent missive from His Grace by midday," Coventry added. "The duke should have received Flaherty's and Garahan's missives by now and will have sent a directive to me, demanding to know what in the bloody hell is going on."

"By then, we will have set the first part of our plans in place,"

King said. "Send word if the duke reacts differently than we expect. We will amend our plans accordingly."

"Aye, King." Coventry turned and nodded to Masterson. "We'll keep in close contact."

➤➤➤◄◄◄

"I DON'T LIKE it, O'Malley." O'Shaughnessy's glare was fierce. "I don't want my wife left alone while I'm off chasing down your kin."

Emmett O'Malley glared at O'Shaughnessy. "How do ye know 'tis me family and not something else entirely?"

"A feeling in my gut. I get them, same as you do," O'Shaughnessy grumbled.

"What else do ye know that ye aren't telling me?" Emmett demanded.

The big Irishman grunted. "I can keep my mouth shut when I've been told to. All I will tell you is that I need to leave immediately with Jackson, Greeves, and Varley, and we're riding south."

"I still don't see—"

"Promise me you'll protect my wife while I'm gone. Mary's still skittish around those she feels are her betters...through no fault of her own. I'm begging you."

Emmett raked a hand through his hair and winced. The muscles in his back had been damaged when he was viciously stabbed a few weeks ago. He was healing, but it would be a few more weeks, mayhap longer, before he was back to full fighting form. "Aye. Michaela and I will ride over, collect Mary, and bring her back here."

O'Shaughnessy hesitated. "She'll give you ten reasons why she cannot stay at Grosvenor Square. Isn't there somewhere else you can take her?"

"Ye trust me, don't ye?"

In answer, the man pulled Emmett in a one-armed hug. "Aye.

Thank you. I expect to return tonight or early in the morning at the latest."

"Go, before King sends another of his runners to find out why you haven't reported in yet."

With a wave, O'Shaughnessy was gone and Michaela slipped out from behind the door to the servants' staircase to join her husband in the hallway. "I have a bad feeling about this, Emmett."

He pulled her into his arms and kissed her forehead. "Let's alert Findley, and have two of the footmen stand guard with him. It won't take long to fetch Mary and bring her back here."

"Give me two minutes," Michaela said. "I'll let Mrs. O'Toole know, and ask her to bake a batch of her lemon teacakes. Mary's partial to them."

Emmett pulled his wife in for a lingering kiss. "I'll have the carriage made ready. Meet me by the stables, instead of out front. We don't want to attract undue attention." Watching his wife rushing toward the kitchen, he smiled and raised his eyes Heavenward. "Thank ye, Lord, for granting me more time with me darling wife."

He stepped outside and gave a short, sharp whistle. Findley came striding toward him from the front of the town house. It was part of their duty not to attract attention by running in and around the town house in response to the whistled warning. Best to act as if nothing was wrong. "Trouble?"

"Could be. Michaela and I are going to collect O'Shaughnessy's wife. She'll be staying with us tonight. Something's happening that we're not privy to—yet—but I have this feeling in me gut."

Findley nodded. "I'll grab two of the footmen and set them at their posts. We'll be ready for anything."

"Thank ye. I'll speak to the stable master. We'll be taking the black carriage—without the duke's seal."

"Wise choice."

"Aye. Watch yer back, Findley."

"Watch yours."

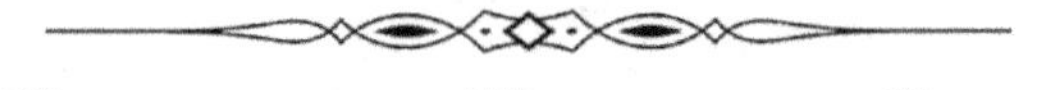

CHAPTER THIRTY-ONE

"P ERSEPHONE!"

The duchess sighed. She had no doubt that her husband had received a handful of missives too. "What a bumble-broth!" she muttered. They had to get to the bottom of this mess and untangle the knotted threads holding it together before they lost Flaherty and Garahan for good!

She opened the door to the nursery suite and waited for her husband to reach her side.

"Why is this happening? What are my men thinking? What in the bloody hell was Chattsworth thinking?"

"Come in, darling. I'll ring for tea." Persephone waited until he closed the door behind him to walk over to the corner of the room and tug on the bellpull.

"I don't want any bloody tea! My guard is on the precipice of falling into ruins. How will I be able to protect you or our children without them? What if the rest of the guard decides to resign in support of their cousins? What will happen to my brother, sister, cousins, and their families?"

She pressed a kiss to his cheek and sighed. He had only spoken of half of those the men in his guard were protecting. Her husband needed a good knock on the head, and she was thinking about using the book on the table when someone knocked. "Answer the door and ask for tea and whisky or brandy—

whatever you wish, Jared."

The duke grumbled, but opened the door and made the request.

⤜⤜⤜✦⤛⤛⤛

PATRICK O'MALLEY RECEIVED two missives. One from his brother, Dermott, and one from his cousin, Michael. He broke the wax seal and read the contents of Dermott's message and then Michael's. Immediately assessing the situation as dire, he folded the notes and tucked them in his waistcoat pocket. Stepping just outside the rear entrance to Wyndmere Hall, he whistled. Three men came running: Aiden Garahan, Eamon O'Malley, and Rory Flaherty.

He nodded at the expectant expressions on their faces. "Men, we have a problem. No doubt the duke has received a similar missive just now. There is a situation in Sussex." When Rory and Aiden stiffened, bracing for the news, Patrick told them, "Yer brothers have left their positions in Sussex and sent their resignations to His Grace."

Rory shook his head. "Why in the bloody hell would Seamus do that?"

"James would have to be a bloody *eedjit*," Aiden added.

"No doubt His Grace is still reeling from the last urgent missive, received two days' past," Patrick said. "Not one of us could conceive of the fact that Mary Kate had been abducted twice, or that it was not connected to any of the previous attacks and attempted abductions. It is unconscionable that she and Seamus were found unconscious, left to die inside a burning barn."

The men agreed, and Rory muttered, "I'm thinking Seamus's actions have more to do with that than the abduction attempt."

"Mayhap 'twas the direct hit to his pride as well," Patrick suggested. "Not being able to protect his wife while on duty for the earl, while she's serving as Lady Calliope's maid at Chattsworth Manor, has to have been a problem he was trying to resolve before this happened."

"James would have a fit if he were not able to protect Melinda," Aiden interjected. "Pride or not, we have to be able to ensure that we are protecting our wives and babes while at the same time protecting the duke's family."

"Aye," Patrick agreed, then nodded at Eamon. "What do ye think?"

"I'm in total agreement with Seamus and James," his cousin replied. "Our wives are equally important. If the duke cannot see that, then 'tis time to we sought other employment. Our reputation is well known—we could find work anywhere."

Patrick held up his hands as if to forestall that action. "Let's not be hasty. We need to come up with a solution that would benefit His Grace, and those under our protection, as well as our wives."

"I'd like to have a few words with the viscount." Rory cracked his knuckles and slowly smiled. "I haven't even had the chance to meet me sister-in-law, and already Mary Kate's had her life threatened more than once."

"Melinda is the sweetest woman," Aiden said. "The thought of any of our wives not being protected—or their protection is being pushed to the side in favor of the duke's family—is burning a hole in me gut right now."

Patrick felt the depth of his cousin's emotions, as it echoed his own. This situation had the potential to dismantle the duke's guard.

He shook his head. Dismantle? More like detonate.

"I cannot even begin to think of Gwendolyn and little Deidre in harm's way. We need a plan. I'll take yer ideas now, as I'm certain His Grace will be summoning me to speak with him shortly."

"We need more men," Rory said. "Didn't His Grace hire additional men in London?"

"Twenty hired on the recommendation of Captain Coventry.

The men are His Grace's eyes and ears around London."

"Then we need to add twenty more men to take over those positions—no doubt on the docks, in the stews, and the Dark Walk," Aiden suggested.

"Aye," Eamon agreed. "Dividing up the twenty men between the six locations—four that the duke owns, plus the viscount's manor, and the baron's manor."

"'Twould be better if we had twenty-four men to even it out," Rory said. "Surely we can ask King to loan four of his men to us until Coventry hires four more."

Patrick nodded. "A quick plan, but it makes sense to me as well. We don't want to lose Seamus or James, but have to be prepared for the fallout if they leave. Are ye willing to stay on, men, even if yer brothers resign?"

Rory and Aiden shared a glance. "That would depend on what the duke decides to do about the importance of protecting our wives and babes," Aiden answered.

"That's how I see it as well," Rory said.

"Ye aren't even married, Rory," Patrick reminded him.

Flaherty shrugged. "That may be, but I'd want equal consideration for me someday-wife's protection."

Aiden nodded. "I'd want the same for Emily and our babe-to-be. Protecting them both is paramount."

"I feel the same about Helen and our babe she's carrying," Eamon added.

"Then we agree," Patrick said. "I'll present our plan to His Grace when he sends for me."

"And if the duke doesn't agree?" Rory asked.

Patrick shook his head. "We cannot let that possibility occur. His Grace is a reasonable man. He will agree. He *has to*!"

"Are yer flasks full?" Rory asked.

"What in God's name does that have to do with any of this?" Patrick demanded.

Rory grinned. "A bit of the Irish always clears the head and soothes the soul."

Aiden shook his head, and Eamon snorted. "Ye aren't wrong, Flaherty."

"We Flahertys are rarely wrong."

"Back to yer posts, men," Patrick said. "I'll let ye know if and when the duke has spoken to me."

"And ye'll not hold anything back?" Rory asked.

Hand to his heart, Patrick promised, "Ye have me word."

CHAPTER THIRTY-TWO

"Lass, 'twould be best if ye and Melinda go with O'Shaughnessy to Grosvenor Square."

Mary Kate shook her head at Flaherty. "I'm staying with you."

He pulled her into his arms and held her close. "Ye're a distraction, lass. I'd be more worried about how ye're feeling, and whether or not ye were hungry, when I should be paying attention to whatever King and Coventry have to say on the matter of fair treatment for the wives and families of the men in the duke's guard."

She laid her head on his shoulder. "You really cannot concentrate when I am near you?"

Flaherty shifted her in his arms until he could trail kisses along the curve of her cheek, then pressed his mouth to hers urgently.

When he ended the kiss, she sagged against him. "Very well, but I do not like being separated. What if they decide to toss you behind bars for leaving your post?"

He chuckled. "Not a likely occurrence. Besides, ye know that I do not like being separated from ye either. 'Tis why I'd hoped we would end up employed together at one of the duke's residences."

"What if the viscount apologizes—would you consider working for him?"

She watched her husband clench his jaw and curl his hands into fists before he relaxed enough to respond, "I don't know."

"I see. You're asking me to set aside a close working relationship with Lady Calliope, who has become a friend, because of the viscount putting his wife before yours?"

"Aye. If ye cannot understand the fact that he did not value yer life as much as his wife's and expected me to feel the same, then there is no way I can expect ye to understand how I feel."

She stroked the side of his face and traced the tips of her fingers along the strong line of his jaw. Rising on her toes, she pressed a kiss to his cheek beneath the stitches. "I do understand. I just wish I did not. I loved working for Lady Calliope and taking care of little William."

"Garahan and I were discussing the possibility of renting rooms in Coventry's building. Two apartments were recently vacated."

He watched for his wife's reaction. It wasn't long in coming. "I thought it was a popular location, being so close to Grosvenor Square."

"Aye, lass, but after what happened to Coventry's man, Masterson—gunned down on the front steps of the building—two of the residents asked to sever their lease agreements. Coventry complied."

"I overheard Garahan mention that Masterson is healing well." Flaherty shrugged, and she continued, "I haven't been in London for a while. Tell me again who else lives in the building?"

"James's brother Darby and his wife Aimee. Then there's four of Coventry's men: Hennessey, Masterson, Bayfield, and Tremayne."

"And the captain and his family?"

"Aye, lass. Miranda and Coventry have a daughter, Emma, who is three—I think—and her son Michael, who is four and ten, mayhap five and ten by now."

Considering the possibility of living in close proximity with

Melinda and Aimee Garahan, and Miranda Coventry, Mary Kate realized she might enjoy residing in Coventry's building. "I think I'd like that."

"Flaherty! Is your wife ready to leave?"

Mary Kate threw her arms around her husband's neck and kissed him lavishly. "I'm coming, Mr. O'Shaughnessy!"

"Just O'Shaughnessy, ma'am. Are you prepared to listen and not argue with me, Mrs. Flaherty?"

"Why would I argue with you, O'Shaughnessy?"

He rolled his eyes. "Yer maiden name is Donovan, is it not?"

"Yes."

"And you're Irish?"

She laughed. "I am."

"And yet you ask why I thought you would argue with me?"

She bit her lip and fought not to smile. "I see your point. Is Melinda ready to go?"

"Aye, she's saying goodbye to Garahan. I hope she doesn't take as long as you did."

"Mary Kate!"

She spun around. "Aye, Seamus?"

"Don't devil O'Shaughnessy with yer insensate questions," Flaherty warned.

"My questions are never foolish and always make sense," she replied.

"Let's get this over with," O'Shaughnessy mumbled. "I'll be standing guard with the others when we arrive at the duke's town house," he warned when Melinda arrived.

He hesitated, and Mary Kate wondered if there was something bothering the man. "Is there something at the town house that has you worried? Should Melinda and I worry?"

"Nay. My wife is there."

"Melinda and I would love to meet your wife, O'Shaughnessy."

"She's on the shy side and has not been as fortunate as you in life," he explained.

She sensed there was quite a bit more to their story, but did not pry. "Then we shall make certain to treat her with extra care. Shan't we, Melinda?"

Garahan's wife agreed. "Everyone deserves to be treated with kindness. Mrs. O'Toole and Mrs. Wigglesworth have been kindness itself the few times I was there."

"They were to me as well," Mary Kate said. "In fact, I cannot remember ever hearing that those two lovely women were anything but kind. I believe they have worked for His Grace's brother, and their father before that."

"Do I have your word that you will look after Mary until I can fetch her later?" O'Shaughnessy prodded her.

"Absolutely," Mary Kate agreed.

"I promisc," Melinda answered.

"You ladies have hearts of gold, just like my Mary."

"We're grateful for your escort, O'Shaughnessy," Mary Kate said.

"Thank you. Next to Garahan and Flaherty, I feel safe with you," Melinda murmured.

"Well then, let's be off. I'm certain that Mrs. O'Toole will have something sweet to serve with a nice cup of tea."

⟫⟫⟫⟩⟨⟨⟨⟪

FLAHERTY AND GARAHAN watched them depart from a distance. "O'Shaughnessy's a good man. My brother Darby and I trust him with our lives—and our wives."

"We'd best start this discussion now," Flaherty urged. "I'm already missing me wife."

"Did ye mention living in Coventry's building to her?" Garahan asked.

"That I did. Mary Kate seemed to like the idea, especially getting to know Aimee and Miranda."

"'Twill be a fine life we can build here in London, Flaherty."

"Aye. Even if we no longer work for the duke."

The men walked toward King's office and were admitted to the room. They nodded to the men gathered and waited for the questions to begin.

KING AND COVENTRY nodded to the two imposing men dressed in black who walked into the room as if they owned it. A glance from King was the signal for Coventry to begin the proceedings. They had an agenda and a duke's life hanging in the balance, along with that of the cousins of the men who stood before them.

A glance at the identical closed expressions on their faces gave Coventry little hope that they would be easily swayed. Bloody hell, the crux of the matter was that he *agreed* with what Flaherty and Garahan were angling for—equal concern and treatment for the wives and families of the men in the duke's guard. By default, that included his own wife and family.

Flaherty placed a fisted hand over the Celtic harp and embroidered Eire—the only color on the unrelieved black of the uniform adopted by the sixteen men guarding the duke. A nod and a heartbeat later, Garahan did the same. Was it their signal that all that they did, they did for the ones they loved, or was it for something even deeper? A love for their native country?

King cleared his throat, and Coventry greeted the men. "Thank you for coming. As you must realize, this situation is a delicate one, with many lives depending on how you answer our questions, and how willingly the duke is to see the situation resolved."

"His Grace should have shared his thoughts with Chattsworth," Flaherty grumbled.

"His lordship," King reminded him.

"A man earns respect, King. Ye have mine," Flaherty replied. "The viscount had mine, but lost it when he showed no care or concern for me wife's condition after nearly dying"—his voice broke, and he shook his head—"beside me."

Flaherty shifted his gaze to Coventry. "Ye know ye've had me respect since the day ye hired meself and me brothers, captain. I cannot believe that ye would not support Garahan and meself in our bid to have our wives treated equally. If we're going to die to protect the duke and his family, we sure as hell are going to do the same for our families—and that includes yers."

"Aye," Garahan said. "Can ye not see how intertwined our lives and yer own have become since ye married Miranda and gained Michael as yer son?"

The captain did not hesitate to agree. "My feelings about the situation are not in question. Your actions and resignation are."

"Well now, 'tis easy to separate yerself," Flaherty said. "I'm thinking that once ye notice the hole in the fabric of the duke's guard, ye'll realize that ye should have spoken up right away about how yer own wife and life are just as much in jeopardy as ours—and Garahan's brothers, me brothers, and our sainted O'Malley cousins."

When Coventry did not comment, Flaherty added, "Would ye put Emma's life below the duke's twins?"

Coventry's single-eyed gaze was riveted on Flaherty's. "You already know the answer. I would not."

"Ah, too bad King doesn't have a wife or family to consider how he would feel," Garahan muttered.

King frowned at Flaherty, Garahan, and Coventry. "You are supposed to be acquiring the information His Grace requires to make a decision."

"There is no need to ask any further questions," Coventry replied. "I stand with Flaherty and Garahan in this. His Grace needs to realign himself with what is right."

King raised an eyebrow. "And?"

Coventry glared at him. "The lives of the wives and families—most of whom are still babes—of the men in his private guard are of equal importance to the duke's twins, the earl's son, the viscount's son, and the baron's soon-to-be heir or daughter."

"What do you propose to resolve this problem, then?" King asked.

Garahan spoke up. "The viscount needs to apologize to Mary Kate and Flaherty."

Flaherty added, "Although Mary Kate loves working for Lady Calliope, I'll not have me wife working in the viscount's household without an apology."

Coventry nodded, and King asked, "And does Mary Kate share your opinion? Is she willing to leave Lady Calliope's employ?"

"We have discussed it. She loves working for Lady Calliope—but she loves me more."

Coventry's lips twitched. "Well then, King, it would appear that the only thing left to do is to summon Viscount Chattsworth here."

"You do not summon a member of the *ton* to your office as if he were a recalcitrant youth you intend to reprimand."

Flaherty snorted and Garahan chuckled.

Coventry turned to glare at the men. "Pride is not to be discounted in this matter. On second thought, I believe we need to return to Chattsworth Manor to discuss this situation."

Flaherty crossed his arms over his chest. "Ye can go without meself and me wife."

"Melinda and I are sticking with Flaherty and Mary Kate," Garahan added.

King stared at the men and shook his head. "Coventry and I can go to Chattsworth Manor, but I want your word that neither of you will leave London. You are to remain until Coventry and I return with the viscount's decision."

"There is no decision to be made by the viscount," Flaherty announced.

"Other than to apologize," Garahan added. "Ye have our word. Seamus and I will remain in our new apartments."

"Oh?" King said. "And where would that be?"

"In Coventry's building. We'll be moving in as soon as we stop to pick up our wives."

King frowned. "I take it they are at Grosvenor Square?"

Flaherty snorted. "As if ye didn't already order it done, King."

"They are," Garahan replied. "Don't be making things more difficult because of the nick to yer pride, Flaherty."

"I'm more concerned with me wife's life—and that of our unborn babe—than ye seem to be with Melinda's."

Garahan rounded on his cousin, who raised his guard, blocking Garahan's jab to his throat.

"That would have left me unable to speak for a day or two, James. Not well done of ye."

"Ye won't malign me wife or me intentions to her and the baby she carries."

King and Coventry shared a look. Coventry nodded, and King said, "If either of you had mentioned your wives' delicate conditions in the first place, this meeting would not have been necessary."

Coventry slapped Flaherty on the back, and then Garahan. "Congratulations, men. I fully understand your need to take drastic action. A woman's first time carrying a babe is the most delicate and uncertain. It is your duty to ensure that every possible precaution is taken for their wellbeing."

Flaherty sighed. "I've been thinking of Gwendolyn and Patrick and the worry that plagued him through her pregnancy, given what happened to her before she was widowed."

Garahan nodded. "We will do whatever it takes to prevent our wives from suffering from a miscarriage because they were overworked or overwrought. If it means leaving the duke's employ—and working with our brothers and cousins performing a duty that we all have felt called to do—then so be it. Our wives and unborn babes deserve nothing less."

King inclined his head to the men and turned to Coventry. "I'll be waiting for your return."

"He's here now," Flaherty began, only to stop and shake his

head. "Forgive me, Coventry—of course ye'll want to be telling yer wife and children that ye'll be away overnight."

"Have no fear," Garahan added. "Ye can add Seamus and me to those you'll have assigned to protect yer family while ye are in Sussex."

The darkness in Coventry's eye lightened, as if an invisible weight had been lifted. "Thank you. I know that you will."

"Ye know where to find us," Flaherty said as he opened King's door.

"Send word if something else comes up," Garahan added, following Flaherty into the hallway. He closed the door behind them and raised his chin, and Flaherty nodded. They would speak later.

Once they were outside and had retrieved their geldings, they made their way back to Grosvenor Square.

Neither man spoke until they turned into the alleyway and Findley hailed them. "You're back earlier than I thought you'd be."

"Turns out Coventry had our backs," Flaherty said.

"Are you leaving for Wyndmere Hall tonight?"

Garahan shook his head. "We're waiting for Coventry and King to return from Chattsworth Manor. We'll be moving into our new apartment in Coventry's building."

Findley shook his head. "I cannot imagine the duke's guard without the two of you in it, but understand and wish you well."

"Thank ye, Findley," Garahan said.

"Is there any chance you'll change your mind?"

Flaherty stared at Findley for a moment before shrugging. "It all depends on what the viscount decides to do."

Findley nodded. "Last I saw, your wives and O'Shaughnessy's were talking up a storm in the kitchen, sampling Mrs. O'Toole's scones and currant cake."

Garahan's eyes bugged out. "Currant cake?"

"Aye, she baked a butter cake, too."

"Bless Mrs. O'Toole for knowing we'd be arriving with an

appetite." Flaherty started for the rear door to the town house.

Garahan shoved him with his shoulder. "Horses first, sweets second."

Flaherty grinned. "Horses first, kissing me wife second. Sweets third."

"Now ye're talking."

CHAPTER THIRTY-THREE

FLAHERTY ELBOWED GARAHAN as they walked down the hallway toward King's office. "Tell me again why ye think the viscount will apologize?"

Garahan shoved him with his shoulder. "Feck no. I've already told ye twice."

"What if he won't apologize? Mary Kate said it wouldn't matter, but she misses Lady Calliope something fierce."

"Coventry's got our back, and King was coming around to our way of thinking. Have a little faith, Flaherty."

They stopped in front of King's door. Flaherty knocked and they were immediately ushered inside. Coventry and King flanked the viscount, who looked uneasy. Flaherty took it as a good sign.

Their eyes locked. He nodded to the viscount, greeting him, "Yer lordship."

"Flaherty."

You could hear a pin drop, but neither he nor the viscount looked away. It was as if they were alone in the room.

"I came here on a mission, Flaherty: to apologize and offer a position guarding my home, my wife, and my son. Calliope is desolate without Mary Kate."

Flaherty waited. The viscount had yet to apologize.

"So it's just Flaherty ye're concerned about?" Garahan asked.

"I intend to ask you to swap places with Flaherty, but he needs to agree first."

Garahan shook his head and poked Flaherty in the side. "Well?"

"I'm waiting," Flaherty grumbled.

Chattsworth sighed. "This is not easy for me."

Garahan snorted, and Flaherty wanted to punch his cousin—but not in King's office. Later. "'Tis why I normally avoid having to apologize," he said.

Chattsworth's pained expression relaxed. "You were right. I was only thinking of my wife and son—not you or Mary Kate. It was not that I think you or she matter less—I don't. It was your brush with death that scared the bloody life out of me. With your talent with weapons—including your fists—it never occurred to me that you could be caught unaware and end up trapped in a burning building, bound and unconscious. How in the bloody hell would I have a hope of escaping if it were me? What would become of Calliope and our son?"

The viscount turned to Garahan and nodded. "The both of you have fought admirably, and at great cost to yourselves to protect and defend my family." Meeting Flaherty's gaze once again, Chattsworth continued, "An apology does not seem quite enough." He hesitated, then added, "You have my eternal gratitude, and Calliope's. Whatever you need, consider it yours. Please accept my sincere apology for not thinking beyond myself and my family."

"I'd be thinking yer pride had a bit to do with it," Garahan suggested.

Flaherty winced inwardly, expecting the viscount to turn on his heel and leave. But he didn't—he agreed. "According to my wise and lovely wife, I have more than my fair share of pride. I'm setting it aside and humbly begging you to accept my apology and offer of employment—if Garahan accepts transferring to Lippincott Manor."

Garahan frowned.

"Before you get your back up, Garahan, your skills are equal to Flaherty's. But Mary Kate has been more than a lady's maid to Calliope—she's become a trusted friend." Garahan nodded, and Chattsworth rushed to add, "I've spoken to Lippincott and Lady Aurelia, and they agree. They would love to have you and Melinda at Lippincott Manor. I'm sorry if my stiff-necked pride made you feel as if you and your wife mattered less. That could not be further from the truth."

Flaherty got tired of his cousin's silence. "Accept already, so I can."

Garahan grunted. "I'm certain Melinda would not mind, and it wouldn't be a hardship to work with Sean and Dermott."

Chattsworth offered his hand to Garahan, who shook it. "Flaherty?"

The nick to his pride hadn't healed, but when Flaherty accepted the apology, the crack in the foundation of the duke's guard would be filled...stabilized. "If ye'll accept me apology as well, for not realizing ye were only thinking as I was—of yer wife and family." When the viscount inclined his head, Flaherty added, "Mary Kate will be beyond happy when I share the news. Thank ye."

"Now that that's settled," King said, "you should deliver the news in person."

Coventry agreed and stared at the viscount. "I believe a second round of apologies are in order, Chattsworth."

"Calliope would have my head if I did not apologize to your wives, men," Chattsworth said. "Let's go."

LITTLE EMMA COVENTRY was sitting between Mary Kate and Melinda, sipping from her half-filled cup of tea.

"You are doing so well, Emma," Aimee Garahan said. "I was not quite so steady holding a teacup at your age."

"I usually spilled," Miranda told her daughter. "Papa will be so proud of you."

"Where is he?" Emma asked, setting her empty cup on her saucer with a loud clink. She flinched and lifted it up to inspect the bottom. "I didn't chip it, Mum."

Mary Kate smiled, and Melinda congratulated the little girl.

"Papa's late."

Miranda brushed a strand of hair out of her daughter's face and tucked it behind her ear. "You know that Papa had important business to attend to on behalf of His Grace."

Emma put her elbows on the table and leaned her chin on her hands. "The duke is always taking Papa away from us."

"Your father is proud of his duties to His Grace. You should not doubt that as soon as he is able to, your father will come home." Miranda leaned close and pressed a kiss to the end of her daughter's nose. "I'll bet he can smell the second pan of ginger-bread we just put in the oven."

"Just for him," Emma said with a grin.

"Just for him," Miranda agreed. "Now then—" A loud knock on the door had her rising to see who it was. She opened the door and gasped. "Lady Calliope, Lord Chattsworth!" She stepped to the side. "Please, come in."

The viscount reached for her hand and bowed over it. "Thank you, Mrs. Coventry." His gaze swept the room and landed on Mary Kate. "Ah, Mrs. Flaherty, I am happy to find you here. Might I speak with you a moment?"

She nodded, and the viscount slipped his arm beneath his wife's elbow and escorted Calliope over to the table.

"Please have a seat, your ladyship," Miranda urged.

"Thank you. I confess to being desperate for a cup of tea—if it is not too much trouble."

The women started talking all at once while Miranda reached for the teakettle. "Just give it a few minutes to steep. Would you care for a slice of gingerbread while you wait?"

Calliope smiled. "That sounds lovely, thank you."

Once his wife was seated, the viscount held out his hand to Mary Kate, who stared at it for a moment as if unsure what he expected from her. Finally, she placed her hand in his, and he bowed over it. "I ask your humble forgiveness, Mrs. Flaherty. I never meant to insinuate that your life and that of your babe's were not of the utmost importance to me. You have been with my wife from the beginning and have become an integral part of our lives. She has been distraught without you."

Mary Kate was not sure what to say first—should she accept the apology and tell the viscount how much she missed working for the viscountess?

The door opened and Coventry, Flaherty, and the Garahan brothers walked in. "The viscount and I have come to an understanding," Flaherty said. "'Tis all right to say whatever comes to mind first, Mary Kate. I'll not be the first man to cast a stone—ye of all people know I'm not perfect."

Mary Kate nodded as she wondered if her husband would ever admit to his jealousy and temper. Not wanting to make the viscountess wait, she said, "I have missed you, Lady Calliope, but I promised Seamus that if he resigned, I would find employment wherever necessary. I'm accustomed to working."

The viscountess rushed over to hug her. "Would you reconsider returning to your position if Flaherty changed his mind?"

She looked to Seamus for a hint as to what he wanted her to do. After all, she'd given him her word and would not go back on it.

He met her questioning look with a nod. "Answer with yer heart, lass. Ye know ye want to."

Confused, Mary Kate was not sure what had been discussed, but she had the distinct feeling that her husband *wanted* her to return to her position at Chattsworth Manor.

"Let me assure you, Mrs. Flaherty," the viscount said, "that your husband and I have both admitted to making more than one mistake in life. The second biggest mistake I made was not thinking beyond my worry for my wife and son."

"Oh?" Mary Kate said. "What was the first?"

Flaherty smacked a hand to the middle of his forehead. "Lass, ye aren't supposed to be asking that!"

"Well, you and his lordship may have come to an understanding, but I haven't. I gave you my word—are you asking me to rescind it?"

Flaherty sighed. "I am."

"Then you are admitting that you were wrong to make me leave without telling Lady Calliope goodbye?"

"Aye, lass. I have already apologized to her ladyship."

Mary Kate frowned at him. "Have you apologized to his lordship? He was only thinking of his wife and son, and you cannot fault him for that. Can you?"

"I came to that conclusion meself, but had to bring up the point to his lordship so we could come to an understanding," Flaherty admitted.

Mary Kate sensed how difficult that discussion must have been for her proud husband—mayhap even more so for the viscount. "Forgiving someone not only heals whatever happened between two people, Seamus, but it lightens the heavy burden one carries inside when one does not forgive those we believe have wronged us."

Flaherty walked over and hugged her. "Faith, but I married a wise woman. To answer yer question, lass, yes, I apologized to his lordship and admitted that me jealousy where ye are concerned often triggers me temper."

Mary Kate's eyes welled with tears. Her husband had surprised her, though after all they had been through in the last few weeks, it should not have been a surprise at all. He was a man of integrity and honesty—and those qualities far outweighed the temper and jealousy in her mind.

"He did," the viscount agreed, "after I apologized."

Miranda motioned to the men. "Please, have a seat." All but Darby Garahan sat. "The tea is ready, and so is a fresh pan of gingerbread." She opened the oven to retrieve the promised treat.

"There is still some of the other gingerbread left while we wait for the new pan to cool."

Darby waited, while Miranda and Aimee served. When Aimee sat, he sat beside her.

The viscount said, "Flaherty, Garahan—James, that is—and I have come to an agreement. We have discussed it with Earl Lippincott and the O'Malleys, and sent a written copy of it to His Grace for his edification, though I am quite certain he will be in full agreement, as it aligns with the missive I received from him."

Mary Kate hesitated. "May I ask what the agreement involved?"

"Of course," the viscount replied. "Edward and I wanted it in writing that we hold the wives and families of the men in the duke's guard in the highest esteem and value them as we do our own wives and families. It was my worry for my wife that clouded my better judgment."

"And you believe His Grace will accept this as well?"

"I can guarantee it," Captain Coventry announced from where he stood with his daughter in his arms.

She hadn't noticed that he'd picked Emma up, but then, she was distracted. "What if Seamus does not wish to return to his position working for the earl?" she asked the viscount.

"It is, of course, his decision to discuss with you. Edward and I have discussed the possibility of Flaherty and Garahan swapping places—with both Mary Kate and Flaherty working at Chattsworth Manor."

"Fortunately, for those of us who miss you to pieces, Mary Kate," Lady Calliope began, "Flaherty has already agreed to not only withdraw his resignation, but also to switch places with Garahan as one of the guards at Chattsworth Manor."

Mary Kate glanced at Melinda where she sat beside her husband. "What of Garahan? Did he decide to move to Lippincott Manor?"

"Aye, Seamus and I agreed," James Garahan answered. "Melinda and I spoke of the possibility, and as a matter of fact, 'twas a good thing we brought the matter up before any of the O'Malley wives were in harm's way. Ye know how high-handed the sainted O'Malleys can be. Then it would have been the five of us living in Coventry's building."

Flaherty's mirthful snort triggered Mary Kate's laughter. Before long, Melinda and the others joined in.

"Gingerbread, anyone?" Miranda asked as the laughter died down.

"I need two pieces, my dear," Coventry said. "After all, I missed my daily dose yesterday, and I have been craving more than a slice."

"That's not all he said—" Garahan began, only to be elbowed in the gut by his wife.

"James!"

"Would ye have me lie and not say—" His eyes were twinkling with laughter as Melinda clapped her hand over his mouth.

From where she sat beside her husband, Mary Kate felt her world right itself once more. "I would love to return to Chattsworth Manor, your lordship, your ladyship. Thank you for giving me a second chance."

"Life is all about second chances," Darby Garahan said, slipping his arm around his wife.

"There are no guarantees in life as to how many days, months, or years each of us has," James Garahan added.

"Life is precious." Flaherty pressed a kiss to Mary Kate's temple. "*Ye're* precious, lass. I would challenge the world to see ye safe and well cared for. Swallowing me pride and apologizing to his lordship, agreeing to move back to Chattsworth Manor, was the right thing to do."

"I love you, Seamus."

"I know." Her laughter was cut off when his lips met hers in an all-too-brief kiss. "I'll kiss ye properly later, lass. We aren't alone."

"You are a rogue, Seamus Flaherty."

"Faith, it's a good thing ye love me, lass."

"And?"

Flaherty finally gave her the words. "I love ye more than life itself, Mary Kate."

"I know."

EPILOGUE

Nine months later...

FLAHERTY PULLED HIS wife into the shelter of his arms and confessed, "I thought nearly dying in that barn fire was the most terrifying moment of me life."

Mary Kate sighed and leaned against her husband's strength. "It still is the most terrifying moment to me."

Flaherty leaned back and stared down into the blue-violet eyes that had bewitched him from the start. "Lass, how can ye say that when ye struggled for hours to birth our son?"

She brushed the tip of her finger over the top of their new-born babe's head and then the curve of his cheek. "He's beautiful, isn't he, Seamus?"

His throat constricted for a moment as emotions he had successfully held off during his son's birth came to a head. "God in Heaven, lass. I thought I would lose the both of ye. The birthing took forever."

Mary Kate kissed their babe's brow and snuggled closer to Flaherty. "Don't you remember the midwife saying that it went quickly for a first birth? Only fourteen hours."

"Fourteen hours," Seamus rasped. "I promise to never make ye go through that again, lass."

Mary Kate smiled as she closed her eyes. Their babe was wrapped in her arms, and they were both safe and warm in the circle of her husband's arms. "Did I forget to tell you that I'd like half a dozen children?"

The choking sound he made had her laughing softly. "Ye have a mean streak, wife. 'Tis a good thing I learned of it now. I'll not be getting ye pregnant again."

"Well, if you are certain that you no longer wish to make love with me, then I'll have to find someone else willing to have a family with me."

"Over me dead body!" Flaherty proclaimed.

"If you wish," she said sweetly.

"Are you trying to drive me daft, woman?"

She snickered. "Mayhap just a little. I love you, Seamus. I would never want to look elsewhere for the perfect da for our children."

"Son—we have *one* son."

"Ah, but he'll need a little sister to watch over and protect. After all, James and Melinda have twins—a son and a daughter. We need to catch up." When he didn't answer right away, she whispered his name and slipped a hand around his nape, pulling him closer. "Kiss me, Seamus."

Their lips met and time stood still. "Just one more babe, Mary Kate. And then, by God, that is all we'll be having!"

"Yes, Seamus."

Eleven months later...

SEAMUS FLAHERTY BENT down and gently kissed Mary Kate's forehead, all the while keeping their son from grabbing on to his new sister. "Ah, lass, ye're going to be the death of me."

"Isn't she beautiful?"

"Was yer hair that red when ye were born?"

She laughed. "It was."

"Ye've gone and saddled me with a daughter who will no doubt be as feisty as her ma."

Mary Kate sighed. "She will be the sweetest little angel."

"Do ye promise?"

She crossed her fingers and smiled at her husband. "I promise."

He frowned. "Are yer fingers crossed?"

She lifted them out from beneath their daughter and laughed. "I didn't want you to fret over having to be on your toes while chasing after our son and daughter."

"I'll chase after these two, and hope to bloody hell that they listen to their da—but no more than these two babes. I'm meaning what I'm saying, lass."

"Yes, Seamus."

Eight years later…

SEAMUS FLAHERTY STOOD with his arm around his wife, watching their daughter, and her five brothers, lead Garahan's six sons across the field in their quest to chase and capture fireflies. Their laughter filled the soft summer-night air.

"Did ye ever think we'd be so lucky as to have such fine sons?" Garahan asked from where he stood holding his wife at his side.

"We were only having one babe," Flaherty reminded his cousin. "Ended up with one daughter and five sons—and aye, they are all fine."

Garahan laughed. "Funny, that's what Melinda said to me—one babe, and look at us with six sons."

Melinda and Mary Kate shared a telling look, then smiled. "Have you told James yet?" Mary Kate asked.

Melinda shook her head. "Have you told Seamus?"

The men turned and stared at their wives. Garahan was the first to laugh, then Flaherty joined in. "Here we go again."

Dear Reader

I am so grateful to you for coming along with me on the biggest adventure of my thirty-two-year writing career. Although I have written trilogies, I have never tackled a series this large before. You embraced the sixteen men in the Duke of Wyndmere's private guard from the start and rooted for them as each and every man met the other half of their heart—offered the protection of his strength and his name, while being shot at, stabbed, clubbed over the head, etc.—while falling *arse* over head in love with the feisty women who battled with scars from their past, whether they were physical or emotional.

You buoyed my strength when it was lagging, and when the O'Malleys, Garahans, and Flahertys gave me a hard time by ignoring my plots. As the end of the series is drawing closer, I need to thank you again. Without your constant support, I would not be so close to finishing this series.

I'll be debuting my new series, Wyndmere's Warriors, in 2026.

Don't worry, there will always be one of the Garahans, Flahertys, or O'Malleys interrupting where he is not supposed to be, or answering the call from Captain Coventry, if and when the men he has hired to work undercover need assistance.

About the Author

If we have not met yet, I'm delighted to meet you. Here's a little bit about me...

I have been writing romance novels for almost half my life—well, at least for the last thirty years. I'm a die-hard romantic and have to confess the broad shoulders and wicked glint in the brilliant green eyes of a stranger had my breath snagging in my breast, my heart beating madly, and my future flashing before my eyes. At the age of seventeen, I'd met the man I knew I was going to spend the rest of my life with.

I write Historical & Contemporary Romance featuring characters that I know so well: hardheaded heroes and feisty heroines! They rarely listen to me and in fact, I think they enjoy messing with my plans for them. Over the years I have learned to listen to them. I have always used family names in my books and love adding bits and pieces of my ancestors and ancestry in them, too! Visit my website to learn more about my books.

<u>C.H.'s Social Media Links:</u>
Website: www.chadmirand.com
Amazon: amazon.com/stores/C.-H.-Admirand/author/B001JPBUMC
BookBub: bookbub.com/authors/c-h-admirand
Facebook Author Page: facebook.com/CHAdmirandAuthor
GoodReads:
goodreads.com/author/show/212657.C_H_Admirand
Dragonblade Publishing: dragonbladepublishing.com/team/c-h-admirand
Instagram: instagram.com/c.h.admirand
Youtube:
youtube.com/channel/UCRSXBeqEY52VV3mHdtg5fXw

9 781967 169634